the autumn
of the
patriarch

By Gabriel García Márquez

No One Writes to the Colonel
One Hundred Years of Solitude
Leaf Storm and Other Stories
The Autumn of the Patriarch
Innocent Eréndira and Other Stories
In Evil Hour
Chronicle of a Death Foretold
Collected Stories
The Story of a Shipwrecked Sailor
Clandestine in Chile: The Adventures of Miguel Littín
Love in the Time of Cholera
Collected Novellas
The General in His Labyrinth
Strange Pilgrims
Of Love and Other Demons
News of a Kidnapping
Living to Tell the Tale
Memories of My Melancholy Whores

gabriel garcía márquez

the autumn
of the
patriarch

Translated from the Spanish by Gregory Rabassa

HARPER**PERENNIAL** ● MODERN**CLASSICS**

NEW YORK ● LONDON ● TORONTO ● SYDNEY

HARPER**PERENNIAL** ● MODERN**CLASSICS**

First Harper Perennial edition published 1991.

First Perennial Classics edition published 1999.

First Harper Perennial Modern Classics edition published 2006.

The Library of Congress has catalogued the first Perennial Classics edition as follows:
García Márquez, Gabriel.
    [Otoño del patriarca. English]
    The autumn of the patriarch / Gabriel García Márquez ; translated from the Spanish by Gregory Rabassa.—1st Perennial Classics edition.
    p. cm.
  ISBN 0-06-093267-8
  I. Rabassa, Gregory. II. Title
  PQ8180.17.A730813 1999
  863—dc21   99-34253

ISBN 978-0-06-088286-0 (pbk.)

23 24 25 26 27 LBC 22 21 20 19 18

the autumn
of the
patriarch

the leftovers of the Sunday lunch that had been interrupted by panic, in shadows we saw the annex where government house had been, colored fungi and pale irises among the unresolved briefs whose normal course had been slower than the pace of the dryest of lives, in the center of the courtyard we saw the baptismal font where more than five generations had been christened with martial sacraments, in the rear we saw the ancient viceregal stable which had been transformed into a coach house, and among the camellias and butterflies we saw the berlin from stirring days, the wagon from the time of the plague, the coach from the year of the comet, the hearse from progress in order, the sleep-walking limousine of the first century of peace, all in good shape under the dusty cobwebs and all painted with the colors of the flag. In the next courtyard, behind an iron grille, were the lunar-dust-covered rosebushes under which the lepers had slept during the great days of the house, and they had proliferated to such a degree in their abandonment that there was scarcely an odorless chink in that atmosphere of roses which mingled with the stench that came to us from the rear of the garden and the stink of the henhouse and the smell of dung and urine ferment of cows and soldiers from the colonial basilica that had been converted into a milking barn. Opening a way through the asphyxiating growth we saw the arches of the gallery with potted carnations and sprigs of astromelias and pansies where the concubines' quarters had been, and from the variety of domestic leftovers and the quantity of sewing machines we thought it possible that more than a thousand women had lived there with their crews of seven-month runts, we saw the battlefield disorder of the kitchens, clothes rotting in the sun by the wash basins, the open slit trench shared by concubines and soldiers, and in back we saw the Babylonian willows that had been carried alive from Asia Minor in great seagoing hothouses, with their own soil, their sap, and their drizzle, and behind the willows we saw government house, immense and sad, where the vultures were still entering through the chipped blinds. We did not have to knock down the door, as we had thought, for the main door seemed to open by itself with just the push of a voice, so we went up to the main floor along a bare stone stairway where the opera-house carpeting had been torn by the hoofs of the cows, and from the first vestibule on down to the private bedrooms we saw the ruined offices and protocol salons through which the brazen cows wandered, eating the velvet curtains and nibbling at the trim on the chairs, we saw heroic portraits of saints and soldiers thrown to the floor among broken furniture and fresh cow flops, we saw a dining room that had been eaten up by the cows, the music room profaned by the cows' breakage, the domino tables destroyed and the felt on the billiard tables cropped by the cows, abandoned in a corner we saw the wind machine, the one which counterfeited any phenomenon from the four points of the compass so that the people in the house could bear up under their nostalgia for the sea that had gone away, we saw birdcages hanging everywhere, still covered with the sleeping clothes put on some night the week before, and through the numerous windows we saw the broad and sleeping animal that was the city, still innocent of the historic Monday that was beginning to come to life, and beyond the city, up to the horizon, we saw the dead craters of harsh moon ash on the endless plain where the sea had been. In that forbidden corner which only a few people of privilege had ever come to know, we smelled the vultures' carnage for the first time, we caught their age-old asthma, their premonitory instinct, and guiding ourselves by the putrefaction of their wing flaps in the reception room we found the wormy shells of the cows, their female animal hindquarters repeated many times in the full-length mirrors, and then we pushed open a side door that connected with an office hidden in the wall, and there we saw him, in his denim uniform without insignia, boots, the gold spur on his left heel, older than all old men and all old animals on land or sea, and he was stretched out on the floor, face down, his right arm bent under his head as a pillow, as he had slept night after night every night of his ever so long life of a solitary despot. Only when we turned him over to look at his face did we realize that it was impossible to recognize him, even though his face had not been pecked away by vultures, because none of us had ever seen him, and even though his profile was on both sides of all coins, on postage stamps, on condom labels, on trusses and scapulars, and even though his engraved picture with the flag across his chest and the dragon of the fatherland was displayed at all times in all places, we knew that they were copies of copies of portraits that had already been considered unfaithful during the time of the comet, when our own parents knew who he was because they had heard tell from theirs, as they had from theirs before them, and from childhood on we grew accustomed to believe that he was alive in the house of power because someone had seen him light the Chinese lanterns at some festival, someone had told about seeing his sad eyes, his pale lips, his pensive hand waving through the liturgical decorations of the presidential coach, because one Sunday many years ago they had brought him the blind man on the street who for five cents would recite the verses of the forgotten poet Rubén Darío and he had come away happy with the nice wad they had paid him for a recital that had been only for him, even though he had not seen him, of course, not because he was blind, but because no mortal had ever seen him since the days of the black vomit and yet we knew that he was there, we knew it because the world went on, life went on, the mail was delivered, the municipal band played its retreat of silly waltzes on Saturday under the dusty palm trees and the dim street lights of the main square, and other old musicians took the places of the dead musicians in the band. In recent years when human sounds or the singing of birds were no longer heard inside and the armored doors were closed forever, we knew that there was someone in government house because at night lights that looked like a ship's beacons could be seen through the windows of the side that faced the sea, and those who dared go closer could hear a disaster of hoofs and animal sighs from behind the fortified walls, and one January afternoon we had seen a cow contemplating the sunset from the presidential balcony, just imagine, a cow on the balcony of the nation, what an awful thing, what a shitty country, and all sorts of conjectures were made about how it was possible for a cow to get onto a balcony since everybody knew that cows can't climb stairs, and even less carpeted ones, so in the end we never knew if we had really seen it or whether we had been spending an afternoon on the main square and as we strolled along had dreamed that we had seen a cow on the presidential balcony where nothing had been seen or would ever be seen again for many years until dawn last Friday when the first vultures began to arrive, rising up from where they had always dozed on the cornices of the charity hospital, they came from farther inland, they came in successive waves, out of the horizon of the sea of dust where the sea had been, for a whole day they flew in slow circles over the house of power until a king with bridal feathers and a crimson ruff gave a silent order and that breaking of glass began, that breeze of a great man dead, that in and out of vultures through the windows imaginable only in a house which lacked authority, so we dared go in too and in the deserted sanctuary we found the rubble of grandeur, the body that had been pecked at, the smooth maiden hands with the ring of power on the bone of the third finger, and his whole body was sprouting tiny lichens and parasitic animals from the depths of the sea, especially in the armpits and the groin, and he had the canvas truss on his herniated testicle, which was the only thing that had escaped the vultures in spite of its being the size of an ox kidney, but even then we did not dare believe in his death because it was the second time he had been found in that office, alone and dressed and dead seemingly of natural causes during his sleep, as had been announced a long time ago in the prophetic waters of soothsayers' basins. The first time they found him had been at the beginning of his autumn, the nation was still lively enough for him to feel menaced by death even in the solitude of his bedroom, and still he governed as if he knew he was predestined never to die, for at that time it did not look like a presidential palace but rather a marketplace where a person had to make his way through barefoot orderlies unloading vegetables and chicken cages from donkeys in the corridors, stepping over beggar women with famished godchildren who were sleeping in a huddle on the stairs awaiting the miracle of official charity, it was necessary to elude the flow of dirty water from the foul-mouthed concubines who were putting fresh flowers in the vases in the place of nocturnal flowers and swabbing the floor and singing songs of illusory loves to the rhythm of the dry branches that beat rugs on the balconies and all of it in the midst of the uproar of tenured civil servants who found hens laying eggs in desk drawers, and the traffic of whores and soldiers in the toilets, and a tumult of birds, and the fighting of street dogs in the midst of audiences because no one knew who was who or by whom in that palace with open doors in the grand disorder of which it was impossible to locate the government. The man of the house not only participated in that marketplace disaster but he had set it up himself and rules over it, for as soon as the lights in his bedroom went on, before the cocks began to crow, the reveille of the presidential guard gave the notice of the new day to the nearby Conde barracks, and from there it was repeated for the San Jerónimo base, and from there to the harbor fort, and there it would be repeated in the six successive reveilles that would first awaken the city and then the whole country, while he mediated in the portable latrine trying to stifle with his hands the buzzing in his ears, which was beginning to show itself at that time, and watching the passage of the lights of ships along the fickle topaz sea which in those days of glory was still beneath his window. Every day, ever since he had taken possession of the house, he had supervised the milking in the cow barns to measure with his own hand the quantity of milk that the three presidential wagons would carry to the barracks in the city, in the kitchen he would have a mug of black coffee and some cassava without knowing too well the direction in which the whimsical winds of the new day would blow him, always attent on the gabbling of the servants, who were the people in the house who spoke the same language as he, whose serious blandishments he respected most, and whose hearts he best deciphered, and a short time before nine o'clock he would take a slow bath in water with boiled leaves in the granite cistern built in the shadow of the almond trees of his private courtyard, and only after eleven o'clock would he manage to overcome the drowsiness of dawn and confront the hazards of reality. Previously, during the occupation by the marines, he would shut himself up in his office to decide the destiny of the nation with the commandant of the forces of the landing and sign all manner of laws and decrees with his thumbprint, for in those days he did not know how to read or write, but when they left him alone with his nation and his power again he did not poison his blood again with the sluggishness of written law, but governed orally and physically, present at every moment and everywhere with a flinty parsimony but also with a diligence inconceivable at his age, besieged by mobs of lepers, blind people and cripples who begged for the salt of health from his hands, and lettered politicians and dauntless adulators who proclaimed him the corrector of earthquakes, eclipses, leap years and other errors of God, dragging his great feet of an elephant walking in the snow all through the house as he resolved problems of state and household matters with the same simplicity with which he gave the order take that door away from here and put it over there for me, they took it away, put it back again for me, they put it back, the clock in the tower should not strike twelve at twelve o'clock but two times so that life would seem longer, the order was carried out, without an instant of hesitation, without a pause, except for the mortal hour of siesta time when he would take refuge in the shade of the concubines, he would choose one by assault, without undressing her or getting undressed himself, without closing the door, and all through the house one could hear his heartless panting of an urgent spouse, the craving tinkle of his gold spur, his dog whimper, the surprise of the woman who wasted her time at love in trying to get rid of the squalid stares of the seven-month runts, her shouts of get out of here, go play in the courtyard, this isn't for children to see, and it was as if an angel had flown across the skies of the nation, voices were muffled, life came to a halt, everybody remained stone-still with a finger to his lips, not breathing, silence, the general is screwing, but those who knew him best had no faith even in the respite of that sacred moment, for it always seemed that he was in two places at once, they would see him playing dominoes at seven o'clock at night and at the same time he had been seen lighting cow chips to drive the mosquitoes out of the reception room, nor did anyone harbor any illusions until the lights in the last of the windows went out and they heard the noise of the three crossbars, the three locks, the three bolts on the door of the presidential bedroom, and they heard the thump of the body as it collapsed from fatigue onto the stone floor, and the breathing of a decrepit child that grew deeper as the tide rose, until the nocturnal harp of the wind silenced the cicadas and their fiddling and a broad big sea wave swept through the streets of the ancient city of viceroys and buccaneers and poured into government house through all the windows like a tremendous August Saturday that caused barnacles to grow on the mirrors and left the reception room at the mercy of the sharks and it rose higher than the highest levels of prehistoric oceans and overflowed the face of the land and space and time, and only he remained floating face down on the lunar water of his dreams of a solitary drowned man, in his denim private soldier's uniform, his boots, his gold spur, and his right arm folded under his head to serve as a pillow. That simultaneous presence everywhere during the flinty years that preceded his first death, that going up as he went down, that going into ecstasy in the sea while in agony in unsuccessful loves, were not a privilege of his nature, as his adulators proclaimed, or a mass hallucination, as his critics said, but his luck in counting on the complete service and doglike loyalty of Patricio Aragonés, his perfect double, who had been found without anyone's searching for him when they came to him with the news general sir a false presidential coach was driving around to Indian villages doing a prosperous business of impostoring, they had seen the taciturn eyes in the morguelike shadows, they had seen the pale lips, the hand of a sensitive bride with a velvet glove that went along throwing handfuls of salt to sick people kneeling in the street, and behind the coach followed two bogus cavalry officers collecting hard cash for the favor of health, just imagine general sir, what a sacrilege, and he gave no order against the impostor, but asked instead that they bring him secretly to the presidential palace with his head stuck in a burlap bag so that people would not get them mixed up, and then he suffered the humiliation of seeing himself in such a state of equality, God damn it, this man is me, he said, because it really was as if he were, except for the authority of the voice, which the other one never managed to imitate, and for the clearness of the lines on the hand where the life line went along without obstacles all around the base of the thumb, and if he did not have him shot immediately it was not because he was interested in keeping him as his official impostor, that occurred to him later, but because the illusion that the cipher of his own fate should be written on the hand of an impostor bothered him. When he became convinced of the vanity of that dream Patricio Aragonés had already impassively survived six assassination attempts, had acquired the habit of dragging his feet which had been flattened out with a mallet, his ears buzzed, and his hernia ached at dawn in the winter, and he had learned to take off and put on the golden spur as if the straps were tangled up simply to gain time at audiences muttering God damn it these buckles Flemish blacksmiths make aren't even good for this, and from the jokester and gabbler that he had been when he was a glassblower in his father's carquaise he became thoughtful and somber and paid no attention to what people were saying to him but scrutinized the shadows of their eyes to guess what they were not saying to him, and he never answered a question without first asking in turn what do you think and from the slothful wastrel he had been in his business as a vendor of miracles, he became diligent to the point of torture and an implacable walker, he became tight-fisted and rapacious, he resigned himself to sleeping on the floor, his clothes on, face down and with no pillow, and he renounced his precocious presumption of an identity of his own and all hereditary vocation for the golden flightiness of simply blowing and making bottles, and he confronted the most terrible risks of power laying cornerstones where the second stone was never to be laid, cutting ribbons in enemy territory and bearing up under so many soft-boiled dreams and so many repressed sighs of impossible illusions as he crowned and did not so much as touch all those ephemeral and unattainable beauty queens, for he had become resigned forever to live a destiny that was not his, even though he did not do it out of greed or conviction but because he had exchanged his life for his in the lifetime job of official impostor with a nominal salary of fifty pesos a month and the advantage of living like a king without the calamity of being one, what more could you ask? That mix-up of identities reached its high point one night when the wind was long and he found Patricio Aragonés sighing out toward the sea amidst the fragrant vapor of the jasmines and he asked him with legitimate alarm if they had put wolfbane in the food because he was drifting off as if pierced by evil air, and Patricio Aragonés answered him no general, it's worse than that, on Saturday he had crowned a carnival queen and had danced the first waltz with her and now he couldn't find any exit out of that memory, because she was the most beautiful woman on earth, the kind you never get for yourself general, if you could only see her, but he answered with a sigh of relief and what the hell, this is the kind of trouble a man gets into when he gets all tied up with women, he proposed abducting her as he had done with so many good-looking women who had become his concubines, I'll have her held down by force on the bed with four troopers at her arms and legs while you take care of her with your soup ladle, God damn it, you can take her while she's bulldogged, he told him, even the tightest of them roll around with rage at first and then they beg you don't leave me like this gen-

eral like a sad rose apple whose seed has fallen off, but Patricio
Aragonés didn't want as much as that he wanted more, he
wanted them to love him, because this girl is one of those who
know where the tune comes from general, you'll see when you
get a look at her, so as a formula for relief he pointed out the
nocturnal pathways to the rooms of his concubines to him and
authorized him to make use of them as if it were he himself, by
assault and quickly and with his clothes on, and Patricio Aragonés in good faith sank into that morass of loves even believing
that he could put a gag on his urges through them, but such was
his anxiety that sometimes he forgot the conditions of the loan,
he would unbutton his fly absentmindedly, linger over details,
carelessly stumble across the hidden jewels of the basest of
women, draw out their deepest sighs, and even make them
laugh with surprise in the shadows, you old devil general, they
would tell him, you're growing greedy on us in your old age,
and from then on neither of them or any of the women either
ever knew whose child was whose or by whom, because Patricio
Aragonés's children were seven-monthers just like his. So it
came to pass that Patricio Aragonés became the man most essential to the seat of power, the most beloved and also perhaps the
most feared, and he had more time available to take care of the
armed forces, not because the armed forces were what sustained
his power, as we all thought, quite the contrary, because they
were his most feared natural enemy, so he made some officers
believe that they were being watched by others, he shuffled their
assignments to prevent their plotting, every army post received
a ration of eight blank cartridges for every ten live rounds and
he sent them gunpowder mixed with beach sand while he kept
the good ammunition within reach in an arsenal in the presidential palace the keys to which hung on a ring with other keys that
had no duplicates and opened other doors that no one else could

open, protected by the tranquil shadow of my lifelong comrade General Rodrigo de Aguilar, an artilleryman and academy graduate who was also his minister of defense and at the same time commander of the presidential guard, director of the state security services, and one of the very few mortals authorized to beat him in a game of dominoes, because he had lost his right arm trying to defuse a dynamite charge minutes before the presidential berlin was to pass by the site of the assassination attempt. He felt so safe under the protection of General Rodrigo de Aguilar and with the presence of Patricio Aragonés that he began to relax his concern with self-preservation and was becoming more and more visible, he dared take a ride through the city with only one aide in a covered wagon bearing insignia looking through the peepholes at the arrogant gilt stone cathedral which he had declared by decree the most beautiful in the world, he peeped at the ancient stone mansions with entranceways from times when all was drowsy and the sunflowers turned seaward, the cobbled streets with the smell of snuff in the viceregal quarter, the pale young ladies making bobbin lace with inelectable decency among the pots of carnations and the bunches of pansies in the light of balconies, the checkerboard convent of the Biscayan sisters with the same harpsichord exercise at three in the afternoon with which they had celebrated the first passage of the comet, he went through the Babelic labyrinth of the commercial district, its lethal music, the labara of lottery tickets, the pushcarts with cane juice, the strings of iguana eggs, the Turks and their sunlight-faded bargains, the fearsome tapestry of the woman who had been changed into a scorpion for having disobeyed her parents, the alley of misery of women without men who would emerge naked at dusk to buy blue corbinas and red snappers and exchange mother-directed curses with the women selling vegetables while their clothes were drying on the carved wooden balconies, he smelled the rotten shell-fish wind, the everyday light of the pelicans around the corner, the disorder of colors of the Negro shacks on the promontories of the bay, and suddenly there it was, the waterfront, alas, the waterfront, the dock and its spongy planks, the old battleship of the marines longer and gloomier than truth, the black dock-worker woman who was too late in getting out of the way of the fearsome little wagon and felt touched by death with the sight of the sunset old man who was contemplating the water-front with the saddest look in the world, it's him, she exclaimed with surprise, hurray for the stud, she shouted, hurray, shouted the men, the women, the children who came running out of the Chinese bars and lunchrooms, hurray, shouted the ones who held the horses' legs and blocked the coach's way so they could shake the hand of the power that was, a maneuver so swift and unforeseen that he barely had time to push aside the armed hand of his aide scolding him in a tense voice, don't be a damned fool, lieutenant, let them love me, so overwhelmed by that out-pouring of love and by similar ones during the days that fol-lowed that it was hard for General Rodrigo de Aguilar to make him get out of his head the idea of riding about in an open carriage so that the patriots of the nation could see me full length, what the hell, because he didn't even suspect that the assault at the waterfront may have been spontaneous but that the ones that followed had been organized by his own security services in order to please him but without any risks, so honeyed by the breezes of love on the eve of his autumn that he dared go out of the city after many years, he started up the old train painted with the colors of the flag again and went creeping and crawling about the cornices of his vast mournful realm, opening a path through orchid sprigs and Amazonian balsam apples, rousing up monkeys, birds of paradise, jaguars sleeping on the tracks, even the glacial and deserted villages of his native barren uplands where they waited for him at the station with mournful-music bands, tolling death bells, displaying signs of welcome for the nameless patriot who sits at the right hand of the Holy Trinity, they recruited rustics from the back reaches who came down to meet the hidden power in the funereal shadows of the presidential coach, and those who managed to get close enough only saw the quivering lips, the palm of a hand with no origins which waved from the limbo of glory, while a member of the escort tried to get him away from the window, be careful, general, the nation needs you, but he would reply sleepily don't worry, colonel, these people love me, as it was on the train in the barren lands so it was the same on the wooden paddle-wheeler that went along leaving a wake of player-piano waltzes in the midst of the sweet fragrance of gardenias and rotting salamanders of the equatorial tributaries, eluding prehistoric dragons in their leather gun cases, providential isles where sirens lay down to give birth, sunsets which were the disasters of immense disappeared cities, even the burning and desolate shantytowns where the inhabitants appeared on the riverbank to see the wooden boat painted with the national colors and they could just make out an anonymous hand with a velvet glove which waved from a window of the presidential stateroom, but he saw the groups on shore who were waving malanga leaves for lack of flags, he saw those who jumped into the water with a live tapir, a gigantic yam that was as big as an elephant's foot, a cage of partridges for the presidential stewpot, and he sighed with emotion in the ecclesiastical penumbra of the stateroom, see how they come, captain, see how they love me. In December, when the Caribbean world turned to glass, he would take the closed carriage on a climb along the cornices of crags until he came to the house perched on top of the reefs and he would spend the afternoon playing dominoes with the former dictators of other nations of the continent, the dethroned fathers of other countries to whom he had granted asylum over the course of many years and who were now growing old in the shadow of his mercy dreaming in chairs on the terrace about the chimerical vessel of their second chance, talking to themselves, dying dead in the rest home he had built for them on the balcony of the sea after having received all of them as if each were the only one, for they all appeared at dawn in the dress uniform they had put on inside out over their pajamas, with a chest of money they had pilfered from the public treasury and a suitcase with a box of decorations, newspaper clippings pasted into old ledgers, and a photograph album they would show him at the first audience, as if they were credentials, saying look general, that's me when I was a lieutenant, this was the day I was inaugurated, this was the sixteenth anniversary of my taking power, here, look general, but he would give them asylum without paying any more attention to them or inspecting credentials because the only document of identity for an overthrown president should be his death certificate, he would say, and with the same disdain he would listen to the illusory little speech of I accept for this short time your noble hospitality while the justice of the people brings the usurper to account, the eternal formula of puerile solemnity which a while later he would hear from the usurper, and then from the usurper's usurper as if the God-damned fools didn't know that in this business of men if you fall, you fall, and he put all of them up for a few months in the presidential palace, made them play dominoes until he had fleeced them down to their last cent, and then he took me by the arm over to the window looking out onto the sea, he helped me grieve over this meat-beating life that only goes in one direction, he consoled me with the illusion that I go over there, look, over there to that big house that looked like an ocean liner aground on the top of the reefs where I have some lodgings with good light and good food, and plenty of time to forget along with other companions of misfortune, and with a terrace overlooking the sea where he liked to sit on December afternoons not so much for the pleasure of playing dominoes with that bunch of boobs but to enjoy the base good fortune of not being one of them, to look at himself in the instructive mirror of their misery while he wallowed in the great slough of felicity, dreaming alone, tiptoeing like an evil thought in pursuit of the tame mulatto girls who swept government house in the dimness of dawn, he sniffed out their public dormitory and drugstore hairgrease trail, he would lie in wait for the chance to catch one alone and make rooster love to her behind office doors while they would burst with laughter in the shadows, what a devil you are general, such a great man and still so horny, but he would be sad after making love and would start singing to console himself where no one could hear him, bright January moon, he would sing, see how sad I am standing on the gallows by your window, he would sing, so sure of his people's love on those Octobers with no evil omens that he would put up a hammock in the courtyard of the suburban mansion where his mother Bendición Alvarado lived and sleep his siesta in the shade of the tamarind trees, without an escort, dreaming about the errant fish who swam in the colored waters of the bedrooms, a nation is the best thing that was ever invented, mother, he would sigh, but he never waited for the answer from the only person in the world who dared scold him for the rancid onion smell of his armpits, but he returned to the presidential palace through the main door in exaltation with that miraculous season of the Caribbean in January, that reconciliation with the world at the end of old age, those mellow soft afternoons after he had made peace with the papal nuncio and the latter would visit him without an appointment to attempt to convert him to the faith of Christ while they had chocolate and cookies, and bursting with laughter he would allege that if God is the man you say he is tell him to rid me of this beetle that's buzzing in my ear, he would tell him, he would unbutton the nine buttons of his fly and show him his huge tool, tell him to deflate this creature, he would tell him, but the nuncio went along with his shepherd's work with patient stoicism, tried to convince him that everything that is truth, no matter who says it, comes from the Holy Spirit, and he would see him to the door when the first lights went on, dying with laughter as had rarely been seen, don't waste your gunpowder on buzzards, father, he told him, why should you want to convert me since everything I'm doing is just what you people want, what the hell. That floating calmness shattered its hull suddenly at a cockpit on a faraway plain when a bloodthirsty cock tore the head off his adversary and ate it, pecking at it before an audience that was maddened by blood and a drunken brass band that celebrated the horror with festive music, and he was the only one who spotted the evil omen, and he sensed that it was so clear and so imminent that he secretly ordered his escort to arrest one of the musicians, that one, the one playing the tuba, and, indeed, they found a sawed-off shotgun on him and under torture he confessed that he had planned to shoot him during the confusion as the people left, it was quite obvious, of course, he explained, because I was looking at everybody and everybody was looking back at me, but the only one who didn't dare look at me one single time was that son of a bitch with the tuba, poor devil, and still he knew that that wasn't the ultimate reason for his anxiety, because he kept on feeling it at night in government house even after his security service had shown that there was no reason for worry general sir, everything was in order, but he had clung to Patricio Aragonés as if he were himself after he had received the omen at the cockpit, he gave him his own food to eat, he gave him his own honey to drink with the same spoon so that he would at least die with the consolation that they had both died together in case the things had been poisoned, and they went like fugitives through forgotten rooms, walking on the rugs so that no one would hear their great furtive Siamese elephant steps, navigating together in the intermittent light from the beacon as it came in through the windows and flooded the rooms of the house every thirty seconds with green amidst the vapor from cow flops and the mournful greetings of nocturnal ships on the sleeping seas, they would spend whole afternoons watching it rain, counting swallows on languid September afternoons like two aged lovers, so far removed from the world that he himself did not realize that his fierce struggle to exist twice was feeding the contrary suspicion that he was existing less and less, that he was lying in a lethargy, that the guard had been doubled and no one was allowed in or out of the presidential quarters, that someone had still managed to get through that strict filter and had seen the birds silent in their cages, the cows drinking at the baptismal font, the lepers and cripples sleeping in the rose beds, and everybody at midday seemed to be waiting for dawn to come since he had died as had been announced in the prophetic basins of natural causes during his sleep but the high command was delaying notice while they tried to settle in bloody secret meetings their postponed quarrels. Although he did not know of those rumors he was aware that something was about to occur in his life, he would interrupt the slow domino games to ask General Rodrigo de Aguilar how the mess was going, friend, everything under control sir, the nation was calm, he watched for signs of premonition in the funeral pyres of cow chips that burned on the courtyard corridors and in the wells with their ancient waters but he could find no answer for his anxiety, he visited his mother Bendición Alvarado in the suburban mansion when the heat died down, they would sit and take in the cool afternoon breezes under the tamarinds, she in her maternal rocking chair, decrepit but with her soul intact, tossing handfuls of grain to the hens and the peacocks who pecked about the courtyard, and he in the large wicker chair, fanning himself with his hat, following with his look of old hunger the big mulatto women who brought him colored fruit juices to quench his hot thirst, general, thinking oh Bendición Alvarado, my mother, if you only knew that I can't stand the world any more, that I'd like to go away I don't know where, mother, far away from so much injustice, but not even his mother was shown the inside of his sighs but he would return to the presidential palace with the first lights of evening, go in through the service entrance hearing the clicking of sentries' heels as he went along the corridors and they saluted him all's well general sir, everything in order, but he knew that it wasn't true, that they were dissembling from habit, that they lied to him out of fear, that nothing was true in that crisis of uncertainty which was rendering his glory bitter and had been taking away his old desire to command ever since that fateful night at the cockpit, until very late he would stay stretched out face down on the floor without sleeping, through the open window facing the sea he could hear the distant drums and sad bagpipes that were celebrating some wedding among the poor with the same uproar with which they would have celebrated his death, he could hear the farewell of a vagabond steamer that was weighing anchor at two o'clock in the morning without permission from the port captain, he could hear the paper sound of the roses as they opened at dawn, without one moment of rest, sensing with a woodsman's instinct the imminence of the afternoon when he would be on his way back from the suburban mansion and be surprised by a mob in the street, an opening and closing of windows and a panic of swallows in the diaphanous December sky and he peeped through the curtain of the carriage to see what was going on and he said to himself this is it, mother, this is it, he said to himself, with a terrible feeling of relief, seeing the colored balloons in the sky, the red and green balloons, the yellow balloons like great blue oranges, the innumerable wandering balloons that took flight in the midst of swallows' fright and floated for an instant in the crystal light of four o'clock and suddenly broke with a silent and unanimous explosion releasing thousands and thousands of bits of paper over the city, a blizzard of broadsides which the coachman took advantage of in order to slip through the tumult of the public market without anyone's recognizing the coach of power, because everybody was busy in the scramble for the papers from the balloons general sir, they were shouting out the words on them from the balconies, from memory they repeated down with oppression, they shouted death to the tyrant, and even the sentries along the corridors of the presidential palace were reading aloud about the union of all without distinction of class against the despotism of centuries, patriotic reconciliation against the corruption and the arrogance of the military, no more blood, they shouted, no more pillaging, the whole country was awakening from its age-old sleep at the moment he was going through the coach house door and he ran into the terrible news general sir that Patricio Aragonés had been fatally wounded by a poisoned dart. Years before one night of bad moods he had proposed to Patricio Aragonés that they gamble their lives on heads or tails, heads you die, tails I die, but Patricio Aragonés made him see that they would both meet death in a tie because all coins had both their faces on both sides, he then proposed that they gamble their lives at the domino table, the best out of twenty games, and Patricio Aragonés accepted with great honor general sir, with the proviso that you grant me the privilege of being allowed to beat you, and he accepted, agreed, so they played one game, they played two, they played twenty, and Patricio Aragonés always won because he only used to win because it was forbidden to beat him, a long and bloody battle was joined and they reached the last game without his having won a single match, and Patricio Aragonés dried the sweat of his brow with his shirt sleeve sighing I'm deeply sorry general but I don't want to die, and then he went about picking up the pieces, placed them in order in the little wooden box while he said like a schoolmaster chanting a rote lesson that he had no need to die at the domino table either but in his own time and his own place from natural causes in his sleep as had been predicted ever since the beginning of his days by the sibylline basins, and not even that way, when you come to think of it, because Bendición Alvarado didn't bring me into the world to pay any heed to basins but to command, and after all I am what I am, and not you, so give thanks to God that this was only a game, he told him laughing, not having imagined then or ever that the terrible joke was to come true the night he went into Patricio Aragonés's room and found him facing the demands of death, hopeless, with no chance of surviving the poison, and he greeted him from the door with his hand outstretched, God save you, stud, it's a great honor to die for your country. He stayed with him during his slow agony, the two of them alone in the room, giving him the spoonfuls of anodyne with his own hand, and Patricio Aragonés took them without gratitude telling him between spoonfuls I will leave you here for a while my general with your world of shit because my heart tells me that quite soon we shall meet again in the depths of hell, I all twisted up worse than a mullet because of this poison and you with your head in your hand looking for a place to put it, let it be said without the least bit of respect general sir, that I can tell you now that I never loved you as you think but that ever since the days of the filibusters when I had the evil misfortune to chance into your domains I've been praying that you would be killed, in a good way even, so that you would pay me back for this life of an orphan you gave me, first by flattening my feet with tamping hands so that they would be those of a sleepwalker like yours, then by piercing my nuts with a shoemaker's awl so I would develop a rupture, then by making me drink turpentine so I would forget how to read and write after all the work it took my mother to teach me, and always obliging me to go through the public ceremonies you didn't dare face, and not because the nation needs you alive as you say but because even the toughest man can feel his ass freeze up when he crowns a beauty whore and doesn't know from what direction death will explode in on him, let it be said without the least respect general, but he wasn't bothered by the insolence but rather by the ingratitude of Patricio Aragonés who I set up in life like a king in a palace and I gave you what no one has ever given anybody in the world even lending you my own women, although we'd best not talk about that general because it's better to be gelded by a mace than to go about laying mothers on the ground as if it were a matter of branding calves, just because those poor heartless bitch waifs don't even feel the brand or kick or twist or complain like calves, and they don't smoke from the haunches or smell of singed flesh which is the least one asks of good women, but they lay down their dead-cow bodies so a person can do his duty while they go on peeling potatoes and shouting to the other women please keep an eye on the kitchen for me while I take a breather here so my rice doesn't burn, only you would think that stuff like that is love general, because it's the only kind you know, without the least respect of course, and then he began to roar shut up, God damn it, shut up or you'll pay for it, but Patricio Aragonés kept on saying without the slightest intention of a joke why should I shut up when all you can do is kill me and you're already killing me, it would be better now to take advantage and look truth in the face general, so you can know that no one has ever told you what he really thinks but that everyone tells you what he knows you want to hear while he bows to your face and thumbs his nose at you from behind, you might even thank fate that I'm the man who most pities you in this world because I'm the only one who looks like you, the only one honorable enough to sing out to you what everyone says that you're president of nobody and that you're not on the throne because of your big guns but because the English sat you there and the gringos kept you there with the pair of balls on their battleship, because I saw you scurrying like a cockroach this way and that, back and forth when the gringos shouted to you we're leaving you here with your nigger whorehouse so let's see if you can put it all together without us, and if you never got out of your chair since that time or have never gotten out it's probably not because you don't want to but because you can't, recognize it, because you know that the moment they see you on the street dressed as a mortal they're going to fall on you like a pack of dogs to collect from you in one case for the killings at Santa María del Altar, in another for the prisoners thrown into the moat of the harbor fort to be eaten by crocodiles, in another for the people you skin alive and send their hides to their families as a lesson, he said, dipping into the bottomless well of his long-postponed rancor and drawing out the string of atrocities of his regime of infamy, until he could no longer tell him any more because a fiery rake tore his guts apart, his heart softened again and he ended with no intent of offense but almost one of supplication I'm serious general, take advantage of the fact that I'm dying now and die with me, no one has more right than I to tell you this because I never had any intention of looking like anyone much less a national hero but only a sad little glassblower making bottles like my father, take a chance, general, it doesn't hurt as much as it seems, and he said it with an air of such serene truth that the rage to answer did not overcome him but rather he tried to hold him up in his chair when he saw that he was starting to twist about and hold his belly in his hands and was sobbing with tears of pain and shame I'm so sorry general but I'm shitting in my pants and he thought he meant it in a figurative sense that he was dying of fear, but Patricio Aragonés answered him no, I mean real shit shitting general and he managed to beseech him hold on Patricio Aragonés, hold on, we generals of the fatherland have to die like men even if we pay for it with our lives, but he said it too late because Patricio Aragonés fell face down and on top of him kicking with fear and soaked in shit and tears. In the office next to the hearing room he had to scrub the body with a dishrag and soap to get rid of the bad smell, he dressed it in the clothes he was wearing, he put the canvas truss on, the boots, the gold spur on the left heel, feeling as he did it that he was changing into the most solitary man on earth, and last of all he erased all traces of the farce and reproduced the perfection down to the tiniest details that he had seen with his own eyes in the premonitory waters of the basins so that at dawn on the next day the cleaning women would find the body as they did find it stretched out face down on the floor of the office, dead for the first time of natural causes in his sleep with his denim uniform with no insignia, boots, the gold spur, and his right arm folded under his head as a pillow. They did not spread the news immediately that time either, contrary to what he expected, but many prudent hours passed with clandestine investigations, secret agreements among the heirs of the regime who were trying to gain time by denying the rumor of death with all manner of contrary versions, they brought his mother Bendición Alvarado out into the commercial district to show that she was not wearing a mourning face, they dressed me in a flowered dress like a chippy, sir, they made me buy a macaw-feather hat so that everybody would see me happy, they made me buy every piece of junk to be found in the stores in spite of my telling them no, sir, it wasn't a time for buying but for crying because even I believed that it was really my son who had died, and they forced me to smile when people took full-length pictures of me because the military men said it had to be done for the good of the country while he wondered confused in his hiding place what's happening out in the world since nothing had changed with the trick of his death, how was it that the sun had risen and had risen again without stumbling, why that Sunday look, mother, why the same heat without me, he was wondering in surprise when a sudden cannon shot sounded from the fortress on the harbor and the main bells of the cathedral began to toll and all the way up to government house came the surge of the crowds that were rising up out of the age-old morass with the greatest piece of news in the world, and then he half-opened the bedroom door and peeped into the audience room and saw himself laid out more dead and more decorated than all the dead popes of Christendom, wounded by the horror and the shame of his own body of a military stud lying among the flowers, his face pale with powder, his lips painted, the hard hands of a dauntless young lady crossed over the chest armored with military decorations, the showy dress uniform with the ten pips of general of the universe, a rank someone had invented for him after death, the king-of-spades saber he never used, the patent leather boots with

two gold spurs, the vast paraphernalia of power and the lugubrious martial glories reduced to his human size of a fagot lying in
state, God damn it, that can't be me, he said to himself in a fury
it's not right, God damn it, he said to himself, contemplating
the procession that was parading around his corpse, and for an
instant he forgot the murky reasons for the farce and felt raped
and diminished by the inclemency of death toward the majesty
of power, he saw life without him, he saw with a certain compassion how men were bereft of his authority, he saw with a
hidden uneasiness those who had only come to decipher the
enigma of whether it really was or was not he, he saw a very old
man who gave the masonic salute from the days of the federalist
war, he saw a man in mourning who kissed his ring, he saw a
schoolgirl who laid a flower on him, he saw a fishwife who could
not resist the truth of his death and strewed her basket of fresh
fish all over the floor and embraced the perfumed corpse sobbing aloud that it was him, my God, what's going to become of
us without him, she wept, so it was him, they shouted, it was
him, shouted the throng suffocated by the sun in the main
square and then the bells of the cathedral stopped tolling their
knell and those of all the churches announced a Wednesday of
jubilation, Easter rockets exploded, Roman candles, drums of
liberation, and he watched the assault groups that came in
through the windows in the face of the silent complacency of
the guard, he watched the ferocious leaders who dispersed the
procession with clubs and knocked down the inconsolable
fishwife, he watched the ones who attacked the corpse, the eight
men who took it out of its immemorial state and its chimerical
time of agapanthus lilies and sunflowers and dragged it down
the stairs, those who gutted the insides of that paradise of opu-
lence and misfortune thinking they were destroying the lair of
power forever, knocking over the papier-mâché Doric capitals,

velvet curtains and Babylonic columns crowned with alabaster palm trees, throwing birdcages out the window, the throne of the viceroys, the grand piano, breaking the funeral urns with the ashes of unknown patriots and Gobelin tapestries of maidens asleep in gondolas of disillusion and enormous oil paintings of bishops and archaic military men and inconceivable naval battles, annihilating that world so that in the memory of future generations not the slightest memory of the cursed line of men of arms would remain, and then he peeped into the street through the slats in the blinds to see what degree the ravages of defenestration had reached and with just one glance he saw more infamy and more ingratitude than had ever been seen and wept over by my eyes since the day I was born, mother, he saw his merry widows leaving the building through the service entrance leading the cows from my stables by the halter, carrying off government furniture, the jars of honey from your hives, mother, he saw his seven-month runts making music of jubilation with kitchen pots and treasures from the crystal set and the table service for pontifical banquets singing with street-urchin shouts my papa is dead, hurray for freedom, he saw the bonfire that had been lighted on the main square to burn the official portraits and the almanac lithographs that had been in all places and at all times every since the beginning of his regime, and he saw his own body dragged by as it left behind along the street a trail of medals and epaulets, dolman buttons, strands of brocade and frog embroidery and tassels from playing-card sabers and the ten sad pips of the king of the universe, mother, look what they've done to me, he said, feeling in his own flesh the ignominy of the spitting and the sickbed pans that were thrown on him from the balconies as he went by, horrified with the idea of being quartered and devoured by dogs and vultures amidst the delirious howls and the roar of fireworks celebrating the carnival of my death. When the cataclysm had passed he still heard the distant music of the windless afternoon, he went on killing mosquitoes and with the same slaps trying to kill the katydids in his ears which hindered him in his thinking, he still saw the light of the fires on the horizon, the lighthouse that tinted him with green every thirty seconds through the slits in the blinds, the natural breathing of daily life which was getting to be the same again while his death was changing into a different death more like so many others in the past, the incessant torrent of reality which was carrying him off toward the no-man's-land of compassion and oblivion, God damn it, fuck death, he exclaimed, and then he left his hiding place exalted by the certainty that his grandest hour had struck, he went through the sacked salons dragging his thick phantom feet in the midst of the ruins of his former life in the shadows that smelled of dying flowers and burial candlewicks, he pushed open the door of the cabinet room, heard through the smoky air the thin voices around the long walnut table, and saw through the smoke that all the ones he wanted to be there were there, the liberals who had sold the federalist war, the conservatives who had bought it, the generals of the high command, three of his cabinet ministers, the archbishop primate and Ambassador Schontner, all together in one single plot calling for the unity of all against the despotism of centuries so that they could divide up among themselves the booty of his death, so absorbed in the depths of greed that no one noticed the appearance of the unburied president who gave a single blow with the palm of his hand on the table, and shouted aha! and that was all he had to do, for when he lifted his hand from the table the stampede of panic was over and all that was left in the room were the overflowing ashtrays, the coffee mugs, the chairs flung on the floor, and my comrade of a lifetime General Rodrigo de Aguilar in battle dress, minute, impassive, wafting away the smoke with his one hand and indicating to him to drop to the floor general sir because now the fun is going to begin, and they both dropped to the floor at the instant the machine guns' death jubilation started up by the front of the building, the butcher feast of the presidential guard who with great pleasure and great honor general sir carried out his fierce orders that no one should escape alive from the meeting where treason was being hatched, any who tried to escape through the main door were mowed down with machine-gun bursts, the ones who were hanging out the windows were shot down like birds from a blind, the ones who were able to escape the encirclement and took refuge in nearby houses were degutted with phosphorus grenades, and they finished off the wounded in accordance with the presidential criterion that any survivor is a dangerous enemy as long as he lives, while he remained lying face down on the floor two feet away from General Rodrigo de Aguilar tolerating the hail of glass and plaster that came through the windows with every explosion, murmuring without pause as if he were praying, that's it, old friend, that's it, the trouble's over, from now on I'm going to rule alone with no dogs to bark at me, tomorrow we'll have to see what good has come out of this mother fucking mess and what hasn't and if we don't have anything to sit on in the meantime we'll get six leather stools of the cheapest sort, some straw mats and put them here and there to cover up the holes, we'll buy a few more odds and ends, and that's it, no plates, no spoons, no nothing, I'll bring it all from the barracks, because I'm not going to have any military men or officers around, God damn it, all they're good for is to waste more milk and when there's trouble, as we've seen, they spit on the hand that feeds them, I'll only keep the presidential guard who are straight shooters and brave fellows and I'm not going to name any cabinet, God damn it, just a good minister of health which is the only thing anyone really needs in life, and maybe another one with a good hand for what has to be put in writing, and that way we can rent out the ministries and barracks and save the money for help, because what's needed here isn't people but money, we'll get two good maids, one for cleaning and cooking and the other to wash and iron, and I'll take care of the cows and the birds myself when we get some, and no more of jumping whores in the toilets or lepers in the rosebushes or doctors of philosophy who know everything or wise politicians who see everything, because after all this is a presidential palace and not a nigger whorehouse as Patricio Aragonés said the gringos said, and I'm more than enough all alone to keep on ruling until the comet comes by again, and not just once but ten times, because the way I am I don't intend to die again, God damn it, let other people die, he said, talking without any pauses to think, as if he were reciting by heart, because he had known ever since the war that thinking aloud was driving off the fear of the dynamite charges that were shaking the building, making plans for tomorrow in the morning and for the coming century at dusk until the last coup de grace rang out in the street and General Rodrigo de Aguilar crawled over to the window and gave the order to get the garbage wagons and take away the dead bodies and he left the room saying have a good night general, the same for you old friend, he answered, thank you very much, lying face down on the funereal marble of the cabinet room, and then he folded his right arm to serve as a pillow and fell asleep at once, more alone than ever, lulled by the sound of the trail of yellow leaves of his autumn of pain which had begun forever that night with the smoking bodies and the puddles of red moons of the massacre. He did not have to take any of the predicted measures because the army broke up on its own, the troops scattered, the few officers who resisted until the last moments in the garrisons in the city and in another six in the countryside were wiped out by the presidential guards with the help of civilian volunteers, the surviving ministers fled into exile at dawn and only the two most faithful remained, one who was also his private physician and the other who had the best handwriting in the country, and he did not have to kowtow to any foreign power because the government coffers were overflowing with wedding rings held as surety by instant partisans, nor did he have to buy any mats or leather stools of the cheapest sort to repair the ravages of defenestration, because even before the pacification of the country was over the audience room was restored and more sumptuous than ever, and there were birdcages everywhere, chattering macaws, royal lory parrots who sang in the cornices for Spain and not for Portugal, discreet and serviceable women who kept the building as neat and clean as a battleship, and in through the windows came the music of glory, the same Roman candles of excitement, the same bells of jubilation that had begun celebrating his death and went on celebrating his immortality, and there was a great permanent rally on the main square with shouts of eternal support and large signs saying God Save the Magnificent who arose from the dead on the third day, an endless celebration that he did not have to prolong with any secret maneuvers as he had done at other times, because affairs of state took care of themselves without any help, the nation went along, he alone was the government, and no one bothered the aims of his will whether by word or deed, because he was so alone in his glory that he no longer had any enemies left, and he was so thankful for his comrade of a lifetime Rodrigo de Aguilar that he did not get nervous again over the expense of the milk but ordered the private soldiers who had distinguished themselves by their ferocity and sense of duty to form in the courtyard, and pointing to them according to the impulses of his inspiration he promoted them to the highest ranks knowing that he was restoring the armed forces who were going to spit in the hand that fed them, you to captain, you to major, you to colonel, what am I saying, to general, and all the rest to lieutenant, what the hell old friend, here's your army, and he was so moved by those who had been grieved by his death that he had them fetch the old man with the masonic salute and the gentleman in mourning who had kissed his ring and he decorated them with the medal of peace, he had them bring in the fishwife and he gave her what she said she needed most which was a house with a lot of rooms where she could live with her fourteen children, he had them bring in the schoolgirl who had laid a flower on the corpse and granted her what I most want in this world which was to get married to a man of the sea, but in spite of those acts of relief his confused heart did not have a moment of rest until in the courtyard of the San Jerónimo barracks he saw bound and spat upon the assault groups who had sacked the presidential palace, he recognized them one by one with the remorseless memory of rancor and he went about separating them into different groups according to the intensity of the offense, you here, the one who led the assault, you over there, the ones who had thrown the inconsolable fishwife to the floor, you here, the ones who had taken the corpse out of the coffin and dragged it down the stairs and through the mire, and all the rest on this side, you bastards, although he was really not interested in the punishment but in proving to himself that the profanation of the body and the attack on the building had not been a spontaneous and popular act but an infamous mercenary deal, so he took charge of the interrogation of the prisoners physically present and doing the talking himself to get them to tell him willingly the illusory truth that his heart needed, but he could not manage it, he had them hung from a horizontal beam like parrots tied hand and foot with their heads down for hours on end, but he could not manage it, he had one thrown into the moat of the courtyard and the others saw him quartered and devoured by the crocodiles, but he could not manage it, he chose one out of the main group and had him skinned alive in the presence of all and they saw his flesh tender and yellow like a newborn placenta and they felt the soaking of the warm blood broth of the body that had been laid bare as it went through its throes thrashing about on the courtyard stones, and then they confessed what he wanted that they had been paid four hundred gold pesos to drag the corpse to the dung heap in the marketplace, that they didn't want to do it for love nor money because they had nothing against him, all the less so since he was dead, but that at a secret meeting where they even saw two generals from the high command they had all been frightened with every manner of threat and that was why we did it general sir, word of honor, and then he exhaled a great mouthful of relief, ordered them to be fed, that they be allowed to rest that night and in the morning they would be thrown to the crocodiles, poor deceived boys, he sighed and went back to the presidential palace with his heart free of the hair shirt of doubt, murmuring you all saw it, God damn it, you all saw it, these people love me. Resolved to dissipate even the dregs of the uneasiness that Patricio Aragonés had sown in his heart, he decided that those acts of torture would be the last of his regime, the crocodiles were killed, the torture chambers where it was possible to crumble every bone in the body one by one without killing were dismantled, he proclaimed a general amnesty, he looked to the future with the magical idea that came to him that the trouble with this country is that the people have too much time to think on their hands, and looking for a way to keep them busy he restored the March poetry festival and the annual

contest for the election of a beauty queen, he built the largest
baseball stadium in the Caribbean and imparted to our team the
motto of victory or death, and he ordered a free school established in each province to teach sweeping where the pupils fanat-
icized by the presidential stimulus went on to sweep the streets
after having swept their houses and then the nearby highways
and roads so that piles of trash were carried back and forth from
one province to another without anyone's knowing what to do
with it in official processions with the national flag and large
banners saying God Save the All Pure who watches over the
cleanliness of the nation, while he dragged his slow feet of a
meditative beast about in search of new formulas to keep the
civilian population busy, opening a way among the lepers and
blind men and cripples who begged the salt of health from his
hands, baptizing with his name at the font in the courtyard the
children of his godchildren among persistent adulators who proclaimed him the one and only because now he could not count
on the resources of any look-alike and he had to make himself
double in a marketplace of a palace where every day cages and
more cages of rare birds arrived ever since the secret was let
out that his mother Bendición Alvarado followed the trade of
birdwoman, and even though some sent them out of adulation
and others sent them as a joke after a short time there was no
room to hang any more cages, and he tried to attend to so many
public matters at the same time that among the crowds in the
courtyards and the offices it was impossible to tell who were the
servants and who were the ones served, and they knocked down
so many walls to make more room and opened so many windows for a view of the sea that the simple act of going from one
room to another was like crossing the deck of a sailboat adrift
in a crosswind autumn. They were the March trade winds which
had always come in through the windows of the building, but

now they said they were the winds of peace general sir, it was
the same buzzing in the eardrums that he had had for many
years, but even his physician told him that it was the buzz of
peace general sir, because ever since they had found him dead
the first time all things on heaven and earth had changed into
things of peace general sir, and he believed it, and he believed it
so much that in December he went back to going up to the
house on the reef to seek solace in the misfortune of the brotherhood of nostalgic former dictators who would interrupt the
game of dominoes to tell him that he was for example the double six and let's say that the doctrinaire conservatives were double three, only I wasn't aware of the clandestine alliance between
Masons and priests, who in hell would have thought of it, without worrying about the soup that was jelling in the plate while
one of them explained that for example this sugar bowl was the
presidential palace, here, and the only cannon the enemy had
left had a range of four hundred yards with the wind in its favor,
here, so if you people see me in this state it's only because of
nineteen inches of bad luck, that is to say, and even those most
encrusted by the barnacles of exile wasted their hopes scanning
the horizon and spotting ships from their homelands, they could
recognize them from the color of their smoke, from the rust on
their foghorns, they would go down to the harbor in the drizzle
of early dawn in search of the newspapers the crewmen had used
to wrap up the lunch they took ashore, they found them in the
garbage cans and read them up and down and left to right down
to the last lines to predict the future of their countries from the
news of who had died, who had got married, who had invited
whom and whom they had not invited to a birthday party, deci-
phering their destiny according to the direction of a providential
storm cloud that was going to roar down on their country in an
apocalyptic tempest that would overflow the rivers which would

burst the dams that would devastate the fields and spread misery and plague in the cities, and they will come here to beg me to save them from disaster and anarchy, you'll see, but while they waited for the great hour they had to call aside the youngest exile and ask him to do them the favor of threading their needles to patch these pants that I don't want to throw away for sentimental reasons, they washed their clothes in secret, they honed the razor blades that the new arrivals had used, they would shut themselves up in their rooms to eat so that the others would not see that they were living off leftovers, so that they would not see the shame of pants stained by senile incontinence, and on some unexpected Thursday we would use pins to fasten medals on the last shirt of one of them, wrap his body in his flag, sing his national anthem, and send him off to govern the forgotten people at the base of the sea cliffs with no other ballast than that of his own eroded heart and without leaving any more gap in the world than an easy chair on the terrace without horizons where we would sit down to cast lots for the dead man's possessions, if there were any left general, just imagine this life as civilians after so much glory. On another distant December when the house was inaugurated, he had seen from that terrace the line of the hallucinated isles of the Antilles which someone pointed out to him in the showcase of the sea, he had seen the perfumed volcano of Martinique, over there general, he had seen the tuberculosis hospital, the gigantic black man with a lace blouse selling bouquets of gardenias to governors' wives on the church steps, he had seen the infernal market of Paramaribo, there general, the crabs that came out of the sea and up through the toilets, climbing up onto the tables of ice cream parlors, the diamonds embedded in the teeth of black grandmothers who sold heads of Indians and ginger roots sitting on their safe buttocks under the drenching rain, he had seen the solid gold cows on Tanaguarena beach general, the blind visionary of La Guayra who charged two reals to scare off the blandishments of death with a one-string violin, he had seen Trinidad's burning August, automobiles going the wrong way, the green Hindus who shat in the middle of the street in front of their shops with genuine silkworm shirts and mandarins carved from the whole tusk of an elephant, he had seen Haiti's nightmare, its blue dogs, the oxcart that collected the dead off the streets at dawn, he had seen the rebirth of Dutch tulips in the gasoline drums of Curaçao, the windmill houses with roofs built for snow, the mysterious ocean liner that passed through the center of the city among the hotel kitchens, he had seen the stone enclosure of Cartagena de Indias, its bay closed off by a chain, the light lingering on the balconies, the filthy horses of the hacks who still yawned for the viceroys' fodder, its smell of shit general sir, how marvelous, tell me, isn't the world large, and it was, really, and not just large but insidious, because if he went up to the house on the reefs in December it was not to pass the time with those refugees whom he detested as much as his own image in the mirror of misfortune but to be there at the moment of miracles when the December light came out, mother—true and he could see once more the whole universe of the Antilles from Barbados to Veracruz, and then he would forget who had the double-three piece and go to the overlook to contemplate the line of islands as lunatic as sleeping crocodiles in the cistern of the sea, and contemplating the islands he evoked again and relived that historic October Friday when he left his room at dawn and discovered that everybody in the presidential palace was wearing a red biretta, that the new concubines were sweeping the parlors and changing the water in the cages wearing red birettas, that the milkers in the stables, the sentries in their boxes, the cripples on the stairs and the lepers in the rose beds were going about with the red birettas of a carnival Sunday, so he began to look into what had happened to the world while he was sleeping for the people in his house and the inhabitants of the city to be going around wearing red birettas and dragging a string of jingle bells everywhere, and finally he found someone to tell him the truth general sir, that some strangers had arrived who gabbled in funny old talk because they made the word for sea feminine and not masculine, they called macaws poll parrots, canoes rafts, harpoons javelins, and when they saw us going out to greet them and swim around their ships they climbed up onto the yardarms and shouted to each other look there how well-formed, of beauteous body and fine face, and thick-haired and almost like horsehair silk, and when they saw that we were painted so as not to get sunburned they got all excited like wet little parrots and shouted look there how they daub themselves gray, and they are the hue of canary birds, not white nor yet black, and what there be of them, and we didn't understand why the hell they were making so much fun of us general sir since we were just as normal as the day our mothers bore us and on the other hand they were decked out like the jack of clubs in all that heat, which they made feminine the way Dutch smugglers do, and they wore their hair like women even though they were all men and they shouted that they didn't understand us in Christian tongue when they were the ones who couldn't understand what we were shouting, and then they came toward us in the canoes which they called rafts, as we said before, and they were amazed that our harpoons had a shad bone for a tip which they called a fishy tooth, and we traded everything we had for these red birettas and these strings of glass beads that we hung around our necks to please them, and also for these brass bells that can't be worth more than a penny and for chamber pots and eyeglasses and other goods from Flanders, of the cheapest sort general sir, and since we saw

rumors of his death seemed, he would appear even more alive and authoritarian at the least expected moment to impose other unforeseen directions to our destiny. It would have been easier for a person to let himself be convinced by the immediate indications of the ring with the presidential seal or the supernatural size of his feet of an implacable walker or the strange evidence of the herniated testicle which the vultures had not dared peck, but there was always someone who had memories of other similar indications in the case of other less important dead men in the past. Nor did the meticulous scrutiny of the house bring forth any valid element to establish his identity. In the bedroom of Bendición Alvarado, about whom we only remembered the tale of her canonization by decree, we found broken-down birdcages with little bird bones changed to stone by the years, we saw a wicker easy chair nibbled by the cows, we saw watercolor sets and glasses with paintbrushes of the kind used by birdwomen of the plains so they could sell faded birds by passing them off as orioles, we saw a tub with a balm bush that had kept on growing in neglect and its branches had climbed up the wall and peeped out through the eyes of the portraits and had gone out through the window and ended up getting all entangled with the wild bushes in the rear courtyards, but we couldn't find the most insignificant trace of his ever having been in that room. In the bridal bedroom of Leticia Nazareno, of whom we had a clearer image, not just because she had reigned in a more recent period but also because of the éclat of her public acts, we saw a bed good for the outrages of love with the embroidered canopy converted into a nesting place for hens, in the closets we saw what the moths had left of blue-fox stoles, the wire framework of hoopskirts, the glacial powder of the petticoats, the Brussels lace bodices, the men's high-cut shoes that she wore in the house and the velvet high-heeled pumps with straps that she wore at receptions, the full-length shroud with felt violets and taffeta ribbons from her gala funeral as first lady and the homespun novice's habit like the hide of a gray sheep in which she had been kidnapped from Jamaica inside a crate of party crystal to be placed upon her throne as wife of a hidden president, but we didn't find any vestige in that room either, nothing which would allow us to establish at least whether that kidnapping by corsairs had been inspired by love. In the presidential bedroom, which was the part of the house where he spent the greater part of his last years, we found only an unused barracks bed, a portable latrine of the kind that antiquarians removed from the mansions abandoned by the marines, an iron coffer with his ninety-two medals, and a denim suit just like the one the corpse had on, perforated by six large-caliber bullets that had left singe damage as they entered through the back and came out through the chest, which made us think there was truth to the legend going around that a bullet shot into his back would go right through without harming him, and if shot from the front it would rebound off his body back at the attacker, and that he was only vulnerable to a coup de grace fired by someone who loved him so much that he would die for him. Both uniforms were too small for the corpse, but it was not for that reason that we put aside the possibility that they were his, because it had also been said at one time that he had kept on growing until the age of one hundred and at one hundred fifty he grew a third set of teeth, although in truth the vulture-ravaged body was no larger than that of any average man of our day and it had some healthy teeth, small and stubby that looked like milk teeth, the skin was the color of gall speckled with liver spots without a single scar and empty pouches all over as if he had been quite fat in some other day, there were only empty sockets for the eyes that had been taciturn, and the only thing that seemed out of proportion, except for the herniated testicle, was the pair of enormous feet, square and flat with the calluses and twisted talons of a hawk. Contrary to what his clothing showed, the descriptions made by his historians made him very big and official schoolboy texts referred to him as a patriarch of huge size who never left his house because he could not fit through the doors, who loved children and swallows, who knew the language of certain animals, who had the virtue of being able to anticipate the designs of nature, who could guess a person's thoughts by one look in the eyes, and who had the secret of a salt with the virtue of curing lepers' sores and making cripples walk. Although all trace of his origins had disappeared from the texts, it was thought that he was a man of the upland plains because of his immense appetite for power, the nature of his government, his mournful bearing, the inconceivable evil of a heart which had sold the sea to a foreign power and condemned us to live facing this limitless plain of harsh lunar dust where the bottomless sunsets pain us in our souls. It was calculated that in the course of his life he must have sired five thousand children, all seven-monthers, by the countless number of loveless beloveds he had who succeeded each other in his seraglio until the moment he was ready to enjoy them, but none bore his name or surname, except for the one he had by Leticia Nazareno, who was appointed a major general with jurisdiction and command at the moment of his birth, for he considered no one the son of anyone except his mother, and only her. That certainty seemed valid even for him, as he knew that he was a man without a father like the most illustrious despots of history, that the only relative known to him and perhaps the only one he had was his mother of my heart Bendición Alvarado to whom the school texts attributed the miracle of having conceived him without recourse to any male and of having received in a dream the hermetical keys to his messianic destiny, and whom he proclaimed matriarch of the land by decree with the simple argument that there is no mother but one, mine, a strange woman of uncertain origins whose simpleness of soul had been the scandal of the fanatics of presidential dignity during the beginnings of the regime, because they could not admit that the mother of the chief of state would hang a pouch of camphor around her neck to ward off all contagion and tried to jab the caviar with her fork and staggered about in her patent leather pumps, nor could they accept the fact that she kept a beehive on the terrace of the music room, or bred turkeys and watercolor-painted birds in public offices or put the sheets out to dry on the balcony from which speeches were made, nor could they bear the fact that at a diplomatic party she had said I'm tired of begging God to overthrow my son, because all this business of living in the presidential palace is like having the lights on all the time, sir, and she had said it with the same naturalness with which on one national holiday she had made her way through the guard of honor with a basket of empty bottles and reached the presidential limousine that was leading the parade of celebration in an uproar of ovations and martial music and storms of flowers and she shoved the basket through the window and shouted to her son that since you'll be passing right by take advantage and return these bottles to the store on the corner, poor mother. That lack of a sense of history would have its night of splendor at the formal banquet with which we celebrate the landing of the marines under the command of Admiral Higgingson when Bendición Alvarado saw her son in dress uniform with his gold medals and velvet gloves which he continued to wear for the rest of his life and she could not repress her impulse of maternal pride and exclaimed aloud in front of the whole diplomatic corps that if I'd known my son was going to be president of the republic I'd have sent him to school, yes sir, how shameful it must have been after that when they exiled her to the suburban mansion, an eleven-room palace that he had won on a good night of dice when the leaders of the federalist war had used the gaming tables to divide up the splendid residential district of the fugitive conservatives, except that Bendición Alvarado disdained the imperial décor which makes me feel I'm the wife of the Pope himself and she preferred the servants' quarters next to the six barefoot maids who had been assigned to her, she set up her sewing machine and her cages of painted-up birds in a forgotten back room where the heat never reached and it was easier to drive off the six o'clock mosquitoes, she would sit down to sew across from the lazy light of the main courtyard and the medicinal breeze of the tamarinds while the hens wandered through the parlors and the soldiers of the guard lay in wait for the housemaids in the empty bedrooms, she would sit down to paint orioles and lament with the servants over the misfortunes of my poor son whom the marines had set up in the presidential palace so far from his mother, lord, without a loving wife who could take care of him if he woke up with an ache in the middle of the night, and all involved with that job of president of the republic for a measly salary of three hundred pesos a month, poor boy. She knew quite well what she was talking about because he visited her every day while the city sloshed in the mire of siesta time, he would bring her the candied fruit she liked so much and he took advantage of the occasion to unwind with her about his bitter position as the marines' pratboy, he told her how he had to sneak out the sugar oranges and syrup figs in napkins because the occupation authorities had accountants who in their books kept track even of lunch leftovers, he lamented that the other day the captain of the battleship came to the presidential palace with some kind of land astronomers who took measurements of everything and didn't even say hello but put their tape measure around my head while they made their calculations in English and shouted at me through the interpreter to get out of here and he got out, for him to get out of the light, and he got out, go somewhere where you won't be in the way, God damn it, and he didn't know where to go without getting in the way because there were measurers measuring everything down to the size of the light from the balconies, but that wasn't the worst, mother, they threw out the last two skinny concubines he had left because the admiral had said they weren't worthy of a president, and he was really in such want of women that on some afternoons he would pretend that he was leaving the suburban mansion but his mother heard him chasing after the maids in the shadows of the bedrooms, and her sorrow was such that she roused up the birds in their cages so that no one would find out about her son's troubles, she forced them to sing so that neighbors would not hear the sounds of the attack, the shame of the struggle, the repressed threats of quiet down general or I'll tell your mama, and she would ruin the siesta of the troupials and make them burst with song so that no one would hear his heartless panting of an urgent mate, his misfortune of a lover with all his clothes on, his doggish whine, his solitary tears that came on like dusk, as if rotting with pity amidst the cackling of the hens in the bedrooms aroused by that emergency love-making in the liquid glass air and the godforsaken August of three in the afternoon, my poor son. That state of scarcity was to last until the occupation forces left the country frightened off by an epidemic when they still needed so many years to fulfill the terms of the landing, they broke down the officers' residences into numbered pieces and packed them up in wooden crates, they dug up the blue lawns in one piece and carried them off all rolled up like carpets, they wrapped up the rubber cisterns with the sterile water sent

from their country so that they would not be eaten up inside by
the water worms of our streams, they took their white hospitals
apart, dynamited their barracks so that no one would know how
they were constructed, at the dock they left the old battleship
from the landing and on the deck of which the ghost of a lost
admiral strolled in the squall of June nights, but before bearing
off that portable paradise of war in their flying trains they decorated him with the medal of the good neighbor, rendered him
the honors of chief of state, and said to him aloud so that everybody could hear we leave you now with your nigger whorehouse so let's see how you shape things up without us, but they
left, mother, God damn it, they've gone, and for the first time
since his head-down days of occupation ox he went up the stairs
giving orders in a loud voice and in person through a tumult of
requests to reestablish cockfights, and he so ordered, agreed,
that kite-flying be allowed again, and many other diversions that
had been prohibited by the marines, and he so ordered, agreed,
so convinced of being master of all his power that he inverted
the colors of the flag and replaced the Phrygian cap on the shield
with the invader's defeated dragon, because after all we're our
own dogs now, mother, long live the plague. All her life Bendición Alvarado would remember those surprises of power and
the other more ancient and bitter ones of poverty, but she never
brought them back with so much grief as after the death farce
when he was wallowing in the fen of prosperity while she went
on lamenting to anyone who wanted to listen to her that it was
no good being the president's mama with nothing else in the
world but this sad sewing machine, she lamented, looking at
him there with his gold-braided hearse, my poor son didn't have
a hole in the ground to fall dead into after all those years of
serving his country, lord, it's not fair, and she did not go on
complaining out of habit or disillusionment but because he no

longer made her a participant in his shake-ups nor did he hurry over as before to share the best secrets of power with her, and he had changed so much since the times of the marines that to Bendición Alvarado he seemed to be older than she, to have left her behind in time, she heard him stumble over words, his concept of reality became entangled, sometimes he drooled, and she was struck with the compassion that was not a mother's but a daughter's when she saw him arrive at the suburban mansion loaded down with packages and desperate to open them all at the same time, he cut the twine with his teeth, broke his fingernails on the hoops before she could get the scissors from her sewing basket, dug everything out from the underbrush of debris with flailing hands as he drowned in his high-flying anxiety, look at all this wonderful stuff, mother, he said, a live mermaid in a fishbowl, a lifesize wind-up angel who flew about the room striking the hour with its bell, a gigantic shell in which the listener didn't hear the sound of the waves and the sea wind but the strains of the national anthem, what fancy stuff, mother, now you can see how nice it is not to be poor, he said, but she couldn't feed his enthusiasm and began chewing on the brushes used to paint orioles so her son would not notice that her heart was crumbling with pity thinking back on a past that no one knew as well as she, remembering how hard it had been for him to stay in the chair he was sitting in, but not these days, lord, not these easy times when power was a tangible and unique matter, a little glass ball in the palm of the hand, as he said, but when he was a fugitive shad swimming around without god or law in a neighborhood palace pursued by the voracious swarm of the surviving leaders of the federalist war who had helped overthrow the general-poet Lautaro Muñoz, an enlightened despot whom God keep in His holy glory with his Suetonius missals in Latin and his forty-two pedigreed horses, and in exchange

for their armed help they had taken over the ranches and livestock of the outlawed former owners and had divided the country up into autonomous provinces with the unanswerable
argument that this is federalism general, this is what we have
shed the blood of our veins for, and they were absolute monarchs in their territories, with their own laws, their personal
patriotic holidays, their paper money which they signed themselves, their dress uniforms with sabers encrusted with precious
stones and hussar jackets with gold frogs and three-cornered
hats with peacock-tail plumes copied from ancient prints of viceroys of the country before them, and they were wild and sentimental, lord, they would come into the presidential palace
through the main door, with no one's permission since the
nation belongs to all general, that's why we've sacrificed our
lives for it, they camped out in the ballroom with their respective harems and the farm animals which they demanded as tribute for peace as they went along everywhere so that they would
always have something to eat, they brought along personal
escorts of barbarian mercenaries who instead of boots used rags
to clothe their feet and who could barely express themselves in
Christian tongue but were wise in tricks of dice and ferocious
and skilled in the manipulation of weapons of war, so that the
house of power was like a gypsy encampment, lord, it had the
thick smell of a river at floodtide, the officers of the general staff
had taken the furniture of the republic to their ranches, they
played dominoes gambling away the privileges of government
indifferent to the entreaties of his mother Bendición Alvarado
who did not have a moment's rest trying to sweep up so much
fairground garbage, trying to put just one little bit of order into
that shipwreck, for she was the only one who had made any
attempt to resist the irredeemable debasement of the liberal cru-
sade, only she had tried to drive them out with her broom when

she saw the house perverted by those evil-living reprobates who
fought over the large chairs of the high command with playing-
card altercations, she watched them do sodomite business
behind the piano, she watched them shit in the alabaster amphoras even though she told them not to, lord, they weren't portable
toilets they were amphoras recovered from the seas of Pantelle-
ria, but they insisted that they were rich men's pisspots, lord, it
was humanly impossible to stop General Adriano Guzmán from
attending the diplomatic party celebrating the tenth year of my
rise to power, although no one could have imagined what
awaited us when he appeared in the ballroom wearing an austere
linen uniform chosen especially for the occasion, he came without weapons, just as he had promised me on his word as a soldier, with his escort of escaped French prisoners in civilian
clothes and loaded down with goodies from Cayenne which
General Adriano Guzmán distribute one by one to the wives of
ambassadors and ministers after asking permission from their
husbands with a bow, for that was what his mercenaries had
told him was considered proper in Versailles and so he went
through it with the rare genius of a gentleman, and then he sat
in a corner of the ballroom with his attention on the dance and
nodding his head in approval, very good, he said, these stuck-
ups from Europeland dance good, he said, to each his own, he
said, so forgotten in his easy chair that only I noticed that one
of his aides was filling his glass with champagne after each sip,
and as the hours passed he was becoming more tense and
flushed than he normally was, he opened a button on his sweat-
soaked tunic every time the pressure of a repressed belch came
all the way up to eye level, he was moaning with drowsiness,
mother, and all of a sudden he got up with difficulty during a
pause in the dancing and finally unbuttoned his tunic completely
and then his fly and he stood there wide open and staling away

on the perfumed décolletages of the ladies of the ambassadors
and ministers with his musty old hose of a buzzard's tool, with
his sour war-drunkard's urine he soaked the muslin laps, the
gold brocade bosoms, the ostrich-feather fans, singing impassively in the midst of the panic I'm the gallant swain who waters
the roses of your bower, oh lovely rose in bloom, he sang on,
with no one daring to control him, not even he, because I knew
I had more power than any one of them but much less than two
of them plotting together, still unaware that he saw the others
just as they were while the others were never able to glimpse
the hidden thoughts of the granite old man whose serenity was
matched only by his smooth-sailing prudence and his immense
disposition for waiting, we saw only his lugubrious eyes, his thin
lips, the chaste maiden's hand which did not even tremble on
the hilt of his saber that noon of horror when they came to him
with the news general sir that General Narciso López high on
green pot and anisette had hauled a cadet of the presidential
guard into a toilet and warmed him up as he saw fit with the
resources of a wild woman and then obliged him put it all into
me, God damn it, that's an order, everything, my love, even
your golden little balls, weeping with pain, weeping with rage,
until he found himself vomiting with humiliation on all fours
with his head stuck in the fetid vapors of the toilet bowl, and
then he lifted the Adonic cadet up into the air and impaled him
with a plainsman's lance onto the springtime tapestry of the
audience room like a butterfly and no one dared take him down
for three days, poor man, because all he did was keep an eye on
his former comrades in arms so that they would not hatch plots
but without getting enmeshed in their lives, convinced that they
themselves would exterminate each other among themselves
before they came to him with the news general sir that members
of General Jesucristo Sánchez's escort had been forced to beat

him to death with chairs when he had an attack of rabies that he got from a cat bite, poor man, he scarcely looked up from his domino game when they whispered in his ear the news general sir that General Lotario Sereno had been drowned when his horse had suddenly died under him as he was fording a river, poor man, he barely blinked when they came to him with the news general sir that General Narciso López had shoved a dynamite stick up his ass and blown his guts out over the shame of his unconquerable pederasty, and he said poor man as if he had had nothing to do with those infamous deaths and he issued the same decree of posthumous honors for all, proclaiming them martyrs who had fallen in acts of service and he had them entombed in the national pantheon with magnificent pomp and all on the same level because a nation without heroes is a house without doors, he said, and when there were only six combat generals left in all the land he invited them to celebrate his birthday with a carousal of comrades in the presidential palace, all of them together, lord, even General Jacinto Algarabía who was the darkest and shrewdest, who prided himself on having a son by his own mother and only drank wood alcohol with gunpowder in it, with no one else in the banquet hall like the good old days general, all without weapons like blood brothers but with the men of their escorts crowded into the next room, all loaded down with magnificent gifts for the only one of us who has been able to understand us all, they said, meaning that he was the only one who had learned how to manage them, the only one who had succeeded in getting out of the bowels of his remote lair on the highland plains the legendary General Saturno Santos, a full-blooded Indian, unsure, who always went around like the whore mother that gave me birth with his foot on the ground general sir because we roughnecks can't breathe unless we feel the earth, he had arrived wrapped in a cape with bright-colored prints of strange animals on it, he came alone, as he always went about, without an escort, preceded by a gloomy aura, with no arms except a cane machete which he refused to take off his belt because it wasn't a weapon of war but one for work, and as a gift he brought me an eagle trained to fight in men's wars, and he brought his harp, mother, that sacred instrument whose notes could conjure up storms and hasten the cycles of harvest time and which General Saturno Santos plucked with a skill from his heart that awoke in all of us the nostalgia for the nights of horror of the war, mother, it aroused in us the dog-mange smell of war, it spun around in our souls the war song of the golden boat that will lead us on, they sang it in a chorus with all their heart, mother, I sent myself back from the bridge bathed in tears, they sang, while they ate a turkey stuffed with plums and half a suckling pig and each one drank from his personal bottle, each one his own alcohol, all except him and General Saturno Santos who had never tasted a drop of liquor in all their lives, nor smoked, nor eaten more than what was indispensable for life, in my honor they sang in a chorus the serenade King David sang, with tears they wailed out all the birthday songs that had been sung before Consul Hanemann came to us with the novelty general sir of that phonograph with a horn speaker and its cylinder of happy birthday in English, they sang half-asleep, half-dead from drink, not worrying any more about the taciturn old man who at the stroke of twelve took down the lamp and went to inspect the house before retiring in accordance with his barracks-bred custom and he saw for the last time as he returned on his way through the banquet hall the six generals piled together on the floor, he saw them in embrace, inert and placid, under the protection of the five escort groups who kept watch among themselves, because even in sleep and in embrace they were afraid of each other almost as much as each one of

them was afraid of him and as he was afraid of two of them in
cahoots, and he put the lamp back on the mantel and closed the
three locks, the three bolts, the three bars of his bedroom, and
lay down on the floor face down, his right arm serving as a
pillow at the instant that the foundations of the building shook
with the compact explosion of all the escorts' weapons going off
at the same time, one single time, by God, with no intermediate
sound, no moan, and again, by God, and that was that, the mess
was over, all that was left was a lingering smell of gunpowder in
the silence of the world, only he remained safe forever from the
anxieties of power as in the first mallow-soft rays of the new day
he saw the orderlies on duty sloshing through the swamp of
blood in the banquet hall, he saw his mother Bendición Alvarado seized by a dizzy spell of horror as she discovered that the
walls oozed blood no matter how hard she scrubbed them with
lye and ash, lord, that the rugs kept on giving off blood no
matter how much she wrung them out, and all the more blood
poured in torrents through corridors and offices the more they
worked desperately to wash it out in order to hide the extent of
the massacre of the last heirs of our war who according to the
official statement had been assassinated by their own maddened
escorts and their bodies wrapped in the national flag filled the
pantheon of patriots with a funeral worthy of a bishop, for not
one single man of the escort had escaped alive from the bloody
roundup, not one general, except General Saturno Santos who
was armored by his strings of scapulars and who knew Indian
secrets of how to change his form at will, curse him, he could
turn into an armadillo or a pond general, he could become thunder, and he knew it was true because his most astute trackers
had lost the trail ever since last Christmas, the best-trained jaguar hounds looked for him in the opposite direction, he had
seen him in the flesh in the king of spades in his sibyls' cards,

and he was alive, sleeping by day and traveling by night off the beaten track on land and water, but he kept leaving a trail of prayers that confused his pursuers' judgment and tired out the will of his enemies, but he never gave up the search for one instant day and night for years and years until many years later when he saw through the window of the presidential train a crowd of men and women with their children and animals and cooking utensils as he had seen so many times behind the troops in wartime, he saw them parading in the rain carrying their sick in hammocks strung to poles behind a very pale man in a burlap tunic who says he's a divine messenger general sir, and he slapped his forehead and said to himself there he is, God damn it, and there was General Saturno Santos begging off the charity of the pilgrims with the charms of his unstrung harp, he was miserable and gloomy, with a beat-up felt hat and a poncho in tatters, but even in that pitiful state he was not as easy to kill as he thought for he had decapitated three of his best men with his machete, he had stood up to the fiercest of them with such valor and ability that he ordered the train to stop opposite the cemetery on the plain where the messenger was preaching, and everybody drew apart in a stampede when the men of the presidential guard jumped out of the coach painted with the colors of the flag with their weapons at the ready, no one remained in sight except General Saturno Santos beside his mythical harp with his hand tight on the hilt of his machete, and he seemed fascinated by the sight of the mortal enemy who appeared on the platform of the coach in his denim suit with no insignia, without weapons, older and more remote as if it had been a hundred years since we saw each other general, he looked tired and lonely to me, his skin yellow from liver trouble and his eyes tending toward teariness, but he had the pale glow of a person who was not only master of his power but also the power won from his dead, so I made ready to die without resisting because it seemed useless to him to go against an old man who had come from so far off with no more motives or merits than his barbarous appetite for command, but he showed him the manta-ray palm of his hand and said God bless you, stud, the country deserves you, because it has always known that against an invincible man there is no weapon but friendship, and General Saturno Santos kissed the ground he had trod and asked him the favor of letting me serve you in any way you command general sir while I have the ability in these hands to make my machete sing, and he accepted, agreed, he made him his back-up man but only on the condition that you never get behind me, he made him his accomplice in dominoes and between the two of them they gave a four-handed skinning to many despots in misfortune, he would have him get barefoot into the presidential coach and take him to diplomatic receptions with that jaguar breath that aroused dogs and made ambassadors' wives dizzy, he had him sleep across the doorsill of his bedroom so as to relieve himself of the fear of sleeping when life became so harsh that he trembled at the idea of finding himself alone among the people of his dreams, he kept him close to his confidence at a distance of ten hands for many years until uric acid squeezed off his skill of making his machete sing and he asked the favor that you kill me yourself general sir so as not to leave someone else the pleasure of killing me when he has no right to, but he ordered him off to die on a good retirement pension and with a medal of gratitude on the byways of the plains where he had been born and he could not repress his tears when General Saturno Santos put aside his shame to tell him choking and weeping so you see general the time comes for the roughest of us studs to turn into fairies, what a damned thing. So no one understood better than Bendición Alvarado the boyish excitement with which he got rid of bad times and the lack of sense with which he squandered the earnings of power in order to have as an old man what he had lacked as a child, but it made her angry when they abused his premature innocence by selling him those gringo gewgaws which weren't all that cheap and didn't require as much ingenuity as the faked birds of which she had never managed to sell more than four, it's fine for you to enjoy it, she said, but think about the future, I don't want to see you begging hat in hand at the door of some church if tomorrow or later God forbid they take away the chair you're sitting in, if you only knew how to sing at least, or were an archbishop or a navigator, but you're only a general, so you're not good for anything except to command, she advised him to bury in a safe place the money you have left over from the government, where no one else could find it, just in case you have to leave on the run like those poor presidents of nowhere grazing on oblivion in the house on the reefs and begging a hello from ships, look at yourself in that mirror, she told him, but he didn't pay any attention to her except that he would ease her disconsolation with the magic formula of calm down mother, the people love me. Bendición Alvarado was to live for many years lamenting poverty, fighting with the maids over bills from the market and even skipping lunch in order to economize, and no one dared reveal to her that she was one of the richest women in the land, that everything he accumulated from government business he put in her name, that she was not only the owner of immeasurable land and uncountable livestock but also the local streetcars, the mails, the telegraph service, and the waters of the nation, so that every boat that plied the tributaries of the Amazon or the territorial seas had to pay her a rental fee which she never knew about down to the day she died, just as she was ignorant for so many years of the fact that her son was not so badly off as she supposed when he came to the suburban man-

sion and sank into the wonders of his old-age toys, for in addition to the personal tax that he collected for every head of cattle
for the benefit of the country, in addition to payments for his
favors and gifts which his partisans sent him to help their interests, he had conceived and had been putting to use for a long
time an infallible system for beating the lottery. Those were the
times following his false death, the noisy times, lord, and they
weren't called that as many of us thought because of the underground boom that was felt all over the nation one Saint Heraclius Martyr night and for which there was never any sure
explanation, but because of the constant noise of the projects
begun that were proclaimed at their start as the greatest in the
world and yet were never completed, a peaceful period during
which he summoned councils of government while he took his
siesta in the suburban mansion, he would lie in the hammock
fanning himself with his hat under the sweet tamarind branches,
with his eyes closed he would listen to the doctors with free-
flowing words and waxed mustaches who sat around the hammock discussing things, pale from the heat inside their rough
frock coats and celluloid collars, the civilian ministers he
detested so much but whom he had appointed once more for
convenience and whom he listened to as they argued over matters of state amidst the scandal of roosters chasing after the hens
in the courtyard, and the continuous buzz of the cicadas and the
insomnia-stricken gramophone in the neighborhood that was
singing the song Susana come Susana, they suddenly fell silent,
quiet, the general has fallen asleep, but he would roar without
opening his eyes, without stopping his snoring. I'm not asleep
you God-damned fools, go on, they went on, until he would
feel his way out of the siesta cobwebs and declare that in all this
damned-fool talk the only one who makes any sense is my old
friend the minister of health, by God, the mess was over, the

whole mess was coming to an end, he chatted with his personal
aides walking them back and forth while he ate with plate in one
hand and spoon in the other, he said goodbye to them at the
steps with an indifference of do what you think best because in
the end I'm the one who gives the orders, God damn it, this
farting around and asking whether they wanted to or didn't
want to was over, God damn it, he cut inaugural ribbons, he
showed himself large as life in public taking on the risks of
power as he had never done in more peaceful times, what the
hell, he played endless games of dominoes with my lifetime
friend General Rodrigo de Aguilar and my old friend the minister of health who were the only ones who had enough of his
confidence to ask him to free a prisoner or pardon someone
condemned to death, and the only ones who dared ask him to
receive in a special audience the beauty queen of the poor, an
incredible creature from that miserable wallow we called the
dogfight district because all the dogs in the neighborhood had
been fighting for many years without a moment's truce, a lethal
redoubt where national guard patrols did not enter because they
would be stripped naked and cars were broken up into their
smallest parts with a flick of the hand, where poor stray donkeys
would enter by one end of the street and come out the other in
a bag of bones, they roasted the sons of the rich general sir,
they sold them in the market turned into sausages, just imagine,
because Manuela Sánchez of my evil luck had been born there
and lived there, a dungheap marigold whose remarkable beauty
was the astonishment of the nation general sir, and he felt so
intrigued by the revelation that if all this is as true as you people
say I'll not only receive her in a special audience but I'll dance
the first waltz with her, by God, have them write it up in the
newspapers, he ordered, this kind of crap makes a big hit with
the poor. Yet, the night after the audience, while they were play-

ing dominoes, he commented with a certain bitterness to General Rodrigo de Aguilar that the queen of the poor wasn't even worth dancing with, that she was as common as so many other slum Manuela Sánchezes with her nymph's dress of muslin petticoats and the gilt crown with artificial jewels and a rose in her hand under the watchful eye of a mother who looked after her as if she were made of gold, so he gave her everything she wanted which was only electricity and running water for the dogfight district, but he warned that it was the last time I'll ever receive anybody on a begging mission, God damn it, I'm not going to talk to poor people any more, he said, before the game was over, he slammed the door, left, he heard the metal tolling of eight o'clock, he gave the cows in the stables their fodder, he had them bring up the cow chips, he inspected the whole building eating as he walked with his plate in his hand, he was eating stew with beans, white rice, and plantain slices, he counted the sentries from the entranceway to the bedrooms, they were all there and at their posts, fourteen, he saw the rest of his personal guard playing dominoes at the post in the first courtyard, he saw the lepers lying among the rosebushes, the cripples on the stairs, it was nine o'clock, he put his unfinished plate down on a window sill and found himself feeling around in the muddy atmosphere of the sheds among the concubines who were sleeping as many as three to a bed together with their seven-month runts, he mounted a lump that smelled of yesterday's stew and he separated two heads here six legs and three arms there without ever asking who was who or who was the one who finally suckled him without waking up, without dreaming about him, or whose voice it had been that murmured in her sleep from the other bed not to get so excited general you'll frighten the children, he went back inside the house, checked the locks on the twenty-three windows, lighted the piles of cow chips every twenty feet from

the entranceway to the private rooms, caught the smell of the
smoke, remembered an improbable childhood that might have
been his and which he only remembered at that instant when
the smoke started up and which he forgot forever, he went back
turning out the lights in reverse order from the bedrooms to the
vestibule and covering the cages of the sleeping birds whom he
counted before draping them with pieces of cloth, forty-eight,
once more he covered the whole house with a lamp in his hand,
he saw himself in the mirrors one by one as up to fourteen generals walking with the lighted lamp, it was ten o'clock, everything in order, he went back to the sleeping quarters of the
presidential guard, turned out their lights, good night gentlemen, he made a search of the public offices on the ground floor,
the waiting rooms, the toilets, behind the curtains, underneath
the tables, there was no one, he took out the bunch of keys
which he was able to distinguish by touch one by one, he locked
the offices, he went up to the main floor for a room-by-room
search locking the doors, he took the jar of honey from its hiding place behind a picture and had two spoonfuls before retiring, he thought of his mother asleep in the suburban mansion,
Bendición Alvarado in her drowsiness of goodbyes between the
balm and the oregano with the bloodless hand of a birdwoman
oriole painter as a dead mother on her side, have a good night,
mother, he said, a very good night to you son Bendición Alvarado answered him in her sleep in the suburban mansion, in
front of his bedroom he hung the lamp by its handle on a hook
and he left it hanging by the door while he slept with the absolute order that it was never to be put out because it was the light
for him to flee by, it struck eleven, he inspected the house for
the last time, in the dark, in case someone had sneaked in thinking he was asleep, he went alone leaving a trail in the dust made
by the star of his gold spur in the fleeting dawns of green flashes

of the beams from the turns of the beacon, between two instants of light he saw an aimless leper who was walking in his sleep, he cut him off, led him through the shadows without touching him lighting the way with the lights of his vigilance, put him back among the rosebushes, counted the sentries in the darkness again, went back to his bedroom, seeing as he went past the windows a sea that was the same in every window, the Caribbean in April, he contemplated it twenty-three times without stopping and it was still as it always was in April like a gilded fen, he heard twelve o'clock, with the last toll of the cathedral clappers he heard the twist of the thin whistle of his hernia, there was no other sound in the world, he alone was the nation, he lowered the three crossbars, locked the three locks, threw the three bolts in the bedroom, he urinated sitting down on the portable latrine, he urinated two drops, four drops, seven arduous drops, he fell face down on the floor, fell asleep immediately, did not dream, it was a quarter to three when he awoke drenched in sweat, shaken by the certainty that someone had been looking at him while he slept, someone who had had the ability to get in without taking off the crossbars, who's there, he asked, there was no one, he closed his eyes, again he felt he was watched, he opened his eyes to see with fright, and then he saw, God damn it, it was Manuela Sánchez who went across the room without opening the locks because she came and went as was her will by passing through the walls, Manuela Sánchez of my evil hour with her muslin dress and the hot coal of a rose in her hand and the natural smell of licorice of her breathing, tell me this delirium isn't true, he said, tell me it's not you, tell me that this deadly dizziness isn't the licorice stagnation of your breath, but it was she, it was her rose, it was her hot breath which perfumed the air of the bedroom like an obstinate downwind with more dominion and more antiquity than the snorting

of the sea, Manuela Sánchez of my disaster, you who weren't
written on the palm of my hand, or in my coffee grounds, or
even in the death waters of my basins, don't use up my breathing
air, my dreams of sleep, the confines of this room where no
woman had ever entered or was to enter, extinguish that rose,
he moaned, while he felt around for the light switch and found
Manuela Sánchez of my madness instead of the light, God damn
it, why do I have to find you since you haven't lost me, take my
house if you want, the whole country with its dragon, but let
me put the light on, scorpion of my nights, Manuela Sánchez of
my rupture, daughter of a bitch, he shouted, thinking that the
light would free him from the spell, shouting to get her out of
here, get her off my back, throw her off a sea cliff with an anchor
around her neck so that no one will ever suffer the glow of her
rose, he went shrieking along the corridors, sloshing through
the cow flops in the darkness, wondering in confusion what was
going on in the world because it's going on eight and everybody's asleep in this house of scoundrels, get up, you bastards,
he shouted, the lights went on, they played reveille at three
o'clock, it was repeated at the harbor fort, the San Jerónimo
garrison, in barracks all over the country, and there was the
noise of startled arms, of roses that opened when there were still
two hours left until dew time, of sleepwalking concubines who
shook out rugs under the stars and uncovered the cages of the
sleeping birds and replaced the flowers that had spent the night
in the vases with last night's flowers, and there was a troop of
masons who were building emergency walls and they disori-
ented the sunflowers by pasting gilt paper suns on the windowpanes so that it would not be noticed that it was still nighttime
in the sky and it was Sunday the twenty-fifth in the house and it
was April on the sea, and there was a hubbub of Chinese laun-
drymen who threw the last sleepers out of their beds to take

away the sheets, premonitory blind men who announced love love where there was none, perverse civil servants who found hens laying Monday's eggs while yesterday's were still in the file drawers, and there was an uproar of confused crowds and dogfights in the councils of government urgently called together while he opened a way lighted by the sudden day through the persistent adulators who proclaimed him the undoer of dawn, commander of time, and repository of light, until an officer of the high command dared stop him in the vestibule and came to attention with the news general sir that it's only five after two, another voice, five after three in the morning general sir, and he fetched a ferocious clout with the back of his hand and howled with all his aroused chest so that the whole world would hear him, it's eight o'clock, God damn it, eight o'clock, I said, God's order. Bendición Alvarado asked him when she saw him enter the suburban mansion where are you coming from with that face that looks like a tarantula bit you, why are you holding your hand over your heart, she said to him, but he dropped into the wicker chair without answering her, changed the position of his hand, he had forgotten about her again when his mother pointed at him with the brush for painting orioles and asked in surprise whether he really believed in the Sacred Heart of Jesus with those languid eyes and that hand on his breast, and he hid it in confusion, shit mother, he slammed the door, left, kept walking back and forth at the palace with his hands in his pockets so that on their own they would not put themselves where they shouldn't be, he watched the rain through the window, he watched the water slipping across the cookie-paper stars and the silver-plated moons that had been placed on the windowpanes so that it would look like eight at night at three in the afternoon, he saw the soldiers of the guard numb with cold in the court-yard, he saw the sad sea, Manuela Sánchez's rain in your city without her, the terrible empty parlor, the chairs placed upside down on the tables, the irreparable loneliness of the first shadows of another ephemeral Saturday of another night without her, God damn it, if only I could get rid of what had been danced which is what hurts me most, he sighed, he felt ashamed on his state, he reviewed the places on his body where he could put his hand without its being on his heart, he finally put it on the rupture which had been eased by the rain, it was the same, it had the same shape, the same weight, it hurt the same, but it was even more atrocious like having your own living flesh heart in the palm of your hand, and only then did he understand why so many people in other times had said that the heart is the third ball general sir, God damn it, he left the window, he walked back and forth in the reception room with the unsolvable anxiety of a perpetual president with a fishbone driven through his soul, he found himself in the room of the council of ministers listening as always without understanding, without listening, suffering through a soporific report on the fiscal situation, suddenly something happened in the atmosphere, the treasury minister fell silent, the others were looking at him through the chinks of a cuirass cracked by pain, he saw himself defenseless and alone at the end of the walnut table with his face trembling from his pitiful state of a lifetime president with his hand on his chest having been revealed in broad daylight, his life was singed by the glacial hot coals of the tiny goldsmith eyes of my comrade the minister of health who seemed to be examining him inside as he fingered the chain of his small gold vest-pocket watch, careful, someone said, it might be a pang, but he had already put his siren's hand hardened by rage on the walnut table, he got his color back, along with the words he spat out a fatal wave of authority, you people probably hoped it was a pang, you bastards, go on, they went on, but they spoke without hearing

themselves thinking that something serious must have happened
to him if he flew into such a rage, they whispered it, the rumor
went around, they pointed at him, see how depressed he is, he
has to clutch his heart, he's coming apart at the seams, they
murmured, the story went around that he had had the minister
of health called urgently and that the latter had found him with
his right arm laid out like a leg of lamb on the walnut table and
he ordered him to cut it off for me, old friend, humiliated by his
sad condition of a president bathed in tears, but the minister
answered him no, general, I won't carry out that order even if
you have me shot, he told him, it's a matter of justice, general,
I'm not worth as much as your arm. These and many other
versions of his state were becoming more and more intense
while in the stables he measured out the milk for the garrisons
watching Manuela Sánchez's Ash Tuesday rising in the sky, he
had the lepers removed from the rose beds so that they would
not stink up the roses of your rose, he searched out the solitary
places in the building in order to sing without being heard your
first waltz as queen, so you won't forget me, he sang, so you'll
feel you're dying if you forget me, he sang, he plunged into
the mire of the concubines' rooms trying to find relief from his
torment, and for the first time in his long life of a volatile lover
he turned his instincts loose, he lingered over details, he brought
out sighs from the basest of women, time and again, and he
made them laugh with surprise in the shadows doesn't it bother
you general, at your age, but he knew only too well that that
will to resist was a set of tricks he was playing on himself in
order to waste time, that each step in his loneliness, each stumble in his breathing was bringing him remorselessly to the dog
days of the unavoidable two o'clock in the afternoon when he
went to beg for the love of God for the love of Manuela Sánchez
in the palace of your ferocious dungheap kingdom of a dogfight

district, he went in civilian clothes, without an escort, in the
taxi which slipped away backfiring the smell of rancid gasoline
through a city prostrate in the lethargy of siesta time, he avoided
the Asiatic din of the commercial district alleys, he saw the great
feminine sea of Manuela Sánchez of my perdition with a solitary
pelican on the horizon, he saw the decrepit streetcars with
frosted-glass windows with a velvet throne for Manuela Sánchez, he saw the deserted beach of your sea Sundays and he
ordered them to build little dressing rooms and a flag with a
different color according to the whims of the weather and a steel
mesh fence around a beach reserved for Manuela Sánchez, he
saw the manors with marble terraces and thoughtful lawns of
the fourteen families he had enriched with his favors, he saw one
manor that was larger with spinning sprinklers and stained glass
in the balcony windows where I want to see you living for me,
and they expropriated it forcibly, deciding the fate of the world
while he dreamed with his eyes open in the back seat of the tin-
can car until the sea breeze was gone and the city was gone and
in through the chinks of the window came the satanic din of
your dogfight district where he saw himself and did not believe
it thinking mother of mine Bendición Alvarado look where I am
without you, favor me, but no one recognized in the tumult the
desolate eyes, the weak lips, the languid hand on his chest, the
voice with the sleeping talk of a great-grandfather looking
through a broken glass wearing a white linen suit and a foreman's hat and going around trying to find out where Manuela
Sánchez of my shame lives, the queen of the poor, madam, the
one with the rose in her hand, wondering in alarm where could
you live in that turmoil of sharp bump backbones of satanic
looks of bloody fangs of the string of fleeing howls with the tail
between the legs of the butchery of dogs quartering each other
as they exchanged nips in the mud puddles, where could the

licorice smell of your breath be in this continuous thunder of whore-daughter loudspeakers you'll be the torture of my life of drunks booted out of slaughterhouse saloons, where could you have got lost in the endless binge of the fruits and the hodge-podge school of mullet and ray fish and a salami of penny-pitching and the black penny tossed of the mythical paradise of Black Adán and Juancito Trucupey, God damn it, which house do you live in this clamor of peeling pumpkin yellow walls with the purple trim of a bishop's stole and green parrot windows with fairy blue partitions and columns pink like the rose in your hand, what time can it be in your life since these lowlifes don't know about my order that it's three o'clock now and not eight o'clock yesterday night as it seems to be in this hellhole, which one are you among these women who nod in the empty parlors and ventilate themselves with their skirts holding their legs apart in rocking chairs inhaling the heat from between their legs while he asked through the openings in the window where Manuela Sánchez of my rage lives, the one with the frothy dress with diamond spangles and the solid gold diadem he had given her on the first anniversary of her coronation, now I know who she is, sir, somebody in the tumult said, a big-assed teaty woman who thinks she's the gorilla's own mama, she lives there, sir, there, in a house like all the others, painted at the top of its lungs, with the fresh mark of someone who'd slipped on a lump of dog dirt and left a mosaic carlock, a poor person's house so different from Manuela Sánchez in the chair of the viceroys that it was hard to believe it was her, but it was her, mother of my innards Bendición Alvarado, give me your strength to go in, mother, because it was her, he'd gone around the block ten times to catch his breath, he'd knocked on the door with three knuckle-raps that were like three entreaties, he'd waited in the burning shadows of the entranceway without knowing whether the evil air he was breathing was perverted by the glare of the sun or by anxiety, he waited without even thinking of his own state until Manuela Sánchez's mother had him come into the cool fish leftover smell of the shadows in the broad stark living room of a house asleep that was larger inside than out, he examined the scope of his frustration from the leather stool he had sat on while Manuela Sánchez's mother woke her from her siesta, he saw the walls and the dribbles of past raindrops, a broken sofa, two other stools with leather bottoms, a stringless piano in the corner, nothing else, shit, so much suffering for this trouble, he sighed, when Manuela Sánchez's mother came back with a sewing basket and sat down to make lace while Manuela Sánchez got dressed, combed her hair, put on her best shoes to attend with proper dignity the unexpected old man who wondered perplexed where can you be Manuela Sánchez of my misfortune that I came looking for you and cannot find you in this house of beggars, where is your licorice smell in this pesthole of lunch leftovers, where is your rose, where your love, release me from the dungeon of these dog doubts, he sighed, when he saw her appear at the rear door like the image of a dream reflected in the mirror of another dream wearing a dress of etamine that cost a penny a yard, her hair tied back hurriedly with a back comb, her shoes shabby, but she was the most beautiful and haughtiest woman on earth with the rose glowing in her hand, a sight so dazzling that he barely got sufficient control of himself to bow when she greeted him with her lifted head God preserve your excellency, and she sat down on the sofa opposite him, where the gush of his fetid body odor would not reach her, and then I dared to look at him face to face for the first time spinning the glow of the rose with two fingers so that he would not notice my terror, I pitilessly scrutinized the bat lips, the mute eyes that seemed to be looking at me from the bottom of a pool, the hairless skin like clods of earth tamped down with gall oil which became tighter and more intense on the right hand and the ring with the presidential seal exhausted on his knee, his baggy linen suit as if there were nobody inside, his enormous dead man's shoes, his invincible thought, his occult powers, the oldest ancient on earth, the most fearsome, the most hated, and the least pitied in the nation who was fanning himself with his foreman's hat contemplating me in silence from his other shore, good lord, such a sad man, I thought with surprise, and she asked without compassion what can I do for you your excellency, and he answered with a solemn air that I've only come to ask a favor of you, your majesty, that you accept this visit of mine. He visited her without cease month after month, every day during the dead hours of the heat when he used to visit his mother so that the security service would think he was at the suburban mansion, for only he was unaware of what everyone knew that General Rodrigo de Aguilar's riflemen were protecting him crouched on the rooftops, they raised hell with traffic, they used their rifle butts to clear the streets he would pass along, they put them off limits so that they would seem deserted from two until five with orders to shoot if anyone tried to come out onto a balcony, but even the least curious found some way to spy on the fleeting passage of the presidential limousine painted to look like a taxi with the canicular old man disguised as a civilian inside the innocent linen suit, they saw his orphan paleness, his face that had seen it dawn so many mornings, that had wept in secret, no longer bothered about what they might have thought of the hand on his chest, the archaic taciturn animal who went along leaving a trail of illusions of look at him go since he can't make it any more in the glassy heat of the forbidden streets, until the suspicions of strange illnesses became so loud and repeated they finally stumbled onto the truth that he

was not at his mother's house but in the shadowy parlor of Manuela Sánchez's secret cover under the implacable vigilance of the
mother who knitted without stopping to take a breath, because
it was for her that he bought the ingenious machines that so
saddened Bendición Alvarado, he tried to seduce her with the
mystery of magnetic needles, the January snowstorms captive in
quartz paperweights, apparatuses of astronomers and pharma-
cists, pyrographs, manometers, metronomes and gyroscopes
which he kept on buying from anyone who would sell them
against the advice of his mother, and in opposition to his own
steely avarice, and only for the pleasure of enjoying them with
Manuela Sánchez, he would put to her ear the patriotic shell
that did not have the sound of the sea inside but the military
marches that exalted his regime, he would bring the flame of a
match close to the thermometers so you can see the oppressive
mercury of what I think inside go up and down, he looked at
Manuela Sánchez without asking her for anything, without
expressing his intentions to her, but he would overwhelm her in
silence with those demented presents to try to tell her with them
what he was capable of saying, for he only knew how to show
his most intimate urges with the visible symbols of his uncom-
mon power as on Manuela Sánchez's birthday when he had
asked her to open the window and she opened it and I was
petrified with fright to see what they had done to my poor dogfight district, I saw the white wooden houses with canvas
awnings and terraces with flowers, the blue lawns with their
spinning sprinklers, the peacocks, the glacial insecticide wind, a
vile replica of the former residences of the occupation officials
which had been minutely reproduced at night and in silence,
they had slit the throats of the dogs, they had removed the former inhabitants from their homes for they had no right to be
the neighbors of a queen and sent them off to rot in some other

dungheap, and in that way in a few furtive nights they had built
the new district of Manuela Sánchez so you could see it from
your window on your name day, there it is, queen, so that you
may have many happy years to come, so see whether or not
these displays of power were able to soften your courteous but
unconquerable behavior, my mama is there with the fetters of
my honor, and he drowned in his urges, swallowed his rage,
drank with slow grandfather sips the cool soursop water of pity
which she had prepared to give drink to the thirsty one, he bore
up under the icy jabs in his temples so that the imperfections of
age would not be revealed, so that you will not love me out of
pity after he had exhausted all the resources for her to have loved
him out of love, she left him in such a state of only when I'm
with you I don't have the spirit even to be there, agonizing to
stroke her if only with his breath before the human-size archangel should fly inside the house ringing the bell of my fateful
hour, and he got in one last sip of the visit while she put the
toys away in their original cases so the sea rot would not turn
them to dust, just one minute, queen, he got up from now until
tomorrow, a lifetime, what a mess, he barely had an instant to
take a last look at the untouchable maiden who with the step of
the archangel had remained motionless with the dead rose in her
lap while he took leave, he slipped into the first shadows trying
to hide a shame which was in the public domain and which
everyone commented upon the street, it gave birth to an anonymous song which the whole country knew except him, even the
parrots sang it in courtyards make way women there comes the
general crying green with his hand on his chest, see how he goes
he can't handle his power, he rules in his sleep, he's got a wound
that won't close, wild parrots learned it from having heard it
sung by tame parrots, budgies and mockingbirds learned it from
them and they carried it off in flocks beyond his measureless

realm of gloom, and in all the skies of the nation one could hear at dusk that unanimous voice of fleeting multitudes who sang there comes my ever-loving general giving off crap through his mouth and laws through his poop, an endless song to which everybody even the parrots added verses to mock the security services of the state who tried to capture it, military patrols in full battle dress broke down courtyard doors and shot down the subversive parrots on their perches, they threw whole bushels of parakeets alive to the dogs, a state of siege was declared in an attempt to extirpate the enemy song so that no one would discover that everybody knew that he was the one who slipped like a fugitive of dusk through the doors of the presidential palace, went through the kitchens and disappeared into the manure smoke of the private rooms until tomorrow at four o'clock, queen, until every day at the same hour when he arrived at Manuela Sánchez's house laden with so many unusual gifts that they had to take over the houses next door and knock down the intervening walls in order to have room for them, so that the original parlor had become an immense and gloomy shed where there were uncountable clocks from every period, there was every type of phonograph from primitive ones with cylinders to those with a mirror diaphragm, there were all sorts of sewing machines with cranks, pedals, motors, whole bedrooms full of galvanometers, homeopathic pharmaceuticals, music boxes, optical-illusion instruments, showcase of dried butterflies, Asiatic herbariums, laboratories for physiotherapy and physical education, machines for astronomy, orthopedics and natural sciences, and a whole world of dolls with hidden mechanisms for human traits, forbidden rooms where no one entered not even to sweep because the things stayed where they had been placed when they were brought, no one wanted to hear about them and Manuela Sánchez least of all because she did not wish to know anything about life ever since that black Saturday when the misfortune of being queen befell me, on that afternoon the world ended for me, her former suitors had died one after the other struck down by unpunished collapses and strange illnesses, her girl friends disappeared without a trace, she'd been moved without leaving her house into a district full of strangers, she was alone, watched over in her most intimate aims, the captive of a trap of fate in which she did not have the courage to say no nor did she have sufficient courage to say yes to an abominable suitor who besieged her with a madhouse love, who looked at her with a kind of reverential stupor fanning himself with his white hat, drenched in sweat, so far removed from himself that she had wondered whether he really was looking at her or whether it was only a vision of horror, she had seen him hesitating in broad daylight, she had seen him nibble at fruit juices, had seen him nod with sleep in the wicker easy chair with the glass in his hand when the copper buzz of the cicadas made the parlor shadows denser, she had seen him snore, careful your excellency, she had told him, he would wake up startled murmuring no, queen, I didn't fall asleep, I just closed my eyes, he said, without realizing that she had taken the glass from his hand so that he wouldn't drop it while he slept, she had amused him with subtle wiles until the incredible afternoon when he got to the house gasping with the news that today I'm bringing you the greatest gift in the universe, a miracle of heaven that's going to pass by tonight at eleven-oh-six so that you can see it, queen, only so that you can see it, and it was the comet. It was one of our great moments of disappointment, because for some time a rumor had spread like so many others that the timetable of his life was not controlled by human time but by the cycles of the comet, that he had been conceived to see it once but that he was not to see it again in spite of the arrogant auguries of his adulators, so we had waited like someone waiting for the day when that secular November night is born on which joyous music was prepared, the bells of jubilation, the festival rockets which for the first time in a century did not burst to exalt his glory but to wait for the eleven metal rings of eleven o'clock which would signal the end of his years, to celebrate a providential event that he awaited on the roof of Manuela Sánchez's house, sitting between her and her mother, breathing strongly so that they would not notice the difficulties of his heart under a sky numb with evil omens, breathing in for the first time the nocturnal breath of Manuela Sánchez, the intensity of her inclemency, her open air, he heard on the horizon the conjure drums that were coming out to meet the disaster, he listened to distant laments, the sounds of the volcanic slime of the crowds who prostrated themselves in terror before a creature alien to their power who had preceded and who was to transcend the years of their age, he felt the weight of time, he suffered for an instant the misfortune of being mortal, and then he saw it, there it is, he said, and there it was, because he knew it, he had seen it when it had passed on to the other side of the universe, it was the same one, queen, older than the earth, the painful medusa of light the size of the sky which with every hand measure of its trajectory was returning a million years to its origins, they heard the buzzing of bits of tinfoil, they saw his afflicted face, his eyes overflowing with tears, the track of frozen poisons of its hair disheveled by the winds of space as it left across the world a trail radiant with star debris and dawns delayed by tarry moons and ashes from the craters of oceans previous to the origins of earth time, there it is, queen, he murmured, take a good look at it because we won't see it again for another century, and she crossed herself in terror, more beautiful than ever under the phosphorous glow of the comet and with her head snowy from the soft drizzle of astral trash and celestial sediment, and it was then that it happened, mother of mine Bendición Alvarado, it happened that Manuela Sánchez had seen the abyss of eternity in the sky and trying to cling to life she had reached out her hand into space and the only thing she found to hang on to was the undesirable hand with the presidential ring, his hot stiff hand of rapine cooked in the embers of the slow fire of power. Very few were those who were moved by the biblical passage of the glowing medusa which frightened deer from out of the sky and fumigated the fatherland with a trail of radiant dust of star debris, for even the most incredulous of us were hanging on that uncommonly large death which was to destroy the principles of Christianity and implant the origins of the third testament, we waited in vain until dawn, we returned home more fatigued from waiting than from not sleeping through the post-party streets where the dawn women were sweeping up the celestial trash left by the comet, and not even then did we resign ourselves to believe that it was true that nothing had happened, but that on the contrary we had been the victims of another historic trick, for the official organs proclaimed the passage of the comet as a victory of the regime over the forces of evil, they took advantage of the occasion to deny the suppositions of strange diseases with unmistakable acts of vitality on the part of the man in power, slogans were renewed, a solemn message was made public in which he had expressed my unique and sovereign decision to be in my post of service to the nation when the comet passes again, but on the other hand he heard the music and the rockets as if they did not belong to his regime, he listened without emotion to the clamoring crowd gathered on the main square with large banners saying eternal glory to the most worthy one who will live to tell it, he was not concerned with the troubles of government, he delegated his authority to underlings tormented by the memory of the hot coal that was Manuela Sánchez's hand on his, dreaming of reliving that happy moment even if nature's direction had to be turned off course and the universe be damaged, desiring it with such intensity that he ended up beseeching his astronomers to invent him a fireworks comet, a fleeting morning star, a dragon made of candles, any ingenious star invention that would be terrifying enough to cause a swoon of eternity in a beautiful woman, but the only thing they could come up with in their calculations was a total eclipse of the sun for Wednesday of next week at four in the afternoon general sir, and he accepted it, all right, and it was such a true night in the middle of the day that the stars lit up, flowers closed, hens went to roost, and animals sought shelter with their best premonitory instincts, while he breathed in Manuela Sánchez's twilight breath as it became nocturnal and the rose languished in her hand deceived by the shadows, there it is, queen, it's your eclipse, but Manuela Sánchez did not answer, she did not touch his hand, she was not breathing, she seemed so unreal that he could not resist his urge and he stretched out his hand in the darkness to touch her hand, but he could not find it, he looked for it with the tips of his fingers in the place where her smell had been, but he did not find it either, he kept on looking for it through the enormous house with both hands, waving his arms about with the open eyes of a sleepwalker in the shadows, wondering with grief where can you be Manuela Sánchez of my misfortune as I seek you and cannot find you in the unfortunate night of your eclipse, where can your inclement hand be, your rose, he swam like a diver lost in a pool of invisible waters in whose reaches he found floating the prehistoric crayfish of the galvanometers, the crabs of the musical clocks, the lobsters of your machines of illusory trades, but on the contrary he did not even find the licorice breath of your lungs, and as the darkness of the ephemeral night broke up the light of truth grew brighter in his soul and he felt older than God in the shadows of the six in the afternoon dawn in the deserted house, he felt sadder, lonelier than ever in the loneliness of this world without you, my queen, lost forever in the enigma of the eclipse, nevermore, because never in the rest of the very long years of his power would he find Manuela Sánchez of my perdition again in the labyrinth of her house, she had disappeared in the night of the eclipse general sir, they told him that she'd been seen dancing the plena in Puerto Rico, there where they cut Elena general sir, but it wasn't her, that she'd been seen in the madness of Papa Montero's wake, tricky, lowlife rumba bunch, but it wasn't her either, that she'd been seen in the ticky-tacky of Barlovento over the mine, in the dance of Aracataca, in the pretty wind of the little drum of Panama, but none of them was her, general sir, she just blew the hell away, and if he did not abandon himself to the will of death at that time it was not because he lacked the rage to die but because he knew he was remorsely condemned not to die of love, he had known it ever since one afternoon during the first days of his empire when he went to a sibyl for her to read to him in the water of her basins the keys to his fate which were not written in the palm of his hand, or in the cards, or in his coffee grounds, or in any other means of inquiry, only in that mirror of premonitory waters where he saw himself dead of natural causes during his sleep in the office next to the reception room, and he saw himself lying face down on the floor as he had slept every night of his life since birth, with the denim uniform without insignia, the boots, the gold spur, his right arm folded under his head to serve as a pillow, and at an indefinite age somewhere between 107 and 232 years.

That was how they found him on the even of his autumn, when the corpse was really that of Patricio Aragonés, and that was how we found him again many years later during a moment of such uncertainty that no one could give in to the evidence that the senile body there gouged by vultures and infested with parasites from the depths of the sea was his. The hand turned into a figurine by putrefaction gave no indication that it had ever been held on the chest because of the rebuffs of an improbable maiden during the noisy times, nor had we found any trace of his life that could have led us to the unmistakable establishment of his identity. It didn't seem strange to us, of course, that this should be so in our days, because even during his times of greatest glory there had been reasons to doubt his existence and his own henchmen had no exact notion of his age, for there were periods of confusion in which he seemed to be eighty years old at charity raffles, sixty at civil receptions and even under forty during the celebration of national holidays. Ambassador Palmerston, one of the last diplomats to present his credentials, told in his banned memoirs that it was impossible to conceive of old

age as advanced as his or of a state of disorder and neglect as in
that government house where he had to make his way through
a dungheap of paper scraps and animal shit and the remains of
the meals of dogs who slept in the halls, no one could give me
any information about anything in tax bureaus or offices and I
was forced to have recourse to the lepers and cripples who had
already invaded the first part of the private quarters and who
showed me the way to the reception room where the hens were
pecking at the illusory wheat fields on the tapestries and a cow
was pulling down the canvas with the portrait of an archbishop
so she could eat it, and I realized at once that he was as deaf as
a post not only because I would ask him about one thing and he
would answer about another but also because it grieved him that
the birds were not singing when in fact it was difficult to breathe
with that uproar of birds which was like walking through the
jungle at dawn, and he suddenly interrupted the ceremony of
credentials with a lucid look and cupping his hand behind his
ear he pointed out the window at the dusty plain where the sea
had been and said in a voice to awaken the dead that I should
listen to that troop of mules going along out there, listen my
dear Stetson, it's the sea coming back. It was hard to admit that
that broken-down old man was the same messianic figure who
during the beginnings of his regime would appear in towns
when least expected with no other escort but a barefooted Gua-
jiro Indian with a cane-cutting machete and a small entourage
of congressmen and senators whom he had appointed himself
with his finger according to the whims of his digestion, he
informed himself about the crop figures and the state of health
of the livestock and the behavior of the people, he would sit in
a reed rocking chair in the shadow of the mango trees on the
square fanning himself with the foreman's hat he wore in those
days, and even though he seemed to be dozing because of the

heat he would not let a single detail go by without some explanation in his talks with the men and women he had called
together using their names and surnames as if he had a written
registry of inhabitants and statistics and problems of the whole
nation inside his head, so he called me without opening his eyes,
come here Jacinta Morales, he said to me, tell me what happened
to the boy he had wrestled with himself and given a fall the year
before so he would drink a bottle of castor oil, and you, Juan
Prieto, he said to me, how is your breed bull that he had treated
himself with prayers against sickness so the worms would drop
out of his ears, and you Matilde Peralta, let's see what you're
going to give me for bringing back that runaway husband of
yours in one piece, there he is, pulled along with a rope around
his neck and warned by him in person that he'd rot in the stocks
the next time he tried to desert his legitimate spouse, and with
the same sense of immediate governance he had ordered a
butcher to cut off the hands of a cheating treasurer in a public
spectacle and he would pick the tomatoes in a private garden
and eat them with the air of a connoisseur in the presence of his
agronomists saying that what this soil needs is a good dose of
male donkey shit, it should be spread at government expense,
he ordered, and he interrupted his civic stroll and shouted to me
through the window breaking up with laughter aha Lorenza
López how's that sewing machine he had given me as a present
twenty years earlier, and I answered him that it had already
given up the ghost, general, you have to remember that things
and people we're not made to last a lifetime, but he answered
just the opposite, the world is eternal, and then he set about
dismantling the machine with a screwdriver and an oilcan indifferent to the official delegation that was waiting for him in the
middle of the street, sometimes his desperation was evident
from the bull snorts and even his face was daubed with motor

oil, but after almost three hours the machine was sewing again
as good as new, because in those days there was nothing contrary in everyday life no matter how insignificant which did not
have as much importance for him as the gravest matter of state
and he believed sincerely that it was possible to distribute happiness and bribe death with the wiles of a soldier. It was hard to
admit that that aged person beyond repair was all that remained
of a man whose power had been so great that once he asked
what time is it and they had answered him whatever you command general sir, and it was true, for not only did he alter the
time of day as best suited his business but he would change legal
holidays in accordance with his plans to cover the whole country
from holiday to holiday in the shadow of the barefoot Indian
and the mournful-looking senators and with the crates of splendid cocks who faced the bravest there were in every village
square, he booked the bets himself, he made the foundations of
the cockpit shake with laughter because we all felt obliged to
laugh when he gave off his strange snare-drum guffaws that rang
out above the music and the rockets, we suffered when he was
silent, we would break out in an ovation of relief when his birds
struck ours with lightning ours having been so well trained to
lose that not a single one let us down, except the cock of Dionisio Iguarán's misfortune who struck down the gray one
belonging to the power in an attack so clean and sure that he was
the first to cross the ring and shake the winner's hand, you're a
real man, he told him with a pleasant manner, thankful that
someone had finally done him the favor of an innocuous defeat,
how much do you want for that red one, he said, and Dionisio
Iguarán answered him in a quavering voice it's yours general,
my great honor, and he went home to the applause of the
excited people and the noise of the music and the petards showing everybody the six pedigreed cocks he had been given in

exchange for the undefeated red one, but that night he locked himself up in his bedroom and drank a gourdful of cane liquor all by himself and hanged himself with the rope from his hammock, poor man, for he was not aware of the string of domestic disasters that his jubilant appearances brought on, nor the trail of undesired deaths he left behind, nor the eternal condemnation of comrades in misfortune whom he called by the wrong name in front of solicitous assassins who interpreted the mistake as a deliberate sign of disfavor, he walked all across the country with his strange armadillo step, his trail of strong sweat, his tardy stubble of a beard, he would appear without notice in some kitchen with that air of a useful grandfather which made the people of the house tremble with fear, he would take a drink of water from the bucket with the calabash dipper, he would eat out of the stewpot itself picking up the chunks with his fingers, too jovial, too simple, not suspecting that that house was marked forever with the stigma of his visit, and he did not act that way out of any political calculation or the need for love as was the case in other times but because it was his natural way of being when power was still not the shoreless bog of the fullness of his autumn but a feverish torrent that we saw gush out of its spring before our very eyes so that all he had to do was point at trees for them to bear fruit and at animals for them to grow and at men for them to prosper, and he had ordered them to take the rain away from places where it disturbed the harvest and take it to drought-stricken lands, and that was the way it had been, sir, I saw it, because his legend had begun much earlier than he believed himself master of all his power, when he was still at the mercy of omens and the interpreters of his nightmares and he would suddenly cut short a trip he had just started because he had heard a bird sing above his head and he would change the date of a public appearance because his mother Bendición Alvarado had found an egg with two yolks, and he got rid of the retinue of solicitous senators and congressmen who went with him everywhere and delivered for him the speeches that he never dared deliver, he went without them because he saw himself in the big empty house of a bad dream surrounded by pale men in gray frock coats who were smiling and sticking him with butcher knives, they harried him with such fury that wherever he turned to look he found a blade ready to wound him in the face and eyes, he saw himself encircled like a wild beast by the silent smiling assassins who fought over the privilege of taking part in the sacrifice and enjoying his blood, but he did not feel rage or fear, rather an immense relief that grew deeper as his life trickled away, he felt himself weightless and pure, so he too smiled as they killed him, he smiled for them and for himself in the confines of the dream house whose whitewashed walls were being stained by my spattering blood, until someone who was a son of his in the dream gave him a stab in the groin through which the last bit of breath I had left escaped, and then he covered his face with the blanket soaked in his blood so that no one who had not been able to know him alive would know him dead and he collapsed shaken by such real death throes that he could not repress the urgency of telling it to my comrade the minister of health and the latter ended up by putting him in a state of consternation with the revelation that that death had already occurred once in the history of men general sir, he read him the story of the episode in one of the singed tomes of General Lautaro Muñoz, and it was identical, mother, so much so that in the course of its reading he remembered something that he had forgotten when he woke up and it was that while they were killing him all of a sudden and with no wind blowing all the windows in the presidential palace opened up and they were in fact the same number as the wounds in the dream, twenty-three, a terrifying coincidence which had its culmination that week with an attack on the senate and the supreme court by corsairs along with the cooperative indifference of the armed forces, the august home of our original patriotic forebears was burned to the ground and the flames could be seen until very late in the night from the presidential balcony, but he did not change his expression with the news general sir that they had not even spared the foundation stones, he promised us an exemplary punishment for the perpetrators of the attack who never appeared, he promised us that he would rebuild an exact replica of the house of our forebears but its blackened ruins remained down to our times, he did nothing to disguise the terrible exorcism of the bad dream but took advantage of the occasion to liquidate the legislative and judicial apparatus of the old republic, he heaped honors and fortune upon the senators and congressmen and magistrates whom he no longer needed to keep up the appearances of the beginning of his regime, he exiled them to happy and remote embassies and remained with no other retinue but the solitary shadow of the Indian with his machete who did not abandon him for an instant, who tasted his food and water, kept his distance, watched the door while he stayed in my house giving fuel to the story that he was my secret lover while in fact he visited me once or twice a month to consult me about the cards during those many years when he still thought himself mortal and had the virtue of doubt and knew how to make mistakes and trusted more in the deck of cards than in his rustic instincts, he still arrived as worried and as old as the first time he sat down opposite me and without saying a word stretched out to me those hands with palms as smooth and tight as the belly of a toad such as I had never seen or was ever to see again in my long life as an examiner of the destiny of others, he laid them both on the table at the same time almost like the mute begging of a hopeless case and he seemed so anxious to me and so without illusions that I was not so impressed by his arid palms as by his unalleviated melancholy, the weakness of his lips, his poor heart of an old man eaten by doubt whose fate was not only hermetic in his hands but in all the means of inquiry that we knew in those times, for as soon as he cut the cards they became pools of murky water, the coffee grounds became muddy in the bottom of the cup he had drunk from, the keys to everything that had to do with his personal future, his happiness and the destiny of his acts had been erased, but on the other hand they were crystal clear as concerned the destiny of anyone who had anything to do with him, so we saw his mother Bendición Alvarado painting birds with foreign names at such an advanced age that she could barely distinguish the colors in an air rarefied by a pestilential vapor, poor mother, we saw our city devastated by a hurricane so terrible that it did not deserve its woman's name, we saw a man with a green mask and a sword in his hand and he asked in anguish what part of the world he was in and the cards answered that every Tuesday he was closer to him than on other days of the week, and he said aha, and asked what color eyes he had, and the cards answered that one was the color of juice in the light and the other cane juice in the dark, and he said aha, and he asked what that man's intentions were, and that was the last time I revealed to him the truth of the cards to the very end because I answered him that the green mask was that of perfidy and treason, and he said aha, with a stress of triumph, I already know who he is, God damn it, he exclaimed, and it was Colonel Narciso Miraval, one of his closest aides who two days later put a bullet in his ear with no explanation, poor man, and that was how the destiny of the nation was arranged and its history antici- pated according to the predictions of the cards until he heard tell of a singular sibyl who deciphered death in the error-free waters of her basins and he went to seek her out in secret along mule trails and with no other witness than the angel of the machete all the way up to the settlement on the plains where she lived with a great-granddaughter who had three children and was about to bear another by a husband dead the month before, he found her crippled and half blind in the back of a bedroom almost in darkness, but when she asked him to put his hands over the basin the waters became illuminated with a soft and clear interior glow, and then he saw himself, exactly as he was, lying face down on the floor, wearing a denim uniform without insignia, the boots and the gold spur, and he asked what place that was, and the woman answered examining the sleeping waters that it was a room not much larger than this with something that can be seen here that looks like a desk and an electric fan and a window facing the sea and these white walls with pictures of horses and a flag with a dragon on it, and again he said aha because he had recognized without any doubt the office next to the reception room, and he asked if it was to be in a bad way or from a bad illness, and she answered him no, it was to be during his sleep and without pain, and he said aha, and he asked her trembling when it was to be and she answered him that he could sleep peacefully because it would not take place before you reach my age, which was 107, but also not after 125 years more, and he said aha, and then he murdered the sick old woman in the hammock so that no one else would know the circumstances of his death, he strangled her with the strap from his gold spur, without pain, without a sigh, like a master executioner, in spite of the fact that she was the only being in this world, human or animal, whom he did the honor of killing with his own hand in peace or in war, poor woman. Similar evocations from his fasti of infamy did not twist his conscience during the nights of his autumn, on the contrary they served him as exemplary fables of what should have been done and what had not been, above all when Manuela Sánchez evaporated into the shadows of the eclipse and he wanted to feel himself in the full bloom of his barbarity once more so he could pluck out the rage of deception which was cooking his innards, he would lie down in the hammock under the tinkle bells of the wind in the tamarinds to think about Manuela Sánchez with a rancor that disturbed his sleep while the forces of land, sea and air sought her without any trace even in the unknown confines of the saltpeter deserts, where the fuck have you hidden yourself, he wondered, where the fuck do you think you can hide where my arm can't reach you so that you'll know who gives the orders, the hat on his chest quivered with the drive of his heart, he lay there ecstatic with rage and paying no attention to his mother's insistence as she tried to find out why you haven't spoken a word since the afternoon of the eclipse, but he wouldn't answer, he left, shit mother, he dragged his big orphan feet off bleeding drops of gall with his pride wounded by the irredeemable bitterness that all this trouble is happening to me because I've become such a horse's ass, because I haven't been the director of my destiny the way I was before, because I went into the house of a bitch with her mother's permission and not the way he had gone into the cool and quiet ranch house of Francisca Linero in Vereda de los Santos Higuerones when it was still he in person and not Patricio Aragonés who showed the visible face of power, he had gone in without even touching the door knocker in accordance with the pleasure of his will to the rhythm of the tolling of eleven o'clock on the grandfather clock and I heard the metal of the gold spur from the courtyard terrace and knew that those pile-driver steps with all that authority on the brick floor could not belong to anyone else but him, I sensed him in the flesh before I saw him appear in the doorway of the inner terrace where the curlew was singing out eleven o'clock among the gold geraniums, a troupial disturbed by the fragrant acetone of the bunches of bananas hanging from the eaves, the light of the ominous August Tuesday was taking its ease among the new leaves of the plantain trees in the courtyard and the carcass of the young buck which my husband Poncio Daza had shot at dawn and hung by its hind legs to bleed beside the bunches of bananas tiger-striped by their inner honey, I saw him larger and more somber than in a dream his boots dirty with mud and his khaki jacket soaked with sweat and with no weapons on his belt but protected by the shadow of the barefoot Indian who stood motionless behind him his hand resting on the hilt of his machete, I saw the unavoidable eyes, the hand of a sleeping maiden that plucked a banana from the nearest bunch and ate it with anxiety his whole mouth making a swampy sound without taking his eyes off the provocative Francisca Linero who looked at him without knowing what to do in her modesty of a newly-wed because he had come to give pleasure to his will and there was no power greater than his to stop him, I barely felt the fearful breathing of my husband who sat down beside me and we both remained motionless holding hands and our two post-card hearts were frightened in unison under the tenacious look of the unfathomable old man who kept on eating one banana after another two steps from the door and tossing the peels over his shoulder into the courtyard without having blinked a single time after he had begun to look at me, and only after he had eaten the whole bunch and the bare stalk was left beside the dead buck did he make a signal to the barefoot Indian and ordered Poncio Daza to go with my comrade the one with the machete for a moment because he has some business and although I was dying with fear I maintained enough lucidity to realize that my only means of salvation was to let him do every-thing he wanted to with me on the dinner table, even more, I helped him find me among the lace of the petticoats after he left me gasping for breath with his ammonia smell and he tore off my drawers with a claw and looked for me with his fingers where I wasn't while I thought in confusion oh Blessed Sacra-ment such shame, such misfortune, because that morning I hadn't had time to wash myself being involved with the buck, so he finally did his will after so many months of siege, but he did it fast and poorly, as if he had been older than he was, or much younger, he was so upset that I scarcely noticed when he did his duty as best he could and broke into sobbing with the hot urine tears of a great and solitary orphan, weeping with such deep affliction that not only did I feel pity for him but for every man in the world and I began to rub his head with my fingertips and console him with don't worry about it general, life is long, while the man with the machete took Poncio Daza into the banana groves and cut him up into such thin slices that it was impossible to put his body back together again after it had been scattered by the hogs, poor man, but there was no other way out, he said, because he would have been a mortal enemy for the rest of his life. They were images of his power which came to him from far away and increased the bitterness over how much the brine of his power had been watered down since it hadn't even been of any use to conjure up the evil arts of an eclipse, he was shaken by a thread of black bile at the domino table across from the frozen realm of General Rodrigo de Aguilar who was the only man of arms in whom he had confided his life since uric acid had crystallized the joints of the angel with the machete, and yet he wondered if so much confidence and so much authority delegated to one single person might not have been the cause of his misfortune, if it wasn't my lifetime comrade who had turned him into an ox by trying to shear him of his natural fleece of a backlands leader and convert him into a palace invalid incapable of thinking up an order that hadn't already been carried out ahead of time, by the unhealthy invention of showing in public a face that wasn't his when the barefoot Indian of the good old days had been sufficient and more than enough all by himself to open a path with blows from his machete through the crowds of people shouting make way you bastards here comes the man in charge without being able to distinguish in that thicket of ovations who were the real patriots and who were the tricky ones because we still hadn't discovered that the shadiest ones were those who shout loudest long live the stud, God damn it, long live the general, and quite the opposite now the authority of his weapons wasn't even of any use to him to find the death-breeding queen who had made a mockery out of the unbreakable encirclement of his senile appetites, God damn it, he threw the pieces on the floor, left games half finished for no visible reason depressed by the sudden revelation that everyone ended up finding his place in the world, everyone except him, conscious for the first time that his shirt was soaked in sweat at such an early hour, conscious of the carrion stench that rose up from the vapors of the sea and the soft flute whistle of his rupture twisted by the dampness of the heat, it's the humid weather, he told himself without conviction at the window trying to decipher the strange state of the light of the motionless city where the only living beings seemed to be the flocks of vultures fleeing in fright from the cornices of the charity hospital and the blind man in the main square who sensed the trembling old man at the window of government house and made an urgent signal to him with his staff and shouted something that he couldn't make out and which he interpreted as one more sign in that oppressive feeling that something was about to happen, and yet he repeated to himself for the second time at the end of a long Monday of dejection that it's the humidity, he said that to himself and he fell asleep at once, lulled by the scratching of the drizzle on the frosted glass of the sleeping potion, but suddenly he awoke with a start, who's there, he shouted, it was his own heart oppressed by the strange silence of the cocks at dawn, he felt that the ship of the universe had reached some port while he was asleep, he was floating in a soup of steam, the animals of earth and sky who had the faculty to glimpse death beyond the clumsy omens and best-founded sciences of men were mute with terror, there was no more air, time was changing direction, and as he got up he felt his heart swelling with every step and his eardrums bursting and some boiling matter was running out of his nose, it's death, he thought, his tunic soaked with blood, before realizing no general sir, it was the hurricane, the most devastating of all those that had broken the ancient compact realm of the Caribbean up into a string of scattered islands, a catastrophe so stealthy that only he had detected it with his premonitory instinct long before the panic of dogs and hens began, and so quick that there was scarcely time to find a woman's name for it in the disorder of terrified officials who came to me with the news that now yes it was true general sir, this country had gone to hell, but he ordered them to reinforce the doors and windows with long beams, they tied the sentries to their posts along the corridors, they locked up the hens and the cows in the offices on the first floor, they nailed everything down in place from the main square to the last border stone of his terrorized realm of gloom, the whole nation was anchored in place with the absolute order that with the first show of panic they would shoot twice in the air and the third time shoot to kill, and yet nothing could resist the passage of the tremendous blade of the spinning winds that cut a clean slice through the armored doors of the main entrance and carried off my cows into the air, but he did not realize it in the spell of the impact of where did it come from that roar of horizontal rain that scattered in its wake the volcanic grapeshot of the remains of balconies and beasts from the jungle and the bottom of the sea, nor was he lucid enough to think about the fearful proportions of the cataclysm but he walked about in the midst of the downpour wondering with an aftertaste of musk where can you be Manuela Sánchez of my bad saliva, God damn it, where can you have hidden yourself that this disaster of my vengeance hasn't reached you? In the peaceful pool that came after the hurricane he found himself alone with his closest aides floating in a rowboat in the stew of destruction that had been the reception room, they rowed out the coach house door without bumping into anything through the stumps of the palm trees and the downed lampposts of the main square, they went into the dead lagoon of the cathedral and for an instant he suffered the clairvoyant spark that he had never been nor would he ever be the master of all his power, he was still mortified by the irony of that bitter certainty while the rowboat ran into spaces of densities that differed according to the changes in color of the light from the stained glass in solid gold trim and the clusters of emeralds over the main altar and the gravestones of viceroys buried alive and archbishops dead of disenchantment and the granite promontory of the empty mausoleum for the admiral of the ocean sea with the profile of the three caravels which he had had built in case he wanted his bones to rest among us, we went out through the canal of the presbytery toward an inner courtyard converted into a luminous aquarium in the tiled depths of which schools of mojarra fish wandered among the stalks of spikenards and sunflowers, we cut through the gloomy streams of the cloister of the convent of Biscayan nuns, we saw the abandoned cells, we saw the harpsichord adrift in the intimate pool of the music room, in the depths of the sleeping waters of the refectory we saw the whole community of virgins drowned in their dinner places at the long table with the food served on it, and he saw as he went out through a balcony the broad lakelike expanse under a radiant sky where the city had been and only then did he believe that the news was true general sir that this disaster had happened all over the world only to free me from the torment of Manuela Sánchez, God damn it, how wild God's methods are when compared to ours, he thought smugly, contemplating the muddy swamp where the city had been and on whose limitless surface a world of drowned hens floated and all that rose up out of it were the steeples of the cathedral, the beacon of the lighthouse, the sun terraces of the stone and mortar mansions of the viceregal district, the scattered islands which had been the hills of the former slave port where the shipwrecked refugees from the cyclone were encamped, the last disbelieving survivors as we watched the silent passage of the rowboat painted with the colors of the flag through the sargasso of inert bodies of hens, we saw the sad eyes, the faded lips, the pensive hand which was making the sign of the cross in a blessing so that the rains would cease and the sun shine, and he gave life back to the drowned hens, and ordered the waters to recede and they receded. In the midst of the jubilant bell-ringing, the festival rockets, the music of celebration with which the laying of the first stone of reconstruction was laid, and in the midst of the shouts of the multitude crowded into the main square to glorify the most worthy one who had put the hurricane dragon to flight, someone took him by the arm to lead him out onto the balcony because now more than ever the people needed his words of comfort, and before he could get away he heard the unanimous clamor which got into his innards like the wind of an evil sea, long live the stud, because ever since the first days of his regime he understood the unprotected state of being seen by a whole city at the same time, his words turned to stone, he understood in a flash of mortal lucidity that he did not have the courage nor would he ever have it to appear at full length before the chasm of a crowd, so on the main square we only caught sight of the usual ephemeral image, the glimpse of an ungraspable old man dressed in denim who imparted a silent blessing from the presidential balcony and immediately disappeared, but that fleeting vision was enough for us to sustain the confidence that he was there, watching over our waking and sleeping hours under the historic tamarinds of the suburban mansion, he was absorbed in thought in the wicker rocking chair, with the glass of lemonade untouched in his hand listening to the sound of the kernels of corn that his mother Bendición Alvarado was drying out in the calabash gourd, watching her through the quiver of the three o'clock heat as she grabbed a barred rock hen and stuck it under her arm and twisted its neck with a kind of tenderness while she told me with a mother's voice looking into my eyes you're getting consumptive from so much thinking and not eating well, stay for dinner tonight, she begged him, trying to seduce him with the temptation of the strangled hen that she was holding with both hands so that it would not get away from her in its death throes, and he said all right, mother, I'll stay, he rested until sundown with his eyes closed in the wicker rocking chair, not sleeping, lulled by the soft smell of the hen boiling in the pot, hanging on the course of our lives, for the only thing that gave us security on earth was the certainty that he was there, invulnerable to plague and hurricane, invulnerable to Manuela Sánchez's trick, invulnerable to time, dedicated to the messianic happiness of thinking for us, knowing that we knew that he would not take any decision for us that did not have our measure, for he had not survived everything because of his inconceivable courage or his infinite prudence but because he was the only one among us who knew the real size of our destiny, and he had reached that point, mother, he had sat down to rest at the end of an arduous trip on the last historic stone on the remote eastern frontier where the name and dates of the last soldier killed in defense of the integrity of the nation were carved, he had seen the dismal and glacial city of the neighboring country, he saw the eternal drizzle, the morning mist with the smell of soot, the men in full dress on electric streetcars, the aristocratic funerals in gothic hearses with white Percherons with plumes on their heads, the children sleeping on the steps of the cathedral wrapped in newspapers, God damn it, what strange people, he exclaimed, they look like poets, but they weren't general sir, they're the Goths who hold power, they told him, and he had returned from that trip exalted by the revelation that there is nothing to equal this wind of rotten guavas and this clamor of a marketplace and this deep feeling of mournfulness at dusk in this homeland of misery whose frontiers he was never to cross, and not because he was afraid of moving from the seat where he was sitting, as his enemies said, but because a man is like a tree in the woods, mother, like the animals in the woods who never leave their lairs except to eat, he said, evoking with the mortal lucidity of siesta time the soporific August Thursday of so many years ago when he dared confess that he knew the limits of his ambition, he had revealed it to a warrior from other lands and other times whom he had received alone in the hot shadows of his office, he was a withdrawn young man, troubled by haughtiness and always standing out from the rest with the stigma of solitude, and he had stood motionless in the doorway unable to decide to cross the threshold until his eyes grew accustomed to the half-light which was scented by a brazier of wisteria in all the heat and he was able to make him out sitting in the swivel chair with his fist motionless on the bare desk, so everyday and faded that there was nothing about him of his public image, without escort or weapons, his shirt soaked in the sweat of a mortal man and with salvia leaves stuck to his temples for his headache, and only when I was convinced of the incredible truth that this rusty old man was the same idol of our childhood, the purest incarnation of our dreams of glory, only then did he enter the office and introduce himself by name speaking with the clear firm voice of one who expects to be recognized because of his deeds, and he shook my hand with a soft and miserly hand, the hand of a bishop, and he paid startling attention to the fabulous dream of the foreigner who wanted arms and assistance for a cause which is also yours, excellency, he wanted logistical support and political aid for a war without quarter which would wipe out once and for all every conservative regime from Alaska to Patagonia, and he felt so moved by his vehemence that he had asked him why are you mixed up in this mess, God damn it, why do you want to die, and the foreigner had answered him without a trace of modesty that there was no higher glory than dying for one's country, excellency, and he replied smiling with pity don't be a horse's ass, boy, fatherland means staying alive, he told him, that's what it is, he told him, and he opened the fist that he had resting on the desk and in the palm of his hand showed him this little glass ball which is something a person has or doesn't have, but only the one who has it has it, boy, this is the nation, he said, while he sent him away with pats on the back and not giving him anything, not even the consolation of a promise, and he ordered the aide who closed the door that they were not to bother that man who has just left any more, don't even waste your time keeping him under surveillance, he said, he's got a fever in his quills, he's no good for anything. We never heard that expression again until after the cyclone when he proclaimed a new amnesty for political prisoners and authorized the return of all exiles except men of letters, of course, them never, he said, they've got fever in their quills like thoroughbred roosters when they're moulting so that they're no good for anything except when they're good for something, he said, worse than politicians, worse than priests, just imagine, but let the others come back without distinction of color so that the rebuilding of the nation can be the task of all, so that nobody would be left without proof that he was once more the master of all his power with the fierce support of armed forces that had become once more the same as before since he had distributed the shipments of food and medicine and the material for public relief from foreign aid among the members of the high command, ever since the families of his ministers had Sunday outings at the beach with the Red Cross portable hospitals and field tents, they sold the shipments of blood plasma, the tons of powdered milk to the ministry of health and the ministry of health resold them to charity hospitals, the officers of the general staff gave up their ambitions in return for public works contracts and rehabilitation programs with the emergency loan granted by Ambassador Warren in exchange for unlimited fishing rights for vessels of his nation within our territorial waters, what the hell, only the one who has it has it, he said to himself, remembering the colored marble he had shown that poor dreamer who was never heard of again, so exalted with the reconstruction work that with his own voice and in person he worked on even the tiniest details as in the original days of his power, sloshing through the swamps in the streets with a hat and a pair of duck-hunter's boots so that a city different from the one he had conceived for his glory in his dreams of a solitary drowned man should be built, he ordered his engineers get rid of these houses here for me and put them over there where they won't be in the way, make that tower six feet taller so that people will be able to see the ships on the high seas, they raised it, reverse the course of this river for me, they reversed it, without any mistakes, without any signs of discouragement, and he went about so befogged with that feverish restoration, so absorbed in his task, and so far removed from other minor matters of state that he ran smack into reality when an absent-minded aide mentioned by mistake the problem of the children and he asked from his cloud what children, the children general sir, but which ones, God damn it, because up till then they had hidden from him the fact that the army was keeping in secret custody the children who picked the lottery numbers for fear they would tell why the presidential ticket always won, they told the parents who complained that it wasn't true while they made up a better answer, they told them they were rumors spread by traitors, lies of the opposition, and those who demonstrated in front of the barracks were repulsed with mortar fire and there was a public slaughter that we had also hidden from him so that you wouldn't be bothered general sir, because the fact was that the children were locked up in the dungeons of the harbor fort under the best of conditions, in excellent spirits and very good health, but the trouble is that now we don't know what to do with them general sir, and there were around two thousand of them. The infallible method for winning the lottery had occurred to him without his looking for it, observing the inlaid numbers on billiard balls, and it had been such a simple and dazzling idea that he himself couldn't believe it when he saw the anxious crowd that had overflowed the main square since noontime taking out their numbers in anticipation of the miracle under the broiling sun with a clamor of gratitude and signs painted with glory to the magnanimous one who dis-tributes happiness, anachronistic wheels of fortune and faded animal lotteries, the rubble of other worlds and other times that pillaged in the realm of fortune in an attempt to thrive on the crumbs of so many illusions, they opened the balcony at three o'clock, they brought up the three children under the age of seven chosen at random by the crowd itself so that there would be no doubt concerning the honesty of the method, they gave each child a bag of a different color after showing trustworthy witnesses that there were ten billiard balls numbered from one to zero inside each bag, your attention, ladies and gentlemen, the throng held its breath, each child with his eyes blindfolded will take a ball from each bag, first the child with the blue bag, then the one with the red, and last the one with the yellow, one after the other the three children put their hands into their bags, felt at the bottom nine balls that were just alike and one that was ice-cold, and following the orders we had given them in secret they chose the ice-cold ball, showed it to the crowd, sang it out, and in that way they drew out the three balls that had been kept on ice for several days with the three numbers of the ticket he had reserved for himself, but we never thought about the children's telling it general sir, it occurred to us so late that there was nothing else to do but hide them three by three, and then five by five, and then twenty by twenty, just imagine general sir, so pulling on the thread of the plot he ended up discovering that all of the officers in the high command of the land, sea and air forces were implicated in the miraculous bounty of the national lottery, he found out that the first children went up on the balcony with the consent of their parents and even trained by them in the illusory science of telling the numbers inlaid in ivory by touch, but that the following ones were brought up by force because the rumor had spread that once the children went up they didn't come back down, their parents hid them, they buried them alive while the raiding parties that sought them in the middle of the night passed, the emergency forces did not cordon off the main square to control the public delirium as they had told him, but to hold at bay the crowds that they herded like a drove of cattle with threats of death, the diplomats who had asked for an audience to mediate the conflict ran into the absurd tale that the functionaries themselves told them that the legend of his strange illnesses was true, that he couldn't receive them because toads had proliferated in his belly, that he could only sleep standing up so as not to injure himself with the iguana crest that was growing along his spine, they had hidden the messages of protest and entreaties from all over the world from him, they had kept secret from him a telegram from the Supreme Pontiff in which our apostolic anguish over the fate of the innocents was expressed, there was no room in jail for any more rebellious parents general sir, there were no more children for the Monday drawing, God damn it, what kind of a mess have we got into. In spite of all, he did not measure the true depth of the abyss until he saw the children like cattle in a slaughterhouse in the inner courtyard of the harbor fort, he saw them come out of the dungeons like a stampede of goats blinded by the brilliance of the sun after so many months of nocturnal terror, they were confused in the light, there were so many at the same time that he didn't see them as two thousand separate children but as a huge shapeless animal that was giving off an impersonal stench of sun-baked skin and making a noise of deep waters and its multiple nature saved it from destruction, because it was impossible to do away with such a quantity of life without leaving a trace of horror that would travel around the world, God damn it, there was nothing to do, and with that conviction he called together the high command, fourteen trembling commandants who were never so to be feared because they had never been so frightened, he took his time scrutinizing the eyes of each one,

one by one, and then he saw that he was alone against them all, so he kept his head erect, hardened his voice, exhorted them to unity now more than ever for the good name and honor of the armed forces, absolved them of all blame pounding his fist on the table so that they would not see the tremor of uncertainty and ordered them as a consequence to continue at their posts fulfilling their duties with the same zeal and the same authority as they had always done, because my supreme and irrevocable decision is that nothing has happened, meeting adjourned, I will answer for it. As a simple means of precaution he took the children out of the harbor fort and sent them in nocturnal boxcars to the least-inhabited regions of the country while he confronted the storm unleashed by the official and solemn declaration that it was not true, not only were there no children in the power of the authorities but there was not a single prisoner of any type in the jails, the rumor of the mass kidnapping was an infamous lie on the part of traitors to get people stirred up, the doors of the nation were open so that the truth could be established, let people come and look for it, they came, a commission from the League of Nations came and overturned the most hidden stones in the country and questioned all the people they wanted to and how they wanted to with such minute detail that Bendición Alvarado was to ask who were those intruders dressed like spiritualists who came into her house looking for two thousand children under the beds, in her sewing basket, in her paintbrush jars, and who finally bore public witness to the fact that they had found the jails closed down, the nation in peace, everything in place, and they had not found any indication to confirm the public suspicion that there had been or might have been a violation by intent or by action or by omission of the principles of human rights, rest easy, general, they left, he waved goodbye to them from the window with a handkerchief with embroidered edges and with the feeling of relief over something that was finished for good, goodbye, you horse's asses, smooth sailing and a prosperous trip, he sighed, the trouble's over, but General Rodrigo de Aguilar reminded him no, the trouble wasn't over because the children were still left general sir, and he slapped his forehead with the palm of his hand, God damn it, he'd forgotten completely, what'll we do with the children. Trying to free himself from that evil thought while a drastic formula was taking shape in his mind he had them take the children out of their hiding place in the jungle and carry them off in the opposite direction to the provinces of perpetual rain where there were no treasonous winds to spread their voices, where the animals of the earth rotted away as they walked and lilies grew on words and octopuses swam among the trees, he ordered them taken to the Andean grottoes of perpetual mists so that no one would find out where they were, for them to be transferred from the shady Novembers of putrefaction to the Februaries of horizontal days so that no one would know when they were, he sent them quinine tablets and wool blankets when he found out they were shivering with fever because for days and days they had been hidden in rice paddies with mud up to their necks so that the Red Cross airplanes wouldn't discover them, he had the light of the sun tinted red along with the glow of the stars to cure them of scarlet fever, he had them fumigated from the air with insecticides so that fat banana lice would not devour them, he sent them showers of candy and snowstorms of ice cream from airplanes and parachutes with loads of Christmas toys to keep them happy while a magical solution could occur to him, and in that way he was getting out of the reach of their evil memory, he forgot about them, he sank into the desolate swamp of the uncountable nights all the same of his domestic insomnia, he heard the metal blows strike nine o'clock, he took down the hens who were sleeping on the cornices of government house and took them to the chicken coop, he had not finished counting the creatures sleeping in the scaffolding when a mulatto servant girl came in to collect the eggs, he sensed the sunlight of her age, heard the sound of her bodice, he jumped on top of her, be careful general, she murmured trembling, you'll break the eggs, let them break, God damn it, he said, he threw her down with a cuff without undressing her or getting undressed himself disturbed by the anxiety to flee this Tuesday with its green-shit snow, sleeping creatures, he slipped, he fell into the illusory vertigo of a precipice cut by livid stripes of evasion and outpourings of sweat and the sighs of a wild woman and deceitful threats of oblivion, on the fallen woman he was leaving the curve of the urgent tinkle of the shooting star that was his gold spur, the trace of saltpeter from his wheeze of an urgent spouse, his dog whine, his terror of existing through the flash and the silent thunder of the instantaneous explosion of the deep spark, but at the bottom of the precipice there was the shitted slime again, the hens' insomniac sleep, the affliction of the mulatto girl who got up with her dress all smeared by the yellow molasses of the yolks lamenting now you see what I told you general, the eggs broke, and he muttered trying to tame the rage of another love without love, write down how many they were, he told her, I'll take it out of your wages, he left, it was ten o'clock, he examined one by one the gums of the cows in the stables, he saw one of his women quartered by pain on the floor of her hut and he saw the midwife who took from out of her insides a steaming baby with the umbilical cord wrapped around its neck, it was a boy, what name shall we give him general sir, whatever you feel like, he answered, it was eleven o'clock, as on every night during his regime he counted the sentries, checked the locks, covered the birdcages, put out the lights, it was twelve o'clock, the nation was at peace, the world was asleep, he went to his bedroom through the darkened building across the strips of light from the fleeting dawns of the beacon turns, he hung up the lamp for leaving on the run, he put up the three bars, ran the three bolts, closed the three locks, sat down on the portable latrine, and while he was passing his meager urine he caressed the inclement child of a herniated testicle until the twist was straightened out, it fell asleep in his hand, the pain ceased, but it returned immediately with a lightning flash of panic when in through the window there came the lash of a wind from beyond the confines of the saltpeter deserts which scattered about the bedroom the sawdust of a song about tender-aged throngs who were asking about a gentleman who went to war who were sighing what pain what grief who climbed up onto a tower to see if he was coming who saw him coming back that he came back that well in a velvet box what pain what mourning, and it was a chorus of such numerous and distant voices that he could have gone to sleep with the illusion that the stars were singing, but he got up irate, that's enough, God damn it, he shouted, either them or me, he shouted, and it was them, because before dawn he ordered them to put the children in a barge loaded with cement, take them singing to the limits of the territorial waters, blow them up with a dynamite charge without giving them time to suffer as they kept on singing, and when the three officers who carried out the crime came to attention before him with news general sir that his order had been carried out, he promoted them two grades and decorated them with the medal of loyalty, but then he had them shot without honors as common criminals because there were orders that can be given but which cannot be carried out, God damn it, poor children. Experiences as harsh as that confirmed his very ancient certainty that the most feared enemy is within oneself in the confidence of the heart, that the very men he was arming and raising up so that they would support his regime will end up sooner or later spitting in the hand that feeds them, he wiped them out with one stroke, he took others out of nowhere, raised them to the highest ranks pointing at them according to the impulse of his inspiration, you to captain, you to colonel, you to general, and all the rest to lieutenant, what the hell, he watched them grow in their uniforms until they burst the seams, he lost sight of them, and a casual event like the discovery of two thousand sequestered children permitted him to discover that it was not just one man who had failed him but the whole supreme command of the armed forces who are only good for making me use up more milk and in times of trouble they shit in the plate they've just eaten out of, God damn it, I made them rich, he had won bread and respect for them, and yet he didn't have a moment's rest trying to keep clear of their ambition, he kept the most dangerous closest by to keep a better eye on them, the least bold he sent to frontier garrisons, because of them he had accepted the occupation by the marines, mother, not to fight yellow fever as Ambassador Thompson had written in the official communiqué, nor to protect him from public unrest, as the exiled politicians said, but to show our military men how to be decent people, and that's how it was, mother, to each his own, they taught them to walk with shoes on, to wipe themselves with paper, to use condoms, they were the ones who taught me the secret of maintaining parallel services to stir up distractive rivalries among the military, they invented for me the office of state security, the general investigation agency, the national department of public order, and so many other messes that I couldn't even remember them myself, identical organisms that he made look different in order to rule with more relaxation in the midst of the storm making them believe that some were being watched by others, mixing beach sand in with the gunpowder in the barracks and confusing the truth of his intentions with images of the opposite truth, and yet there were uprisings, he would storm into the barracks chewing the froth of his bile, shouting get out of the way you bastards here comes the one who gives the orders to the fright of the officers who were holding target practice with pictures of me, disarm them, he ordered without stopping but with so much authority that they disarmed themselves, take off those men's clothes you're wearing, he ordered, they took them off, the San Jerónimo base is in revolt general sir, he went in through the main gate dragging his huge feet of an old man in pain through a double file of mutinous guards who rendered him the honors of general supreme chief, he appeared in the post of the rebel command, without escort, without a weapon, but shouting with an explosion of power get down flat on the floor because the one who can do everything has arrived, on the floor, you bastards, nineteen officers of the general staff fell to the floor, face down, he paraded them eating dirt through the coastal villages so that the people could see how much a military man without a uniform is worth, sons of bitches, he heard over the other shouts in the aroused barracks his own irrevocable orders for the organizers of the revolt to be shot in the back, they displayed their corpses hanging by the heels in sun and dew so that nobody would fail to know how those who spit on God end up, tricky bastards, but the trouble didn't end with those bloody purges because with the least bit of carelessness he would find himself once more under the menace of that tentacular parasite he thought he had pulled out by the roots and which was proliferating again in the north winds of his power, in the shadow of the obligatory privileges and the crumbs of authority and the confidence of interest that he had to concede to the bravest officers even against his own will because it was impossible for him to maintain himself without them but also with them, condemned forever to live breathing the same air which asphyxiated him, God damn it, it wasn't fair, as it wasn't possible either to live with the perpetual surprise of the pureness of my comrade General Rodrigo de Aguilar who had come into my office with the face of a dead man anxious to know what had happened to those two thousand children of my first prize because everybody says we drowned them in the sea, and he said without changing expression not to believe rumors spread by traitors, old friend, the children are growing up in God's peace, he told him, every night I can hear them singing over there, he said, pointing with a broad sweep of his hand to an indefinite place somewhere in the universe, and he left Ambassador Evans himself wrapped in an aura of uncertainty when he replied to him impassively I don't know what children you're talking about since your own country's delegate to the League of Nations has made a public statement that the children in the schools are all there and in good health, what the hell, the mess is over, and yet he could not stop them from waking him up in the middle of the night with the news general sir that the two largest garrisons in the country were in revolt and also the Conde barracks two blocks away from the presidential palace, an insurrection of the most dangerous kind led by General Bonivento Barboza who had dug himself in with fifteen hundred very well armed and well supplied troops with matériel obtained as contraband through consuls sympathetic to the opposition politicians, so things are in no shape for licking one's fingers general sir, now we really are fucked up. In other times that volcanic subversion would have been a stimulant for his passion for risks, but he knew better than anyone what the real weight of his age was, that he barely had enough will to resist the ravages of his secret world, that on winter nights he could not get to sleep without first placating the herniated testicle in the hollow of his hand with a coo of tenderness of sleep my sweet to the child of painful whistles, that his spirits were slipping away as he sat on the toilet pushing out his soul drop by drop as through a filter thickened by the mold of so many nights of solitary urination, that his memory was unraveling, that he was not really sure he knew who was who, or from whom, at the mercy of an inescapable fate in that pitiful house which for some time he would have liked to exchange for another, far away from here, in some Indian settlement where no one would know that he had been the only president of the nation for so many and such long years that not even he himself had counted them, and still, when General Rodrigo de Aguilar offered himself as a mediator to negotiate a decorous compromise with the subversion he did not find himself in the presence of the dotty old man who would fall asleep at audiences but with the bison of old who without thinking about it for one instant answered not on your life, that he wasn't leaving, although it wasn't a question of leaving or not leaving but that everything is against us general sir, even the church, but he said no, the church is with the one in charge, he said, the generals of the high command having been meeting for forty-eight hours now already had not been able to reach an agreement, it doesn't matter he said, you'll see what they decide when they find out who pays them the most, the leaders of the civilian opposition have finally shown their faces and were conspiring openly in the street, all the better, he said, hang one from each lamppost on the main square so they'll know who the one is who can do anything, there's no way general sir, the people are with them, that's a lie, he said, the people are with me, so they won't get me out of here except dead, he decided, pounding the table with his rough maiden's hand as he only did in final decisions, and he slept until milking time when he found the reception room a shambles, because the insurrectionists in the Conde barracks had catapulted rocks which had not left one window intact in the eastern gallery and tallow balls which came in through the broken windows and kept the inhabitants of the building in a state of panic all through the night, if you could have seen general sir, we haven't closed an eye running back and forth with blankets and buckets of water to put out the puddles of fire that were lighting up in the least expected corner, but he scarcely paid any attention, I already told you not to pay them any heed, he said, dragging his graveyard feet along the corridors of ashes and scraps of carpets and singed tapestries, but they're going to keep it up, they told him, they had sent word that the flaming balls were just a warning, that the explosions will come after general sir, but he crossed the garden without paying attention to anyone, in the last shadows he breathed in the sound of the newborn roses, the disorders of the cocks in the sea wind, what shall we do general, I already told you not to pay any attention to them, God damn it, and as on every day at that hour he went to oversee the milking, so as on every day at that hour the insurrectionists in the Conde barracks saw the mule cart with the six barrels of milk from the presidential stable appear, and in the driver's seat there was the same lifetime carter with the oral message that the general sends you this milk even though you keep on spitting in the hand that feeds you, he shouted it out with such innocence that General Bonivento Barboza gave the order to accept it on the condition that the carter taste it first so that they could be sure it wasn't poisoned, and then they opened the iron gates and the fifteen hundred rebels looking down from the inside balconies saw the cart drive in to the center of the paved courtyard, they saw the orderly climb up onto the driver's seat with a pitcher and a ladle to give the carter the milk to taste, they saw him uncork the first barrel, they saw

him floating in the ephemeral backwash of a dazzling explosion
and they saw nothing else to the end of time in the volcanic heat
of the mournful yellow mortar building in which no flower ever
grew, whose ruins remained suspended for an instant in the air
from the tremendous explosion of the six barrels of dynamite.
That's that, he sighed in the presidential palace, shaken by the
seismic wind that blew down four more houses around the barracks and broke the wedding crystal in cupboards all the way to
the outskirts of the city, that's that, he sighed, when the garbage
trucks removed from the courtyards of the harbor fort the
corpses of eighteen officers who had been shot in double rows in
order to save ammunition, that's that, he sighed when General
Rodrigo de Aguilar came to attention before him with the news
general sir that once again there was no more room in the jails
for political prisoners, that's that, he sighed, when the bells
began to peal in celebration, the festival rockets, the music of
glory that announced the advent of another hundred years of
peace, that's that, God damn it, the mess is over, he said, and he
was so convinced, so careless about himself, so negligent about
his personal safety that one morning he was crossing the courtyard on his way back from the milking and his instinct failed
him as he did not see in time the bogus leper who rose up out
of the rosebushes to cut off his path in the slow October drizzle
and only too late did he see the sudden glimmer of the flourished revolver, the trembling index finger that began to squeeze
the trigger when he shouted with his arms opened wide offering
him his chest, I dare you you bastard, I dare you, dazzled by the
surprise that his time had come contrary to the clearest forecasts
of the basins, shoot if you've got any balls, he shouted, in the
imperceptible instant of hesitation in which a pale star lighted
up in the eyes of the attacker, his lips withered, his will trembled,
and then he let go with both fists as hammers on his eardrums,

he dropped him, he moved him on the ground with a pile-driver kick on the jaw, from another world he heard the uproar of the guard who came running to his shouts, he passed through the blue explosion of the continuous thunder of the five explosions of the false leper writhing in a pool of blood having shot himself in the stomach with the five bullets in his revolver so that he would not be taken alive by the fearsome interrogators of the presidential guard, he heard over the other shouts in the aroused building his own terminating orders that the body be quartered as a lesson, they sliced it up, they displayed the head smeared with rock salt in the main square, the right leg in the eastern confines of Santa María del Altar, the left one in the limitless saltpeter deserts of the west, one arm on the plains, the other in the jungle, the pieces of torso fried in hog fat and exposed to sun and dew until all that was left was naked bone as chancy and difficult as things were in this nigger whorehouse so that there would be no one who didn't know how those who raised their hands against their father ended up, and still green with rage he went among the rosebushes that the presidential guard had cleaned of lepers at bayonet point to see if at last they would show their faces, sneaky bastards, he went up to the main floor kicking aside the cripples to see if at last they would learn who it was who put their mothers to birth, sons of bitches, he went along the corridors shouting for them to get out of the way, God damn it, here comes the one who gives the orders in the midst of the panic of office workers and the persistent adulators who proclaimed him the eternal one, all through the house he left the rocky trail of his blacksmith-oven wheeze, he disappeared into the hearing room like a fugitive lightning flash toward the private quarters, he went into the bedroom, shut the three crossbars, the three bolts, the three locks, and with his fingertips he took off the pants he was wearing that were soaked in shit. He did not find a moment of rest as he sniffed round about to find the hidden enemy who had armed the bogus leper, for he felt that there was someone within reach of his hand, someone that close to his life who knew the hiding place of his honey, who had his eye at the keyholes and his ears at the walls every minute and everywhere just like my pictures, a voluble presence who whistled in the January trade winds and he recognized him in the jasmine embers on hot nights, one who had pursued him months on end in the fright of his insomnia dragging his fearful ghostly feet through the most hidden rooms of the darkened building, until one night at dominoes he saw the omen materialize in a pensive hand that finished the game with the double five, and it was as if an inner voice had revealed that that hand was the hand of treason, God damn it, it's him, he said to himself perplexed, and then he raised his eyes through the flow of light from the lamp hanging over the center of the table and met the handsome artilleryman's eyes of my soul comrade General Rodrigo de Aguilar, what a mess, his strong right arm, his sacred accomplice, it wasn't possible, he thought, all the more pained as he deciphered more deeply the weave of the false truths with which they had diverted his attention for so many years in order to hide the brutal truth that my lifetime comrade was in the service of politicians of fortune whom for convenience's sake he had taken from the darkest corners of the federalist war and had made them rich and had heaped fabulous privileges upon them, he had let himself be used by them, he had tolerated the fact that they were using him to rise up to a point that the old aristocracy swept away by the irresistible breath of the liberal whirlwind had never dreamed of and they still wanted more, God damn it, they wanted the place of the elect of God that he had reserved for himself, they wanted to be me, motherfuckers, with the way lighted by the glacial lucidity and the infinite prudence of the man who had managed to accumulate the most confidence and authority in his regime by taking advantage of the privileges of being the only person from whom he accepted papers to sign, he had him read aloud the executive orders and ministerial laws that only I could put through, he pointed out the amendments, he signed with his thumbprint and underneath he stamped it with the ring which he then put away in a strongbox whose combination only he knew, to your health, comrade, he always said to him when he handed him the signed papers, here's something to wipe yourself with, he told him laughing, and that was how General Rodrigo de Aguilar had succeeded in establishing another system of power within the power as widespread and as fruitful as mine, and not content with that in the shadows he had set up the mutiny of the Conde barracks with the complicity and unreserved assistance of Ambassador Norton, his buddy in matters of Dutch whores, his fencing master, the one who had smuggled in the ammunition in barrels of Norwegian cod under the protection of diplomatic immunity while he would use balm on me at the domino table with the incense candles saying there was no government more friendly, or just and exemplary than mine, and they were also the ones who had put the revolver in the hand of the false leper along with fifty thousand pesos in bills cut in half which we found buried at the attacker's home, and the other half of which was to be turned over after the crime by my own lifetime comrade, mother, what a bitter mess, and still they didn't resign themselves to failure but had ended up conceiving the perfect coup without shedding a drop of blood, not even yours general sir, because General Rodrigo de Aguilar had collected the most unimpeachable evidence that I spent my sleepless nights conversing with vases and oil paintings of patriots and archbishops in the darkened building, that I took the

cow's temperature with a thermometer and gave them phenace-
tin to eat in order to bring down their fever, that I had had a
tomb built for an admiral of the ocean sea who did not exist
except in my feverish imagination when I myself with my own
blessed eyes had seen the three caravels anchored across the harbor from my window, that I had squandered public funds on
the irrepressible addiction of buying ingenious inventions and
had even tried to get the astronomers to upset the solar system
in order to please a beauty queen who had only existed in the
visions of his delirium, and that during an attack of senile
dementia had ordered two thousand children put on a barge
loaded with cement that was dynamited at sea, mother, just
imagine, what sons of bitches, and it was on the basis of that
solemn testimony that General Rodrigo de Aguilar and the high
command of the presidential guard in plenary session had
decided to intern him in the asylum for illustrious old men on
the reefs at midnight of March first next during the annual banquet in honor of the Holy Guardian Angel, the patron saint of
bodyguards, or within three days general sir, just imagine, but
in spite of the imminence and scope of the conspiracy he showed
no sign that might have aroused the suspicion that he had
uncovered it, but at the appointed hour as every year he received
his personal guard as guests and had them sit at the banquet
table for apéritifs until General Rodrigo de Aguilar arrived to
make the toast of honor, he chatted with them, laughed with
them, one after the other, the officers furtively looked at their
watches, put them to their ears, wound them, it was five minutes
to twelve and General Rodrigo de Aguilar hadn't arrived, it was
as hot as a ship's boiler and there was a perfume of flowers, it
smelled of gladioli and tulips, it smelled of live roses in the
closed room, somebody opened a window, we breathe, we look
at our watches, we feel a soft sea breeze with the smell of the

delicate stew of a wedding feast, they were all sweating except him, we were all suffering from the drowsiness of the moment under the firm glow of the age-old animal who blinked with open eyes in a space of his own reserved in another age of the world, health, he said, the hand with no appeal like a languid lily raised again the glass with which he had toasted all evening without drinking, the visceral sound of watch works in the silence of a final abyss, it was twelve o'clock but General Rodrigo de Aguilar was not arriving, someone started to get up, please, he said, he turned him to stone with the fatal look of nobody move, nobody breathe, nobody live without my permission until twelve o'clock finished chiming, and then the curtains parted and the distinguished Major General Rodrigo de Aguilar entered on a silver tray stretched out full length on a garnish of cauliflower and laurel leaves, steeped with spices, oven brown, embellished with the uniform of five golden almonds for solemn occasions and the limitless loops for valor on the sleeve of his right arm, fourteen pounds of medals on his chest and a sprig of parsley in his mouth, ready to be served at a banquet of comrades by the official carvers to the petrified horror of the guests as without breathing we witness the exquisite ceremony of carving and serving, and when every plate held an equal portion of minister of defense stuffed with pine nuts and aromatic herbs, he gave the order to begin, eat hearty gentlemen.

He had skirted the reefs of so many earthly disorders, so many ominous eclipses, so many flaming tallow balls in the sky that it seemed impossible for someone from our time to trust still the prognostications of the cards regarding his fate. Yet, while the plans for reassembling and embalming the body went forward, even the most candid among us waited without so confessing for the fulfillment of ancient predictions, such as the one that said that on the day of his death the mud from the swamps would go back upriver to its source, that it would rain blood, that hens would lay pentagonal eggs, and that silence and darkness would cover the universe once more because he was the end of creation. It was impossible not to believe all of this since the few newspapers still publishing were still dedicated to proclaiming his eternity and counterfeiting his splendor with material from their files, every day they displayed him to us as during ecstatic times and on the front page in his tenacious uniform with the five sad pips of his days of glory, with more authority and diligence and better health than ever in spite of the fact that many years ago we had lost count of his age, in the usual pictures he was once more dedicating well-known monuments or public installations that no one knew about in real life, he presided over solemn ceremonies which they said had taken place yesterday but which had really taken place during the last century, even though we knew it wasn't true, because no one had seen him in public ever since Leticia Nazareno's atrocious death when he was left alone in that no-man's-land of a house while the daily affairs of government went along all by themselves and only through the momentum of his immense power over so many years, he locked himself up until death in the run-down palace from whose highest windows we were now watching with tight hearts the same gloomy sunset that he must have seen so many times from his throne of illusions, we saw the intermittent beacon of the lighthouse as it flooded the ruined salons with its green and languid waters, we saw the lamps of the poor inside the shell of what had once been the coral reefs of solar glass of the ministries which had been invaded by hordes of poor people when the multicolored huts on the harbor hills had been leveled by another of our numerous cyclones, we saw below the scattered, steamy city, the instantaneous horizon of pale lightning flashes in the crater of ashes of the sea that had been sold, the first night without him, his vast lakelike empire of malarial anemones, its hot villages on the deltas of muddy tributaries, the avid barbed-wire fences of his private provinces where there flourished without count or measure a new species of magnificent cows who were born with the hereditary presidential brand. Not only had we ended up really believing that he had been conceived to survive the third comet but that conviction had infused us with a security and a restful feeling that we tried to hide with all manner of jokes about old age, we attributed the senile characteristics of tortoises and the habits of elephants to him, in bars we told the story that someone had announced to the cabinet that he had died and that they had asked each other in fright who's going to tell him, ha, ha, ha, when the truth was that it wouldn't have mattered to him if he knew it or not or he himself wouldn't have been very sure whether that street joke was true or false, because at that time no one except him knew that all he had left in the pockets of his memory were a few odd scraps of the vestiges of the past, that he was alone in the world, deaf as a post, dragging his thick decrepit feet through dark offices where someone in a frock coat and starched collar had made an enigmatic signal to him with a handkerchief, hello, he said to him, the mistake became law, office workers in the presidential palace had to stand up with a white handkerchief when he passed, the sentries along the corridors, the lepers in the rose beds waved to him with a white handkerchief when he passed, hello general sir, hello, but he didn't hear, he had heard nothing since the sunset mourning rites for Leticia Nazareno when he thought that the birds in his cages were losing their voices from so much singing and he fed them his own honey so they would sing louder, he fed them Cantorina with an eyedropper, he sang them songs from a different age, bright January moon, he sang, for he had not realized that it was not the birds who were losing the strength of their voices but that it was he who was hearing less and less, and one night the buzzing in his eardrums broke all apart, it was over, it had been changed into an atmosphere of mortar through which only the farewell laments of the illusory ships from the shadows of power could pass, imaginary winds passed, the racket of inner birds which finally consoled him for the abyss of silence of the birds of reality. The few people who had access to government house then would see him in the wicker rocking chair enduring the drowsiness of two in the afternoon under the arbor of wild pansies, he had unbuttoned his tunic, had taken off his saber and the belt with the national colors, he had taken off his boots but left on the purple socks from the twelve dozen the Supreme Pontiff had sent him from his private sockery, the girls from a nearby school who would climb over the rear walls where the guard was less rigid had surprised him many times in that heavy insomnia, pale, with medicinal leaves struck to his temples, tiger-striped by the bars of light from the arbor in the ecstasy of a manta ray lying face up at the bottom of a pool, old soursop, they would shout at him, he would see them distorted in the haze of the quivering heat, he would smile at them, wave at them with the hand without the velvet glove, but he couldn't hear them, he caught the shrimp-mud stench of the sea breeze, he caught the pecking of the hens on his toes, but he did not catch the luminous thunder of the cicadas, he couldn't hear the girls, he couldn't hear anything. His only contacts with the reality of this world were by then a few scattered scraps of his largest memories, only they kept him alive after he had been despoiled of the affairs of state and stayed swimming in a state of innocence in the limbo of power, only then did he confront the devastating winds of his excessive years when he wandered at dusk through the deserted building, hid in the darkened offices, tore the margins off ledgers and in his florid hand wrote on them the remaining residue of the last memories that preserved him from death, one night he had written my name is Zacarías, he read it again under the fleeting light of the beacon, he read it over and over and the name repeated so many times ended up seeming remote and alien to him, God damn it, he said to himself, tearing up the strip of paper, I'm me, he said to himself, and he wrote on another strip that he had turned a hundred around the time the comet had passed again although by then he wasn't sure how many times he'd seen it pass, and on another ledger strip he wrote from memory honor the wounded and honor the faithful

soldiers who met death at foreign hands, for there were periods
when he wrote down everything he thought, everything he
knew, he wrote on a piece of cardboard and tacked it to the
door of a toilet that it was fourbidden to do any dirty bizness in
toylets because he had opened that door by mistake and had
surprised a high-ranking officer squatting down and masturbat-
ing into the bowl, he wrote down the few things he remembered
to make sure that he would never forget them, Leticia Nazareno,
he wrote, my only and legitimate spouse who had taught him
to read and write in the ripeness of his old age, he made an effort
to bring back her public image, he tried to see her again with
her taffeta parasol with the colors of the flag and her first lady's
fur piece of silver-fox tails, but all he could manage was to
remember her naked at two in the afternoon under the flour-
haze light of the mosquito netting, he remembered the slow
repose of your soft and pale body surrounded by the hum of the
electric fan, he felt your living teats your smell of a bitch in heat,
the corrosive humors of your ferocious novice nun hands that
curdled milk and rusted gold and withered flowers, but they
were good hands for love, because only she had reached the
inconceivable triumph of take your boots off so you don't soil
my Brabant sheets, and he took them off, take off your saber,
and your truss, and your leggings take everything off my love I
can't feel you, and he took everything off for you as he had never
done before and would never do again for any woman after
Leticia Nazareno, my only and legitimate love, he sighed, he
wrote down the signs on the yellowed ledger margins that he
rolled like cigarettes and hid in the most unlikely chinks in
the house where only he would be able to find them to remember who he was himself when he could no longer remember
anything, where no one ever found them when even the image
of Leticia Nazareno had finally slipped away down the drain of

memory and all that remained was the indestructible memory of his mother Bendición Alvarado on the goodbye afternoons at the suburban mansion, his dying mother who had gathered the hens together by making noise with the kernels of corn in a calabash gourd so that he wouldn't notice that she was dying, who still brought him fruit drinks to the hammock hung between the tamarinds so that he wouldn't suspect that she could barely breathe because of her pain, his mother who had conceived him alone, who had borne him alone, who was rotting away alone until the solitary suffering became so intense that it was stronger than her pride and she had to ask her son to look at my back to see why I feel this hot-ember heat that won't let me live, and she took off her blouse, turned around, and with silent horror he saw that her back had been chewed away by steaming ulcers in whose guava pulp pestilence the tiny bubbles of the first maggots were bursting. Bad times those general sir, there were no secrets of state that were not in the public domain, there was no order that was carried out with complete certainty ever since the exquisite corpse of General Rodrigo de Aguilar had been served up at the banquet table, but he didn't care, he didn't care about the stumbling of power during the bitter months in which his mother was rotting away in a slow fire in the bedroom next to his after the doctors most adept in Asiatic scourges decreed that her illness was not the plague, or scabies, or yaws, or any other Oriental pestilence, but some Indian curse that could only be cured by the one who had cast it, and he understood that it was death and he shut himself up to care for his mother with the abnegation of a mother, he stayed to rot with her so that no one would see her cooking in her stew of maggots, he ordered them to bring her hens to government house, they brought him the peacocks, the painted birds who wandered about at their pleasure through salons and offices so that his mother would not miss the rustic activities of the suburban mansion, he himself burned annato logs in the bedroom so that no one would catch the death stench of his dying mother, he himself with germicidal salves consoled the body that was red with Mercurochrome, yellow with picric, blue with methylene, he himself daubed with Turkish balms the steaming ulcers against the advice of the minister of health who was frightened to death of curses, what the hell, mother, it's better if we die together, he said, but Bendición Alvarado was aware of being the only one who was dying and she tried to reveal to her son the family secrets that she didn't want to carry to her grave, she told him how her placenta had been thrown to the hogs, lord, how it was that I could never establish which of so many backtrail fugitives was your father, she tried to tell him for history that she had conceived him standing up and with her hat on because of the storm of bluebottle flies around the wineskins of fermented molasses in the back room of a bar, she had given birth to him with difficulty in the entranceway to a convent, she had recognized him in the lights of the melancholy harps of the geraniums and his right testicle was the size of a fig and he relieved himself like a bellows and exhaled a bagpipe sigh with his breathing, she wrapped him up in the rags the novices had given her and she displayed him in marketplaces in case she might find someone who knew of a remedy that was better and above all cheaper than honey which was the only thing they recommended to her for his malformation, they consoled her with clichés, you can't get around fate, they told her, because after all the child was good for everything except playing wind instruments, they told her, and only a circus fortuneteller noticed that the newborn baby had no lines on the palm of his hand and that meant he had been born to be a king, and that's how it was, but he wasn't paying any attention to her, he begged her to go to sleep without digging up the past because it was more comfortable for him to believe that those stumbling blocks in national history were feverish deliriums, sleep, mother, he begged her, he wrapped her from head to toe in a linen sheet one of the many he had had made so as not to hurt her sores, he laid her down to sleep on her side with her hand on her heart, he consoled her with don't try to remember that sorry mess, mother, in any case I'm me, sleep softly. The many and ardent official attempts to calm the public rumors that the matriarch of the nation was rotting away in life had been useless, they published contrived medical reports, but the very couriers who carried the bulletins averred that what they themselves denied was true, that the air of corruption was so intense in the dying woman's bedroom that it had even frightened the lepers away, that they had butchered rams in order to bathe her in warm blood, that they took away sheets soaked in iridescent matter that flowed from her sores and no matter how much they washed them they were unable to return them to their original splendor, that no one had seen him again in the milking stalls or in the concubines' rooms where he had always been seen at daybreak even in the worst of times, the primate archbishop himself had offered to administer the last rites to the dying woman but he had left him standing at the door, no one's dying, father, don't believe rumors, he told him, he shared his meals with his mother on the same plate with the same spoon in spite of the pesthouse atmosphere in the room, he bathed her before putting her to bed with thankful-dog soap while his heart stood still with pity from the instructions she gave him with the last threads of her voice for the care of the animals after her death, that the peacocks should not be plucked to make hats, yes mother, he said, and he rubbed her body all over with creolin, don't let them make the birds sing at parties, yes mother, and he wrapped her

in the sleeping sheet, they should take the hens out of their nests
when there's thunder so they don't hatch basilisks, yes mother,
and he laid her down with her hand on her heart, yes mother,
sleep easy, he kissed her forehead, he slept the few hours remaining lying face down next to the bed, hanging on the drift of her
sleep, hanging on the interminable delirium that was becoming
more lucid as it approached death, learning with his accumulated rage gathered each night to bear up under the immense
fury of the Monday of grief when the terrible silence of the
world at dawn awoke him and it was that his mother of my life
Bendición Alvarado had stopped breathing, and then he
unwrapped the loathsome body and saw in the tenuous glow of
the first cock's crow that there was another identical body with
the hand on the heart painted in profile on the sheet, and he saw
that the painted body had no plague wrinkles or ravages of old
age but that it was firm and tight as if painted in oil on both
sides of the shroud and it gave off a natural fragrance of young
flowers that purified the hospital atmosphere of the bedroom
and try as they might by rubbing with nitrate rock and boiling
it in lye they could not erase it from the sheet because it was
integrated front and back into the very material of the linen, and
it was eternal linen, but he had not been calm enough to measure the scope of that miracle but had left the bedroom slam-
ming the door with such rage that it sounded like a shot
throughout the building, and then the bells in the cathedral
began tolling and then those of every church in the nation which
tolled without pause for one hundred days, and those who woke
up to the bells understood with no illusions that he was once
more the master of all his power and that the enigma of his heart
oppressed by the rage over that death was rising up stronger
than ever against the whims of reason and dignity and indul-
gence, because his mother of my life Bendición Alvarado had

died on that early dawn of Monday February twenty-third and a new century of confusion and scandal was beginning in the world. None of us was old enough to have witnessed that death but the fame of the funeral ceremonies had come down to our times and we had trustworthy reports that he did not go back to being what he had been before for the rest of his life, no one had the right to disturb his orphan's insomnia for much more than the hundred days of official mourning, he was not seen again in the house of grief whose confines had been overflown by the immense resonances of the funeral bells, he had no time except for his mourning, he spoke to himself in sighs, the household guard went about barefoot as during the first years of his regime and only the hens could do what they wanted in the forbidden house whose monarch had become invisible, bleeding with rage in the wicker rocking chair while his mother of my soul Bendición Alvarado was going through those wastelands of heat and misery inside a coffin full of sawdust and chopped ice so that her body would not rot more than it had in life, for the body had been carried in a solemn procession to the least-explored corners of his realm so that no one would go without the privilege of honoring her memory, they carried it with hymns of black-ribbon winds to stations on the upland plains where it was received with the same mournful music by the same mournful throngs who in other days of glory had come to see the power hidden in the shadows of the presidential coach, they displayed the body in the convent of the Sisters of Charity where a wandering birdwoman at the beginning of time had given difficult birth to a no-man's-son who became king, they opened the large doors of the sanctuary for the first time in a century, mounted troops made a roundup of Indians in the villages, they herded them along, drove them with rifle butts into the vast nave of the church afflicted by the icy suns of the

stained-glass windows where nine bishops in pontificals sang
Tenebrae, rest in peace in your glory, the deacons sang, the aco-
lytes, rest in your ashes, they sang, outside it was raining on the
geraniums, the novices distributed cane juice and the bread of
the dead, people sold spareribs, rosaries, flasks of holy water
under the stone arcades of the courtyards, there was music in
the sidewalk cafés, there was gunpowder, there was dancing in
the entranceways, it was Sunday, now and forever, they were
years of festivals along the escape trails and the foggy mountain
passes where his mother of my death Bendición Alvarado had
passed into life following the son who was making merry in the
federalist whirlwind, for she had taken care of him during the
war, she had kept the troops' mules from trampling him when
he flopped onto the ground rolled up in a blanket, unconscious,
talking nonsense because of tertian fever, she had tried to incul-
cate in him her ancestral fear of the dangers that lay in wait in
the cities by the shadowy sea for people from the plains, she was
afraid of the viceroys, the statues, the crabs that drink the tears
of the newborn, she had trembled in terror before the majesty
of the house of power which she first saw through the rain on
the night of the attack without having imagined then that it was
the house where she would die, the house of solitude where he
was, where he asked himself in the heat of rage lying face down
on the floor where the hell have you gone, mother, in what
grubby mangrove swamp has your body got entangled, who
shoos the butterflies from your face, he sighed, prostrate with
grief, while his mother Bendición Alvarado floated along under
a canopy of banana leaves through the nauseating vapors of the
swamps to be displayed in backwoods public schools, in barracks on the saltpeter deserts, in Indian corrals, they displayed
her in the main houses along with a picture of her when she was
young, was languid, was beautiful, a diadem had been placed on

her forehead, a lace gorget had been placed around her neck against her will, she had let them put powder on her face and lipstick on her mouth for just that one time, they put a silk tulip in her hand so that she would hold it that way, not like that, madam, like this, casually in her lap when the Venetian photographer of European monarchs took her official portrait as first lady as a final proof against any suspicion of substitution, and they were identical, for nothing had been left to chance, the body was being reconstructed in secret sessions as the cosmetics wore off and the skin wrinkled as the paraffin melted in the heat, they removed the mildew from her eyelids during the rainy season, army seamstresses kept her burial dress in shape as if it had been put on yesterday and they maintained in a state of grace the crown of orange blossoms and the veil of a virgin bride which she had never had during her lifetime, so that no one in this brothel of idolaters would ever dare repeat that you were different from your picture, mother, so that no one will forget who it is who rules till the end of time even in the poorest settlements on jungle sand dunes where after so many years of being forgotten at midnight they saw the return of the ancient riverboat with its wooden paddle wheel with all lights on and they received it with Easter drums thinking that the times of glory had returned, long live the stud, they shouted, blessed be the one who comes in the name of truth, they shouted, they jumped into the water with their fattened armadillos, with a pumpkin the size of an ox, they climbed over the carved wood railings to render the tribute of submission to the invisible power whose dice decided the fate of the nation and they stood breathless before the catafalque of chopped ice and rock salt which was multiplied by the startling glass of the mirrors in the presidential galley, exposed to public judgment under the fan blades in the archaic pleasure boat that traveled month after month among the ephemeral isles of the equatorial tributaries until it got lost in a nightmare age in which gardenias had the use of reason and iguanas flew about in the darkness, the world ended, the wooden wheel ran aground on sandbanks of gold, broke, the ice melted, the salt turned liquid, the swollen body remained floating adrift in a soup of sawdust, and yet it didn't rot, quite the contrary general sir, because then we saw her open her eyes and we saw that her pupils were bright and had the color of January wolfsbane and their usual quality of lunar stones, and even the most incredulous among us had seen the glass cover of the coffin fog over from the vapor of her breath and we had seen living and fragrant perspiration coming from her pores, and we saw her smile. You can't imagine what it was all like general sir, it was fantastic, we've seen mules give birth, we've seen flowers growing in the salt flats, we've seen deaf-mutes confused by the miracles of their own cries of miracle, miracle, miracle, they broke the glass of the coffin general sir and they were at the point of making mincemeat out of the corpse in order to distribute the relics, so we had to use a battalion of grenadiers to hold back the frantic mobs who were arriving in a tumult from the breeding ground of islands which is the Caribbean captivated by the news that the soul of your mother Bendición Alvarado had obtained from God the faculty of going against the laws of nature, they were selling shreds of the shroud, they were selling scapulars, waters from her body, cards with her picture as a queen, but it was such a huge and wild rabblement that it looked more like a torrent of untamed steers whose hoofs devastated everything they found in their path and they made an earthquake roar that even you yourself can hear from here if you listen carefully general sir, listen to it, and he cupped his hand behind his ear which was buzzing less, he listened carefully, and then he heard, mother of mine Bendición Alvarado, he heard the endless thunder, he saw the bubbling swamp of the vast crowd spreading out all the way to the horizon of the sea, he saw the torrent of lighted candles that brought out a different and even more radiant day within the radiant brightness of noon, for his mother of my soul Bendición Alvarado was returning to the city of her ancient terrors as she had arrived the first time with the turmoil of war, with the raw-meat smell of war, but free forever of the risks of the world because he had them tear the pages about the viceroys out of school primers so that they would not exist in history, he had forbidden the statues that disturbed your sleep, mother, so that now she was returning without her congenital fears on the shoulders of a peaceful multitude, she was returning without a coffin, under a clear sky, in an air forbidden to butterflies, overwhelmed by the golden weight of the religious offerings that had been hung on her during the interminable journey from the far reaches of the jungle across his vast and convulsed realm of sorrow, hidden under the pile of small gold crutches that recovered cripples had hung on her, the gold stars of shipwrecked sailors, the gold babies of incredulous barren women who had had to give emergency birth in the bushes, as in the war, general sir, drifting along in the center of the sweeping torrent of the biblical move of a whole nation which could not find a place to put down its kitchenware, its animals, the remains of a life with no more hope of redemption than the very secret prayers that Bendición Alvarado said during combat to turn the direction of the bullets shot at her son, how he had come in the tumult of the war with a red rag on his head shouting during the lull in fighting from the delirium of fever long live the liberal party, God damn it, long live victorious federalism, shitty Goths, even though really drawn along by the atavistic curiosity of knowing the sea, except that the misery-ridden crowd that had invaded the city with the corpse of his mother was more turbulent and frantic than any that had ravaged the country during the adventures of the federalist war, more voracious than that turmoil, more terrible than that panic, the most tremendous thing my eyes had seen in all the uncounted years of his power, the whole world general sir, look, what a wonder. Convinced by the evidence, he came out of the mist of his mourning, he came out pale, hard, with a black armband, resolved to make use of all the resources of his authority to attain the canonization of his mother Bendición Alvarado on the basis of the overwhelming proofs of her qualities as a saint, he sent his ministers of letters to Rome, once more he invited the apostolic nuncio for chocolate and cookies in the shafts of light under the pansy bower, he received him in a familiar way, he lying in his hammock, shirtless, fanning himself with his white hat, and the nuncio sitting opposite him with the cup of steaming chocolate, immune to the heat and the dust inside the lavender aura of his Sunday cassock, immune to the tropical languor, immune to the shitting of the dead mother's birds as they flew free through the puddlelike splotches of sun from the covering, he took measured sips of the vanilla chocolate, chewed the cookies with the modesty of a bride trying to delay the inevitable poison in the last sip, rigid in the wicker chair which he never let anyone sit in, only you, father, as on those mallow-mild afternoons of the days of glory when another old and innocent nuncio tried to convert him to the faith of Christ with Scholastic riddles from Thomas Aquinas, except that now I'm the one who is calling upon you to convert, father, that's the way the world turns, but I believe now, although in reality he didn't believe anything in this world or any other except that his mother of my life had a right to the glory of altars because of the very merits of her vocation for sacrifice and her exemplary modesty, so much so that he wasn't basing his request upon the public excitement over the fact that the north star moved along in the same direction as the funeral cortege and stringed instruments played all by themselves in their cabinets when they heard the corpse pass by but he based it on the virtue of this sheet which he unfurled full sail in the splendor of August so that the nuncio could see what indeed he did see printed on the texture of the linen, he saw the image of his mother Bendición Alvarado with no trace of old age or the ravages of disease lying on her side with her hand on her heart, he felt the dampness of eternal sweat on her fingers, he breathed in the fragrance of living flowers in the midst of the uproar of the birds roused up by the breath of the miracle, you can see what a wonder, father, he said, showing the sheet up and down and on both sides, even the birds recognize her, but the nuncio was absorbed in the cloth with an incisive attention that had been capable of discovering impurities of volcanic ash in the materials worked by the great masters of Christendom, he had known the cracks in character and even the doubts of a faith from the intensity of a color, he had suffered the ecstasy of the roundness of the earth lying face up under the dome of a solitary chapel in an unreal city where time did not pass but floated, until he got enough courage to take his eyes off the sheet and his deep contemplation and declared with a soft but irreparable tone that the body printed on the linen was not an act of Divine Providence to give us one more proof of His infinite mercy, not that or anything like it, your excellency, it was the work of a painter who was very skilled in the good and evil arts and who had abused your excellency's greatness of heart, because that wasn't oil paint it was house paint of the cheapest kind, for painting window frames, your excellency, beneath the smell of the natural resins that had dissolved in the paint the bastard dew of turpentine still remained, plaster crusts remained, a persistent dampness remained that was not the sweat of the last shudder of death as they had made him believe but the fake dampness of linen soaked in linseed oil and kept in dark places, believe me I'm terribly sorry, the nuncio concluded with genuine sadness, but he couldn't bring himself to say anything more as he faced the granite old man who was looking at him without blinking from the hammock, who had listened to him from the slime of his lugubrious Asiatic silences without even moving his mouth to contradict him in spite of the fact that no one knew better than he the truth of the secret miracle of the sheet in which I myself wrapped you with my own hands, mother, I was frightened with the first silence of your death which was as if the world had dawned at the bottom of the sea, I saw the miracle, God damn it, but in spite of his certainty he didn't interrupt the verdict of the nuncio, he only blinked a couple of times without closing his eyes, as iguanas do, he only smiled, it's all right, father, he finally sighed, it's probably the way you say, but I warn you that you carry the burden of your words, I'll repeat it letter by letter so that you won't forget it for the rest of your life you carry the burden of your words, father, I'm not responsible. The world remained in a lethargy during the week of evil omens in which he didn't get out of the hammock even to eat, he used the fan to shoo off the tame birds who alighted on his body, he shooed away the splotches of light coming through the pansies thinking they were tame birds, he received no one, he gave no orders, but the forces of public order remained aloof when the mobs of hired fanatics stormed the palace of the Apostolic Nunciature, sacked its museum of historic relics, surprised the nuncio taking his siesta outdoors in the peaceful backwaters of the inner garden, dragged him naked onto the street, shat on him general sir, just imagine, but he didn't move from the hammock, he didn't blink when they came to him with the news general sir that they were parading the nuncio through the business streets on a donkey under a downpour of dishwater thrown onto him from balconies, shouted pretty boy at him, miss vatican, suffer the little children to come unto me, and only when they left him half dead on the garbage heap in the public market did he get up out of the hammock waving the birds out of the way with his hands, appear in the hearing room waving away the cobwebs of mourning with the black armband and his eyes puffy from poor sleep, and then he gave orders for the nuncio to be placed on a life raft with provisions for three days and they cast him adrift on the lane that cruise ships took to Europe so that the whole world will know what happens to foreigners who lift their hands against the majesty of the nation, and the Pope will learn now and forever that he may be Pope in Rome with his ring on his finger sitting on his golden throne, but here I am what I am, God damn it, them and their shitty petticoats. It was an effective recourse, because before that year was out the process was initiated for the canonization of his mother Bendición Alvarado whose uncorrupted body was displayed for public veneration in the main nave of the cathedral, the Gloria was sung on altars, the state of war that he had declared against the Holy See was revoked, long live peace, the crowds on the main square shouted, long live God, they shouted, while in a solemn audience he received the auditor of the Sacred Congregation of the Rite and promoter and postulator of the faith Monsignor Demetrius Aldous, known as the Eritrene, to whom had been entrusted the mission of scrutinizing the life of Bendición Alvarado until not the slightest trace of doubt remained regarding the evidence of her sainthood, take as long as you like, father, he said to him, holding his hand in his, for he had an immediate confidence in that jaundiced Abyssinian who loved life above all things, he ate iguana eggs, general sir, he loved cockfights, the humor of mulatto women, dancing the cumbia, just like us general sir, the whole bag, and the most heavily guarded doors were opened without restriction by his orders so that the scrutiny of the devil's advocate would not run into difficulties of any kind, because there was nothing hidden just as there was nothing invisible in his measureless nightmare realm that wouldn't be an irrefutable proof that his mother of my soul Bendición Alvarado was predestined to the glory of altars, the nation is yours, father, here it is, and there he had it, of course, the armed forces maintained order at the palace of the Apostolic Nunciature across from which at dawn could be seen the uncountable lines of restored lepers who came to show the newborn skin over their sores, former victims of St. Vitus's dance came to thread needles before the disbelieving, to display their fortunes came those who had been enriched by the roulette table because Bendición Alvarado had revealed the numbers in her dreams to them, those who had had news of lost relatives and friends, those who had found their drowned ones, those who had had nothing and now had everything came, paraded by without cease through the oven-hot office decorated with cannibal-killing muskets and prehistoric tortoises of Sir Walter Raleigh where the tireless Eritrene listened to all without asking any questions, without interrupting, soaked in sweat, alien to the plague of humanity in decomposition that was accumulating in the office where the air was rarefied by the smoke of his cigarettes which were of the cheapest kind, he took detailed notes of the declarations of the witnesses and had them sign here, with your full name, or with an X, or like you general sir with your fingerprint, in one way or another, but they signed, the next one came in, just like the one before, I was consumptive, father, he said, I was consumptive, wrote the Eritrene, and now listen to me, sign, I was impotent, father, and now look how I can go all day long, I was impotent, he wrote in indelible ink so that his careful writing would be safe from changes until the end of humanity, I had a live animal inside my belly, father, I had a live animal inside my belly, he wrote coldly, drunk with cheap bitter coffee, poisoned by the rancid tobacco of the cigarette that he lighted from the butt of the previous one, his collar unbuttoned like an oarsman's general sir, that's a real stud of a priest, yes sir, he said, a real stud, to each his own, working ceaselessly, not eating anything so as not to lose any time until well into the night, but even then he wouldn't take any rest but would appear freshly bathed in the dockside taverns in his rough patched cassock, he would arrive starving, sit down at the long plank table to share the bream stew with the longshoremen, he tore the fish apart with his fingers, he ground it right down to the bone with those Luciferine teeth that had their own glow in the dark, he drank his soup from the edge of the plate like a stevedore general sir, if you only could have seen him mingling with the human scum off the shabby sailing ships that weighed anchor loaded with fags and green bananas, loaded with shipments of unripe whores for the glass hotels of Curaçao for Guantánamo, father, for Santiago de los Caballeros which doesn't even have a sea to get there by, father, for the saddest and most beautiful islands in the world that we go on dreaming about until the first light of dawn, father, remember how different we were when the schooners left, remember the parrot who could guess the future in the house of Matilde Arenales, the crabs that came walking out of the bowls of soup, the shark wind, the distant drums, life, father, bitchy life, boys, because he talks like us general sir, as if he'd been born in the dogfight district, he played ball on the beach, he learned to play the accordion better than the natives, he sang better than they, he learned the flowery language of the queens, he teased them in Latin, he got drunk with them in the fairy joints in the marketplace, he got into a fight with one of them because he said something bad about God, they started punching each other general sir, what shall we do, and he gave the order that nobody should separate them, they formed a circle around them, he won, the priest won general sir, I knew it, he said, pleased, he's a stud, and not as frivolous as everybody thought, because on those wild nights he found more truth than during the wearisome days in the palace of the Apostolic Nunciature, much more than in the shadowy suburban mansion that he had explored without permission one afternoon during a heavy rain when he thought he had tricked the sleepless vigilance of the presidential security services, he scrutinized it down to the last chink soaked by the interior rain from the roof gutters, trapped by the quicksands of malangas and the poisonous camellias of the splendid sleeping quarters that Bendición Alvarado had abandoned to the happiness of the servants, because she was good, father, she was humble, she put them to sleep on percale sheets while she slept on a bare mat on an army cot, she let them wear her first lady's Sunday clothes, they perfumed themselves with her bath salts, they frolicked naked with the orderlies in the colored bubbles in pewter bathtubs with lion's feet, they lived like queens while her life slipped past as she painted birds, cooked her vegetable mush on the wood fire, and cultivated medicinal plants for the emergencies of neighbors who would wake her up in the middle of the night with I've got a stomach spasm, ma'am, and she would give them watercress seeds to chew, that a godson was cross-eyed, and she would give him a worm remedy of epazote tea, I'm going to die, ma'am, but they didn't die because she held health in her hand, she was a living saint, father, she walked about in her own pure space through that mansion of pleasure where it had rained without pity ever since they took her by force to the presidential palace, it rained on the lotus blossoms on the piano, on the alabaster table in the sumptuous dining room which Bendición Alvarado never used because it's like sitting down to eat at an altar, just imagine, father, such a presentiment of sainthood, but in spite of the feverish testimony of the neighbors the devil's advocate found more traces of timidity than humility among the ruins, he found more proofs of poorness of spirit than abnegation among the ebony Neptunes and the pieces of native demons and warlike angels that were floating in the mangrove swamps of the former ballrooms, and on the other hand he did not find the slightest trace of that other difficult god, one and trine, who had sent him from the burning plains of Abyssinia in search of truth where it had never been, because he found nothing general sir, as he said nothing, what a mess. Yet Monsignor Demetrius Aldous was not satisfied merely with the scrutiny of the city but went up on muleback into the glacial limbo of the upland barrens trying to find the seeds of Bendición Alvarado's sainthood where her image might still not be perverted by the splendor of power, he rose out of the mist wrapped in a highwayman's cloak and wearing seven-league boots like a satanic apparition who at first aroused the fear and then the surprise and finally the curiosity of the uplanders who had never seen a human being of that color, but the astute Eritrene urged them to touch to convince themselves that he didn't give off tar, he showed them his teeth in the darkness, he got drunk with them eating cheese with his hand and drinking corn liquor out of the same gourd in order to win their trust in the gloomy little stores along the trails where at the dawn of other centuries they had known a striking birdwoman weighted down by her mad load of cages with chicks painted as nightingales, golden toucans, goatsuckers disguised as peacocks to trick mountain people on the funereal Sundays of upland fairs, she would sit there, father, in the glow of the bonfires, waiting for someone to do her the charity of going to be with her on the wineskins full of molasses in the back of the store, in order to eat, father, only in order to eat, because no one was such a mountain hick as to buy those cheap goods of hers that faded with the first rain and fell apart when they walked, only she was so innocent, father, holy benediction of the birds, or of the barrens, as you wish, because no one knew for certain what her name was then or when she started calling herself Bendición Alvarado which couldn't have been her original name because it's not a name from these parts but for coastal people, what a mess, even that had been checked on by Satan's slippery prosecutor who was uncovering and digging out everything in spite of the presidential security thugs who tangled up the thread of the truth on him and put invisible barriers in his way, what do you think, general sir, they could hound him off a cliff like a deer, they could make his mule stumble on him, he stopped that with the personal order to watch him but to maintain his physical integrity repeat maintain physical integrity permitting absolute freedom all facilities fulfilling his mission by command without appeal from this highest authority obey carry out, signed I, and he repeated, I myself, conscious of the fact that with that decision he was taking on the terrible risk of learning the true image of his mother Bendición Alvarado during the forbidden times when she was still young, was languid, went about dressed in rags, barefoot, and had to use her lower parts in order to eat, but she was beautiful, father, and she was so innocent that she fitted out the cheapest lory parrots with tails from the finest cocks to make them pass for macaws, she repaired crippled hens with turkey-feather fans and sold them as birds of paradise, no one believed it, of course, no one was innocent enough to fall into the snare of the solitary birdwoman who whispered about in the mist of Sunday marketplaces to see who

would say one and take her for nothing, because everybody on
the barrens remembered her for her innocence and her poverty,
and yet it seemed impossible to discover her identity because in
the records of the monastery where she had been baptized her
birth certificate could not be found and on the other hand they
found three different ones for her son and on all three he was
three times different, conceived three times on three different
occasions, given a bad birth three times thanks to the artifices of
national history which had entangled the threads of reality so
that no one would be able to decipher the secret of his origins,
the occult mystery which only the Eritrene managed to track
down by removing the numerous falsehoods superimposed on
it, because he had glimpsed it general sir, he had it within reach
of his hand when there came the immense explosion that kept
echoing along the gray ridges and deep canyons of the mountain
range and one heard the endless wail of fright of the tumbling
mule as it went on falling dizzily and endlessly from the peaks
of perpetual snow through successive and instantaneous climes
out of natural-history prints of the precipice and the birth trickle
of great navigable waters and the high cornices up to which the
learned doctors of the botanical expedition had climbed on
Indian back with their herbal secrets, and the steppes of wild
magnolias where warm-wooled sheep grazed the ones who give
us generous sustenance and cover and good example and the
mansions of the coffee plantations with their paper wreaths on
solitary balconies and their endless invalids and the perpetual
roar of the turbulent rivers of the great natural boundary lines
where the heat began and at dusk there were pestilent waves
from an old dead man dead from treachery dead all alone in
the cacao groves with their great persistent leaves and scarlet
blossoms and berry fruit whose seeds were used as the principal
ingredient of chocolate and the motionless sun and the burning

dust and the seed gourd and the honey gourd and the sad and
skinny cows of the Atlantic province in the only charity school
for two hundred leagues around and the exhalation of the still-
living mule whose guts exploded like a succulent soursop among
the banana trees and frightened pullets at the bottom of the
abyss, God damn it, they deer-hunted him general sir, they had
hunted him down with a jaguar rifle at the pass of the Solitary
Soul in spite of the protection of my authority, sons of bitches,
in spite of my strong telegrams, God damn it, but now they're
going to find out who's who, he bellowed, chewing on his froth
of gall not so much because of rage over the disobedience as
over the certainty that they were hiding something big from him
since they had dared go against the thunderbolts of his power,
he carefully observed the breathing of those who gave him the
information because he knew that only one who knew the truth
would have the courage to lie to him, he scrutinized the secret
intentions of the high command to see which of them was the
traitor, you who I brought up out of nothing, you who I put to
sleep in a golden bed after finding you on the ground, you
whose life I saved, you who I bought for more money than
anyone else, all of you, you dirty mothers' sons, because only
one of them would dare disregard a telegram signed with my
name and countersigned with the wax of the ring of his power,
so he assumed personal command of the rescue operation with
the unrepeatable order that within a maximum of forty-eight
hours you find him alive and bring him to me and if you find
him dead bring him to me alive and if you don't find him bring
him to me, an order so unmistakable and fearsome that before
the time was up they came to him with the news general sir that
they had found him in the underbrush of the precipice with his
wounds cauterized by the golden flowers of the frailejone plant
more alive than any of us general sir, safe and sound by virtue

of his mother Bendición Alvarado who once more was giving a
sign of her clemency and her power in the very person of the
one who had tried to damage her memory, they brought him
down along Indian trails on a hammock hung on a pole with
an escort of grenadiers and preceded by a bullfight master on
horseback who rang a high-mass bell so that everyone would
know that this was a matter of the one who gives the orders,
they put him in the bedroom for honored guests in the presidential palace under the immediate responsibility of the minister of
health until he was able to bring to a close that terrible report
written in his own hand and countersigned with his initials on
the right-hand margin of every one of the three hundred and
fifty folios of every one of these seven volumes which I sign with
my name and my flourish and which I guarantee with my seal
on this fourteenth day of the month of April of this year of Our
Lord, I, Demetrius Aldous, auditor of the Sacred Congregation
of the Rite, postulator and promoter of the faith, by the man-
date of the immense Constitution and for the splendor of justice
of men on earth and the greater glory of God in the heavens I
affirm and show this to be the only truth, the whole truth, and
nothing but the truth, your excellency, here it is. There it was,
indeed, captive in seven lacquered bibles, so unavoidable and
brutal that only a man immune to the spell of glory and alien to
the interests of his power dared expose it in living flesh before
the impassive old man who listened to him without blinking
fanning himself in the wicker rocking chair, who only sighed
after each mortal revelation, who only said aha, repeated it,
using his hat to shoo away the April flies aroused by the lun-
cheon leftovers, swallowing whole truths, bitter truths, truths
which were like live coals that kept on burning in the shadows of
his heart, because everything had been a farce, your excellency, a
carnival apparatus that he himself had put together without

really thinking about it when he decided that the corpse of his mother should be displayed for public veneration on a cata-falque of ice long before anyone thought about the merits of her sainthood and only to contradict the evil tongues that said you were rotting away before you died, a circus trick which he had fallen into himself without knowing it ever since they came to him with the news general sir that his mother Bendición Alva-rado was performing miracles and he had ordered her body car-ried in a magnificent procession into the most unknown corners of his vast statueless country so that no one should be left who did not know the worth of your virtues after so many years of sterile mortification, after so many painted birds without bene-fit, mother, after so much love without thanks, although it never would have occurred to me that the order was to be changed into the jape of the false dropsy victims who were paid to get rid of their water in public, they had paid two hundred pesos to a false dead man who arose from his grave and appeared walking on his knees through the crowd frightened by his ragged shroud and his mouth full of earth, they had paid eighty pesos to a gypsy woman who pretended to give birth in the middle of the street to a two-headed monster as punishment for having said that the miracles had been set up by the government, and that they had been, there wasn't a single witness who hadn't been paid money, an ignominious conspiracy that none the less had not been put together by his adulators with the innocent idea of pleasing him as Monsignor Demetrius Aldous had imagined during his first scrutinies, no, your excellency, it was a dirty piece of business on the part of your proselytes, the most scan-dalous and sacrilegious of all the things they had made prolifer-ate in the shadow of his power, because the ones who had invented the miracles and backed up the testimonies of lies were the same followers of his regime who had manufactured and sold the relics of the dead bride's gown worn by his mother Bendición Alvarado, aha, the same ones who had printed the little cards and coined the medals with her portrait as a queen, aha, the ones who enriched themselves with curls from her head, aha, with the flasks of water drawn from her side, aha, with the shroud of diagonal cloth where they used door paint to sketch the tender body of a virgin sleeping in profile with her hand on her heart and which was sold by the yard in the back rooms of Hindu bazaars, a monstrous lie sustained by the supposition that the corpse remained uncorrupted before the avid eyes of the endless throng that filed through the main nave of the cathedral, when the truth was quite something else, your excellency, it was that body of his mother was not preserved because of her virtues or through the repair work done with paraffin and the cosmetic tricks that he had decided upon out of pure filial pride but that she had been stuffed according to the worst skills of taxidermy just like the posthumous animals in science museums as he found out with my own hands, mother, I opened the glass casket as the funereal emblems fell apart with the air, I took the crown of orange blossoms from your moldy brow where the stiff filly-mane hairs had been pulled out by the roots strand by strand to be sold as relics, I pulled you out from under the damp gauze of your bridal veil and the dry residue and the difficult saltpeter sunsets of death and you weighed the same as a sun-dried gourd and you had an old trunk-bottom smell and I could sense inside of you a feverish restlessness that was like the sound of your soul and it was the scissor-slicing of the moth larvae who were chewing you up inside, your limbs fell off by themselves when I tried to hold you in my arms because they had removed the innards of everything that held together your live body of a sleeping happy mother with her hand on her heart and they had stuffed you up again with rags so that all that was

left of what had been you was only a shell with dusty stuffing
that crumbled just by being lifted in the phosphorescent air of
your firefly bones and all that could be heard were the flea leaps
of the glass eyes on the pavement of the dusk-lighted church,
turned to nothing, it was a trickle of the remains of a demolished
mother which the bailiffs scooped up from the floor with a
shovel to throw it back any way they could into the box under
the gaze of monolithic sternness from the indecipherable satrap
whose iguana eyes refused to let the slightest emotion show
through even when he was all alone in the unmarked berlin with
the only man in this world who had dared place him in front of
the mirror of truth, both looked out through the haze of the
window curtains at the hordes of needy who were finding relief
from the heat-ridden afternoon in the dew-cool doorways where
previously they had sold pamphlets describing atrocious crimes
and luckless loves and carnivorous flowers and inconceivable
fruit that compromised the will and where now one only heard
the deafening racket of the stalls selling false relics of the clothes
and the body of his mother Bendición Alvarado, while he under-
went the clear impression that Monsignor Demetrius Aldous
had read his thoughts when he turned his sight away from the
mobs of invalids and murmured that when all's said and done
something good had come out of the rigor of his scrutiny and it
was the certainty that these poor people love your excellency as
they love their own lives, because Monsignor Demetrius Aldous
had caught sight of the perfidy within the presidential palace
itself, had seen the greed within the adulation and the wily ser-
vility among those who flourished under the umbrella of power,
and he had come to know on the other hand a new form of love
among the droves of needy who expected nothing from him
because they expected nothing from anyone and they professed
for him an earthly devotion that could be held in one's hands

and a loyalty without illusions that we should only want for God, your excellency, but he did not even blink when faced with that startling revelation which in other times would have made his insides twist, nor did he sigh but meditated to himself with a hidden restlessness that this was all we needed, father, all we need is for nobody to love me now that you're going off to take advantage of the glory of misfortune under the golden cupolas of your fallacious world while he was left with the undeserved burden of truth without a loving mother who could help him through it, more lonely than a left hand in this nation which I didn't choose willingly but which was given me as an established fact in the way you have seen it which is as it has always been since time immemorial with this feeling of unreality, with this smell of shit, with this unhistoried people who don't believe in anything except life, this is the nation they forced on me without even asking me, father, with one-hundred-degree heat and ninety-eight-percent humidity in the upholstered shadows of the presidential berlin, breathing dust, tormented by the perfidy of the rupture that whistled like a teakettle during audiences, no one to lose a game of dominoes to, and no one to believe his truth, father, put yourself in my skin, but he didn't say it, he just sighed, he just blinked for an instant and asked Monsignor Demetrius Aldous that the brutal conversation of that afternoon remain between ourselves, you haven't told me anything, father, I don't know the truth, promise me that, and Monsignor Demetrius Aldous promised him that of course your excellency doesn't know the truth, my word as a man. The cause of Bendición Alvarado was suspended for insufficient proof, and the edict from Rome was made public from pulpits with official permission along with the determination of the government to repress any protest or attempt at disorder, but forces of public order did not intervene when hordes of indignant pilgrims built bonfires on the main square with the large wooden doors of the cathedral and broke the stained-glass windows with angels and gladiators of the Apostolic Nunciature with stones, they demolished everything general sir, but he didn't move from the hammock, they laid siege to the convent of the Biscayan nuns to leave them to perish without food and water, they sacked churches, mission houses, they destroyed everything that had to do with priests general sir, but he remained motionless in the hammock under the cool shadows of the pansies until the commandants of his general staff in plenary session declared themselves incapable of calming spirits and reestablishing order without the shedding of blood as had been resolved, and only then did he get up, appear in his office after so many months of indolence, and assume with his own voice and in person the solemn responsibility of interpreting the popular will through a decree which he conceived through his own inspiration and he proclaimed it on his own and at his own risk without advising the armed forces or consulting his ministers and in the first article of which he proclaimed the civil sainthood of Bendición Alvarado by the supreme decision of the free and sovereign people, he named her patroness of the nation, curer of the ill and mistress of birds and a national holiday was declared on her birthday, and in the second article and beginning with the promulgation of the present decree a state of war was declared between this nation and the powers of the Holy See with all the consequences which international law and all extant international treaties have established for such cases, and in the third article there was ordered the immediate, public and solemn expulsion of his grace the archbishop primate followed by that of bishops, apostolic prefects, priests, nuns and all persons native and foreign who had anything to do with the business of God in any condition and under any title within the borders of the country and up to fifty nautical leagues in territorial waters, and ordered in the fourth and last article was the expropriation of all goods of the church, its houses of worship, its convents, its schools, its arable lands with tools and animals thereon, its sugar plantations, factories and workshops and in the same manner everything which really belonged to it even though registered in the name of a third party, which goods would go to form part of the posthumous patrimony of Saint Bendición Alvarado of the Birds for the splendor of her cult and the grandeur of her memory from the date of the present decree promulgated orally and signed with the seal of the ring of this unappealable maximum authority of the supreme power, let it be obeyed and carried out. In the midst of the rockets of celebration, the bell-ringing of glory and the music of pleasure with which the event of the civil canonization was celebrated, he busied himself in person to see that the decree was carried out without any dubious maneuvers so as to be sure they would not make him the victim of new tricks, he picked up the reins of reality again with his firm velvet gloves as in the days of great glory when the people cut off his path on the stairs to beg him to restore horse racing in the streets and he so ordered, agreed, that sack races be revived and he so ordered, agreed, and he would appear in the most miserable of villages to explain how they should put hens in their nests and how calves should be gelded, because he had just been satisfied with his personal test of the minute details of the taking of inventory of church goods but he took charge of the formal ceremonies of expropriation so that there would be no chink between his will and the accomplished acts, he checked the facts on paper against the tricky facts of real life, he oversaw the expulsion of the larger communities to whom had been attributed the intent of smuggling out in bags with double bottoms and trick brassieres the secret treasures of the last viceroy which had been buried in potter's field in spite of the bloodthirsty way in which the federalist leaders had searched for them during the long years of war, and not only did he order that no member of the church was to take with him any more baggage than a change of clothing but he decided beyond appeal that they be embarked naked as the day their mothers bore them, the rough village priests to whom it made no difference whether to wear clothes or go naked as long as they had a change of fortune, the prefects from mission lands who had been devastated by malaria, clean-shaven and dignified bishops, and behind them the women, the timid sisters of charity, the fierce missionary nuns accustomed to taming nature and making vegetables grow in the desert, and the slender Biscayan sisters who played the harpsichord, and the Salesian sisters with thin hands and bodies intact, because even in the naked hide with which they had been thrown into the world it was possible to distinguish their high-class origins, the difference in their condition, and the inequality of their office as they filed past bundles of cacao and sacks of salted catfish in the huge custom-house shed, they went by in a whirling tumult of frightened sheep with their arms crossed over their breasts trying to hide the shame of the ones with that of the others before the old man who looked like stone under the fan blades, who looked at them without breathing, without taking his eyes off the fixed space through which the torrent of naked women would inexorably have to pass, he contemplated them impassively, without blinking, until there was not a single one left in all the national territory, for these were the last of them general sir, and yet he only remembered one whom he had separated with a simple touch of his glance from the troop of frightened novices, he distinguished her among the others in spite of the fact that she was no different, she was small and sturdy, robust, with opulent but-

tocks, large full teats, clumsy hands, protuberant sex, hair cut
with pruning shears, spaced teeth firm as ax heads, snub nose,
flat feet, a novice as mediocre as all of them, but he sensed that
she was the only woman in the drove of naked women, the only
one who on passing in front of him had left the obscure trail of
a wild animal who carried off my vital air and he barely had
time to change his imperceptible look to see her a second time
forevermore when the officer from the identification services
found her name in alphabetical order in the roster and shouted
Nazareno Leticia, and she answered with a man's voice, present.
That was how he had her for the rest of his life, present, until
the last nostalgia trickled away through the fissures in his memory and all that remained was the image of her on the strip of
paper where he had written Leticia Nazareno of my soul look
what has become of me without you, he hid it in the cranny
where he kept the honey, he would reread it when he knew he
was not being observed, he would roll it up again after reliving
for a fleeting instant the unforgettable afternoon of radiant rain
on which they surprised him with the news general sir that they
had repatriated you in fulfillment of his orders which he had not
given, for all he had done was to murmur Leticia Nazareno
while he contemplated the last ash barge as it sank below the
horizon, Leticia Nazareno, he repeated aloud so as not to forget
the name, and that had been enough for the presidential security
services to kidnap her from the convent in Jamaica, gagged and
in a strait jacket inside a pine box with metal hoops and black
letters saying fragile and in English do not drop this side up
and an export license in accordance with the necessary consular
permission for the two thousand eight hundred champagne
glasses of genuine crystal for the presidential wine cellar, for the
return voyage they loaded her aboard among the ship's stores of
a collier and they laid her naked and drugged on the columned

bed in the bedroom for distinguished guests as he had remembered her at three in the afternoon under the flour-haze light of the mosquito netting, she had the restful look of sleep of so many other inert women who had served him without even awakening from the lethargy of the Luminal and tormented by a terrible feeling of abandonment and defeat, except that he did not touch Leticia Nazareno, he contemplated her in sleep with a kind of infantile amazement surprised at how much her nakedness had changed since he had seen her in the harbor shed, they'd curled her hair, they'd made her up right down to the most intimate nooks and crannies, and they'd put crimson polish on her fingernails and toenails and lipstick and rouge on her mouth and cheeks and mascara and she gave off a sweet fragrance that did away with your trace of a wild animal, Jesus, they'd ruined her trying to recreate her, they'd made her so different that he couldn't even see her underneath the clumsy cosmetics while he contemplated her naked in the ecstasy of the Luminal, he saw her come to the surface, he saw her wake up, he saw her see him, mother, it was her, Leticia Nazareno of my bewilderment petrified with terror before the stony old man who was contemplating her mercilessly through the tenuous mists of the netting, frightened with the unforeseeable aims of her silence because he couldn't imagine anything in spite of his uncountable years and his measureless power he was more frightened than she, more alone, more not knowing what to do, as confused and as defenseless as he had been the first time he was a man with a camp follower whom he had surprised in the middle of the night swimming naked in a river and whose strength and size he had imagined from her mare snorts after each dive, he heard her dark and solitary laugh in the darkness, he sensed the joy of her body in the darkness but he was paralyzed with fear because he was still a virgin even though he was

already an artillery lieutenant in the third civil war, until the fear
of losing the chance was more decisive than the fear of the
attack, and then he jumped into the water with all his clothes
on, boots, knapsack, cartridge belt, machete, carbine, buried
under so many military encumbrances and so many secret terrors that the woman thought at first that he was someone who
had ridden his horse into the water, but she realized immediately
that he was only a poor frightened man and she gathered him
into the lagoon of her pity, took him by the hand in the darkness
of his confusion because he couldn't manage to find his way in
the darkness of the lagoon, she indicated to him with a mother's
voice in the darkness to get a good grip on my shoulders so the
current won't knock you over, not to squat down in the water
but to kneel firmly on the bottom breathing slowly so you'll
have enough wind, and he did what she told him with a boyish
obedience thinking mother of mine Bendición Alvarado why in
hell do women do things as if they were inventing them, how
can they be such men about it, he thought, while she was taking
off the useless paraphernalia of other less fearful and desolate
wars than that solitary war with the water up to his neck, he had
died of fright under the protection of that body that smelled
of pine soap when she finished unbuckling his two belts and
unbuttoned his fly and I was twisted with terror because I
couldn't find what I was looking for except for the enormous
testicle swimming like a toad in the darkness, she let go of it
with fright, go back to your mama and have her turn you in for
another one, she told him, you're no good for anything, because
he had been defeated by the same ancestral fear that held him
motionless before the nakedness of Leticia Nazareno in whose
river of unforeseeable waters one was not to enter not even with
everything he had on until she could lend him the aid of her
mercy, he himself covered her with a sheet, played the song of

poor Delgadina ruined by the love of her father on the gramophone until the cylinder wore out, he had felt flowers put into the vases so that they would not wilt like natural ones from the evil touch of her hands, he did everything he could think of to make her happy but he kept the rigors of captivity intact and the punishment of nudity so that she would understand that she would be well taken care of and well loved but that she had no possibility of escaping that fate, and she understood so well that during the first truce of fear she ordered him without saying please to open the window general so that we could have a little air, and he opened it, to close it again because the moon is hitting my face, he closed it, he carried out her orders as if they were from love all the more obedient and sure of himself the closer he got to the afternoon of radiant rain in which he slipped inside the mosquito netting and lay down with his clothes on beside her without waking her up, he participated alone for nights on end in the secret outflow of her body, he breathed in her smell of a mountain bitch that grew warmer with the passage of months, the moss of her womb sprouted, she woke up startled shouting get out of here general and he arose with his heavy parsimony but lay down beside her again while she was sleeping and in that way he enjoyed her without touching her during the first year of captivity until she grew accustomed to awakening beside him without understanding the direction of the currents of that indecipherable old man who had abandoned the flattery of power and the enchantments of the world to devote himself to her contemplation and service, she all the more disconcerted as she came to know the afternoon of radiant rains when he had gone into the water with everything on, the uniform without insignia, the sword belts, the ring of keys, the leggings, the riding boots with the gold spur, a nightmare attack that awakened her in terror trying to get out from under that caparisoned charger, but he was so resolute that she decided to gain time with the last recourse of take your harness off general the buckles hurt my heart, and he took it off, he should take off the spur general it injures my ankles with its gold rowel, that he take off the clump of keys from his belt they keep bumping into my hipbones, and he ended up doing what she ordered although three months were needed to get him to take off his sword belt which hinders my breathing and another month for the leggings which break my soul with their buckles, it was a slow and difficult struggle in which she held him off without exasperating him and he ended up giving in so as to please her, so neither of them ever knew how it was that the final cataclysm occurred a short time after the second anniversary of the kidnapping when his aimless warm and tender hands by chance came upon the hidden gems of the sleeping novice who awoke in shock with a pale sweat and a death quiver and did not try to get away with either good or evil arts from the uncouth animal she had on top of her except that she shocked him by begging him to take off his boots they were dirtying my Brabant sheets and he took them off as best he could, take off your leggings, and pants, and the truss, take it all off my life I can't feel you, until he himself didn't know when he was left as only his mother had known him in the light that filtered through the melancholy harps of the geraniums, freed from fear, free, changed into a battling bison who with the first charge demolished everything he found in his way and fell face down into an abyss of silence where all that could be heard was the schoonerbeam creaking of the clenched back teeth of Nazareno Leticia, present, she had clutched all my hair in her fingers so as not to die alone in the bottomless dizzy fall in which I was already dying sought at the same time and with the same drive by all the urgencies of the body, and none the less he forgot about her, he was alone in the shadows looking for himself

last three civilian ministers, the archbishop primate, all those whom he would not have wanted there were sitting around the long walnut table trying to come to an agreement on the manner in which the news of that enormous death was to be released so as to avoid the premature explosion of mobs in the street, first a bulletin number one at the start of the first night concerning a slight indisposition which had obliged him to cancel all of his excellency's public appearances and civilian and military audiences, then a second medical bulletin in which it was announced that the illustrious patient had been obliged to remain in his private quarters due to an indisposition in keeping with his years, and lastly, without any announcement, the heavy tolling of the cathedral bells on the radiant dawn of the hot August Tuesday of an official death which no one was ever to know for certain that really was his or not. We were defenseless against that evidence, compromised by a pestilential corpse that we were incapable of replacing in the world because he had refused in his senile insistence to take any decision concerning the destiny of the nation after he was gone, with the invincible stubbornness of an old man he had resisted all suggestions made to him ever since the government had been moved to the ministry buildings with their sun-drenched glass and he had stayed behind living alone in the deserted palace of his absolute power, we would find him walking about in dreams, waving his arms in the midst of the cows' destruction with no one to command except the blind men, the lepers and the cripples who were dying not from illness but from old age in the weeds of the rose garden, and yet he was so lucid and stubborn that we could only get evasive answers and postponements out of him every time we brought up the matter of putting his legacy in order, because he would say that thinking ahead about the world that's left after you've gone yourself was something made up of the same ashes

as death itself, God damn it, because when I finally die the politicians will come back and divide up the mess the way it was
during the times of the Goths, you'll see, he said, they'll go back
to dividing everything up among the priests, the gringos and
the rich, and nothing for the poor, naturally, because they've
always been so fucked up that the day shit is worth money, poor
people will be born without an asshole, you'll see, he said, talking to someone about his days of glory, even making fun of
himself when he told us as he choked with laughter that for the
three days he was going to be dead it wouldn't be worth the
trouble taking him to Jerusalem and burying him in the Holy
Sepulcher, and he put an end to all disagreement with the final
argument that it didn't matter whether something back then was
true or not, God damn it, it will be with time. He was right,
because during our time there was no one who doubted the
legitimacy of his history, or anyone who could have disclosed or
denied it because we couldn't even establish the identity of his
body, there was no other nation except the one that had been
made by him in his own image and likeness where space was
changed and time corrected by the designs of his absolute will,
reconstituted by him ever since the most uncertain origins of his
memory as he wandered at random through that house of
infamy where no happy person had ever slept, as he tossed
cracked corn to the hens who pecked around his hammock and
exasperated the servants with orders he pulled out of the air to
bring me a lemonade with chopped ice which he had left within
reach of his hand, take that chair away from over there and put
it over there, and they should put it back where it had been in
order to satisfy in that minute way the warm embers of his enormous addiction to giving orders, distracting the everyday pas-
times of his power with the patient raking up of ephemeral
instants from his remote childhood as he nodded sleepily under

the ceiba tree in the courtyard, he would wake up suddenly when he managed to grasp a memory like a piece in a limitless jigsaw puzzle of the nation that lay before him, the great, chimerical, shoreless nation, a realm of mangrove swamps with slow rafts and precipices that had been there before his time when men were so bold that they hunted crocodiles with their hands by placing a stake in their mouths, like that, he would explain to us holding his forefinger against his palate, he told us that on one Good Friday he had heard the hullabaloo of the wind and the scurf smell of the wind and he saw the heavy clouds of locusts that muddied the noonday sky and went along scissoring off everything that stood in their path and left the world all sheared and the light in tatters as on the eve of creation, because he had seen that disaster, he had seen a string of headless roosters hanging by their feet and bleeding drop by drop from the eaves of a house with a broad and crumbling sidewalk where a woman had just died, barefoot he had left his mother's hand and followed the ragged corpse they were carrying off to bury without a coffin on a cargo litter that was lashed by the blizzard of locusts, because that was what the nation was like then, we didn't even have coffins for the dead, nothing, he had seen a man who had tried to hang himself with a rope that had already been used by another hanged man from a tree in a village square and the rotted rope broke before it was time and the poor man lay in his death throes on the square to the horror of the ladies coming out of mass, but he didn't die, they beat him awake with sticks without bothering to find out who he was because in those days no one knew who was who if he wasn't known in the church, they stuck his ankles between the planks of the stocks and left him there exposed to the elements along with other comrades in suffering because that was what the times of the Goths were like when God ruled more than the government, the evil times of the nation before he gave the order to chop down all trees in village squares to prevent the terrible spectacle of a Sunday hanged man, he had prohibited the use of public stocks, burial without a coffin, everything that might awaken in one's memory the ignominious laws that existed before his power, he had built the railroad to the upland plains to put an end to the infamy of mules terrified by the edges of precipices as on their backs they carried grand pianos for the masked balls at the coffee plantations, for he had also seen the disaster of the thirty grand pianos destroyed in an abyss and of which they had spoken and written so much even outside the country although only he could give truthful testimony, he had gone to the window by chance at the precise moment in which the rear mule had slipped and had dragged the rest into the abyss, so that no one but he had heard the shriek of terror from the cliff-flung mule train and the endless chords of the pianos that fell with it playing by themselves in the void, hurtling toward the depths of a nation which at that time was like everything that had existed before him, vast and uncertain, to such an extreme that it was impossible to know whether it was night or day in the kind of eternal twilight of the hot steamy mists in the deep canyons where the pianos imported from Austria had broken up into fragments, he had seen that and many other things in that remote world although not even he himself could have been sure with no room for doubt whether they were his own memories or whether he had heard about them on his bad nights of fever during the wars or whether he might have seen them in prints in travel books over which he would linger in ecstasy for long hours during the dead doldrums of power, but none of that mattered, God damn it, they'll see that with time it will be the truth, he would say, conscious that his real childhood was not that crust of uncertain recollections that he only remembered when the smoke from the cow chips arose and he forgot it forever except that he really had lived it during the calm waters of my only and legitimate wife Leticia Nazareno who would sit him down every afternoon between two and four o'clock at a school desk under the pansy bower to teach him how to read and write, she had put her novice's tenacity into that heroic enterprise and he matched it with his terrifying old man's patience, with the terrifying will of his limitless power, with all my heart, so that he would chant with all his soul the tuna in the tin the loony in the bin the neat nightcap, he chanted without hearing himself or without anyone's hearing him amidst the uproar of his dead mother's aroused birds that the Indian packs the ointment in the can, papa places the tobacco in his pipe, Cecilia sells seals seeds seats seams scenes sequins seaweed and receivers, Cecilia sells everything, he would laugh, repeating amidst the clamor of the cicadas the reading lesson that Leticia Nazareno chanted to the time of her novice's metronome, until the limits of the world became saturated with the creatures of your voice and in his vast realm of dreariness there was no other truth but the exemplary truths of the primer, there was nothing but the moon in the mist, the ball and the banana, the bull of Don Eloy, Otilia's bordered bathrobe, the rote reading lessons which he repeated at every moment and everywhere just like his portraits even in the presence of the treasury minister from Holland who lost the thread of an official visit when the gloomy old man raised the hand with the velvet glove on it in the shadows of his unfathomable power and interrupted the audience to invite him to sing with me my mama's a mummer, Ismael spent six months on the isle, the lady ate a tomato, imitating with his forefinger the beat of the metronome and repeating from memory Tuesday's lesson with a perfect diction but with such a bad sense of the occasion that the interview ended as he had wanted it to with the postponement of payment of the Dutch debts for a more propitious moment, for when there would be time, he decided, to the surprise of the lepers, the blind men, the cripples who rose up at dawn among the rosebushes and saw the shadowy old man who gave a silent blessing and chanted three times with high-mass chords I am the king and the law is my thing, he chanted, the seer has fear of beer, a lighthouse is a very high tower with a bright beam which guides sailors at night, he chanted, conscious that in the shadows of his senile happiness there was no time but that of Leticia Nazareno of my life in the shrimp stew of the suffocating gambols of siesta time, there were no other anxieties but those of being naked with you on the sweat-soaked mattress under the captive bat of an electric fan, there was no light but that of your buttocks, Leticia, nothing but your totemic teats, your flat feet, your ramus of rue as a remedy, the oppressive Januaries of the remote island of Antigua where you came into the world one early dawn of solitude that was furrowed by the burning breeze of rotted swamps, they had shut themselves up in the quarters for distinguished guests with the personal order that no one is to come any closer than twenty feet to that door because I'm going to be very busy learning to read and write, so no one interrupted him not even with the news general sir that the black vomit was wreaking havoc among the rural population while the rhythms of my heart got ahead of the metronome because of that invisible force of your wild-animal smell, chanting that the midget is dancing on just one foot, the mule goes to the mill, Otilia washes the tub, kow is spelled with a jackass k, he chanted, while Leticia Nazareno moved aside the herniated testicle to clean him up from the last love-making's dinky-poo, she submerged him in the lustral waters of the pewter bathtub with lion's paws and lathered him with Reuter soap, scrubbed him with washcloths, and rinsed

him off with the water of boiled herbs as they sang in duet ginger gibber and gentleman are all spelled with a gee, she would
daub the joints of his legs with cocoa butter to alleviate the rash
from his truss, she would put boric acid powder on the moldy
star of his asshole and whack his behind like a tender mother for
your bad manners with the minister from Holland, plap, plap,
as a penance she asked him to permit the return to the country
of the communities of poor nuns so they could go back to taking
care of orphan asylums and hospitals and other houses of charity, but he wrapped her in the gloomy aura of his implacable
rancor, never in a million years, he sighed, there wasn't a single
power in this world or the other that could make him go against
a decision taken by himself alone and aloud, she asked him during the asthmas of love at two in the afternoon that you grant
me one thing, my life, only one thing, that the mission territory
communities who work on the fringes of the whims of power
might return, but he answered her during the anxieties of his
urgent husband snorts never in a million years my love, I'd
rather be dead than humiliated by that pack of long skirts who
saddle Indians instead of mules and pass out beads of colored
glass in exchange for gold nose rings and earrings, never in a
million years, he protested, insensitive to the pleas of Leticia
Nazareno of my misfortune who had crossed her legs to ask him
for the restitution of the confessional schools expropriated by
the government, the disentailment of property held in mort-
main, the sugar mills, the churches turned into barracks, but he
turned his face to the wall ready to renounce the insatiable torture of your slow cavernous love-making before I would let my
arm be twisted in favor of those bandits of God who for centuries have fed on the liver of the nation, never in a million years,
he decided, and yet they did come back general sir, they returned
to the country through the narrowest slits, the communities of

poor nuns in accordance with his confidential order that they
disembark silently in secret coves, they were paid enormous
indemnities, their expropriated holdings were restored with
interest and the recent laws concerning civil marriage, divorce,
lay education were repealed, everything he had decreed aloud
during his rage at the comic carnival of the process of the declaration of sainthood for his mother Bendición Alvarado may God
keep her in His holy kingdom, God damn it, but Leticia Nazareno was not satisfied with all that but asked for more, she asked
him to put your ear to the lower part of my stomach so that you
can hear the singing of the creature growing inside, because she
had awakened in the middle of the night startled by that deep
voice that was describing the aquatic paradise of your insides
furrowed by mallow-soft sundowns and winds of pitch, that
interior voice that spoke to her of the polyps on your kidneys,
the soft steel of your intestines, the warm amber of your urine
sleeping in its springs, and to her stomach he put the ear that
was buzzing less for him and he heard the secret bubbling of the
living creature of his mortal sin, a child of our obscene bellies
who would be named Emanuel, which is the name by which
other gods know God, and on his forehead he will have the
white star of his illustrious origins and he will inherit his mother's spirit of sacrifice and his father's greatness and his own destiny of an invisible conductor, but he was to be the shame of
heaven and the stigma of the nation because of his illicit nature
as long as he refused to consecrate at the altar what he had vili-
fied in bed for so many years of sacrilegious concubinage, and
then he opened a way through the foam of the ancient bridal
mosquito netting with that snort of a ship's boiler coming from
the depths of his terrible repressed rage shouting never in a million years, better dead than wed, dragging his great feet of a
secret bridegroom through the salons of an alien house whose

splendor of a different age had been restored after the long period of the shadows of official mourning, the crumbling holy-week crepe had been pulled from the cornices, there was sea light in the bedrooms, flowers on the balconies, martial music, and all of it in fulfillment of an order that he had not given but which had been an order of his without the slightest doubt general sir because it had the tranquil decision of his voice and the unappealable style of his authority, and he approved, agreed, and the shuttered churches opened again, and the cloisters and cemeteries were returned to their former congregations by another order of his which he had not given either but he approved, agreed, the old holy days of obligation had been restored as well as the practices of lent and in through the open balconies came the crowd's hymns of jubilation that had previously been sung to exalt his glory as they knelt under the burning sun to celebrate the good news that God had been brought in on a ship general sir, really, they had brought Him on your orders, Leticia, by means of a bedroom law which she had promulgated in secret without consulting anybody and which he approved in public so that it would not appear to anyone's eyes that he had lost the oracles of his authority, for you were the hidden power behind those endless processions which he watched in amazement through the windows of his bedroom as they reached a distance beyond that of the fanatical hordes of his mother Bendición Alvarado whose memory had been erased from the time of men, the tatters of her bridal dress and the starch of her bones had been scattered to the winds and in the crypt the stone with the upside-down letters had been turned over so that even the mention of her name as a birdwoman painter of orioles in repose would not endure till the end of time, and all of that by your orders, because you were the one who had ordered it so that no other woman's memory would cast a shadow on your memory, Leticia Nazareno of my misfortune, bitch-daughter. She had changed it into an age in which no one changed unless it was to die, she had managed with bedroom wiles to do away with his puerile resistance of never in a million years, better dead than wed, she had made him put on his new truss listen to the way it sounds like the bell of a stray sheep in the dark, she made him put on your patent leather boots from the time he had danced the first waltz with the queen, the gold spur on his left heel which had been given him by the admiral of the ocean sea so that he would wear it unto death as a sign of the highest authority, your tunic with gold braid and tasseled ribbons and the statue epaulets which he had not worn since the times when his sad eyes could still be glimpsed, his pensive chin, the taciturn hand with the velvet glove behind the peepholes in the presidential coach, she made him put on his military saber, your man's perfume, your medals with the sash of the order of the knights of the Holy Sepulcher which the Supreme Pontiff sent you for having given back the church its expropriated possessions, you dressed me like a feast-day altar and you took me at early dawn on my own feet to the somber audience room which smelled of dead men's candles from the boughs of orange blossoms hung by the windows and the symbols of the nation hanging on the walls, without any witnesses, harnessed to the yoke of the novice who was stuccoed with a linen petticoat under the light breeze of muslin in order to smother the seven-month shame of hidden unrestraint, they were sweating in the lethargy of the invisible sea which sniffed restlessly about the gloomy ballroom to which access had been forbidden by his orders, the windows had been walled up, all trace of life in the building had been exterminated so that the world would not get even the slightest rumor of the monstrous hidden wedding, you could barely breathe in the heat because of the urgent pressure of the premature male who was swimming among the shadowy lichens on the dunes of your insides, for he had resolved that it would be a boy, and it was, he sang in the subsoil of your being with the same voice of an invisible spring with which the archbishop primate wearing pontificals sang glory to God on high so that the dozing sentries would not hear him, with the same terror of a lost diver with which the archbishop primate commended his soul to the Lord to ask the inscrutable old man what no one until then or ever after until the end of time had dared ask him do you take Leticia Mercedes María Nazareno as your wife, and he only blinked, agreed, on his chest the military medals gave a slight twinkle from the hidden pressure of his heart, but there was so much authority in his voice that the terrible creature in your insides rolled over completely in his equinox of thick waters, corrected his compass and found the direction of the light, and then Leticia Nazareno doubled over sobbing oh my father and my lord have pity on this your humble servant who has taken much pleasure in breaking your holy laws and accepts with resignation this terrible punishment, but biting her lace wristlet at the same time so that the sound of the disjointed bones of her waist would not reveal the dishonor held in by the linen petticoat, she squatted down, she fell to pieces in the steaming puddle of her own waters and withdrew from among the muslin folds the seven-month runt who had the same size and the same forlorn unboiled-animal look of a calf fetus, she lifted him up with both hands trying to recognize him in the dim light of the candles on the improvised altar, and she saw that he was a male, just as the general had decreed, a fragile and timid male who was to bear without honor the name Emanuel, as had been foreseen, and he was appointed a major general with effective jurisdiction and command from the moment he placed him on the sacrifice stone and

cut his umbilical cord with the saber and recognized him as my
only and legitimate son, father, baptize him for me. That
unprecedented decision was to be the prelude of a new epoch,
the first announcement of the evil times in which the army cor-
doned off the streets before dawn and made people close balcony windows and emptied the market with their rifle butts so
that no one would see the fugitive passage of the flashy automobile with armored plates of steel and the gold shackles of the
presidential squiry, and those who dared peek from the forbidden rooftops did not see as in other times the age-old military
man with his chin resting on the pensive hand with the velvet
glove through the peepholes edged with the colors of the flag
but the chubby former novice with her straw hat with felt flowers and the string of blue foxes that hung around her neck in
spite of the heat, we would see her get out across from the public
market on Wednesdays at dawn escorted by a patrol of combat
soldiers leading by the hand the tiny major general no more than
three years old and because of his grace and his languid air it
was impossible not to believe that it was a little girl dressed up
as a soldier in the dress uniform with gold braid which seemed
to be growing on his body, for Leticia Nazareno had put it on
him even before he grew his first teeth, when she would take
him in his baby carriage to preside over official acts as represen-
tative of his father, she carried him in her arms when he
reviewed his troops, she would lift him over her head to receive
the cheers of the crowds in the ball park, she would nurse him
in the open car during parades on the national holiday not concerned with the secret jokes brought on by the public spectacle
of a five-star general clinging ecstatically to his mother's nipple
like an orphaned calf, he attended diplomatic receptions from
the time he was able to take care of himself, and then along with
the uniform he wore the military medals which he had chosen

himself from the jewel case full of decorations which his father had given him to play with, and he was a strange, serious child, he knew how to conduct himself in public from the age of six holding in his hand the glass of fruit juice instead of champagne as he spoke about grown-up matters with a natural propriety and grace that he had not inherited from anyone, although on more than one occasion a dark cloud would cross the ballroom, time would stand still, the pale dauphin invested with the highest powers had fallen into a lethargy, silence, they whispered, the little general is sleeping, his aides-de-camp would carry him out in their arms through the crisp conversations of high-class thugs and modest ladies who scarcely dared murmur repressing the laugh of embarrassment behind feathered fans, how awful, if the general only knew, because he let flourish the belief of his own invention that he was aloof from everything that happened in the world which was not up to the level of his grandeur and for that reason we had the public boldness of the only son he had accepted as his among the countless ones he had bred, or the widespread functions of my only and legitimate wife Leticia Nazareno who would arrive at the market at dawn on Wednesdays leading her toy general by the hand in the midst of the noisy escort of barracks maidservants and assault-troop orderlies who had been transfigured by that rare visible splendor of the awareness which precedes the imminent rising of the sun in the Caribbean, they would wade into the pestilential waters of the bay up to their waists to sack the sloops with patched sails that were anchored in the former slave port loaded with flowers from Martinique and ginger roots from Paramaribo, they swept away all the live fish in their path like a wartime mopping up, they fought over the hogs with rifle butts around the former slave platform still in use where on another Wednesday of another time in the nation before him they had sold at public auction a captive Senegalese woman who brought more than her own weight in gold because of her nightmare beauty, they wiped out everything general sir, it was worse than the locusts, worse than a hurricane, but he remained impassive at the growing scandal which had Leticia Nazareno bursting as he himself would not have dared into the motley gallery of the bird and vegetable market followed by the uproar of street dogs who barked in surprise at the astonished eyes of the blue foxes, she moved with the insolent domination of her authority through slender columns of ironwork with great yellow glass leaves, with pink glass apples, with fabulous cornucopias of riches amidst the blue glass flora of the gigantic dome of lights where she chose the most delicious fruits and the tenderest vegetables which would wither the instant she touched them, unaware of the evil virtue of her hands which made mold grow on bread that was still warm and had blackened the gold of her wedding ring, so that she heaped curses on the vegetable women for having hidden their best wares and for the house of power had only these miserable pig mangoes left, sneak thieves, this pumpkin that sounds like a musician's gourd inside, ill-born wenches, these shitty ribs with wormy blood that a person can see a mile away didn't come from a steer but a donkey dead from some disease, by your evil mothers, she screamed, while the serving girls with their baskets and the orderlies with their troughs cleaned out everything edible in sight, their corsair shouts more strident than the clamor of the dogs maddened by the dampness of the snowy hideaways of the tails of the blue foxes she had had brought alive from Prince Edward Island, more cutting than the bloody reply of the foul-mouthed macaws whose mistresses taught them in secret what they themselves could not have the pleasure of shouting leticia larceny, whorehouse nun, they shrieked roosting up on the iron branches of the dusty colored-

glass foliage of the dome of the market where they knew they
were safe from the devastating wind of that buccaneer zamba-
palo dance which was repeated every Wednesday at dawn during
the turbulent childhood of the miniature hoax of a general
whose voice became more affectionate and his manners sweeter
the more he tried to look like a man with the saber of a playing-
card king that still dragged when he walked, he would stand
unperturbed in the midst of the rapine, he would remain serene,
haughty, with the inflexible decorum his mother had inculcated
in him so that he would deserve the flower of the bloodline that
she herself was squandering in the market with her drive of a
furious bitch and her Arab vendor's curses under the unaffected
look of the old black women in bright-colored rag turbans who
bore the insults and contemplated the sack fanning themselves
without blinking with the canyon-deep calm of sitting idols, not
breathing, ruminating wads of tobacco, wads of coca leaves, the
medicines of poverty which allowed them to live through so
much ignominy as the ferocious assault of the whirlwind passed
and Leticia Nazareno opened a way with her vest-pocket officer
through the frantic dogs whose hair stood on end along their
spines and she would shout from the door send the bill to the
government, as always, and they only sighed, oh Lord, if the
general only knew, if there were only someone capable of telling
him, fooled by the illusion that he would still be unaware until
the hour of his death of what everyone knew to be the greatest
scandal of his memory that my only and legitimate wife Leticia
Nazareno had despoiled the Hindu bazaars of their terrible glass
swans and mirrors with seashell frames and coral ashtrays, had
stripped the Syrian shops of mortuary taffetas and carried off by
the fistful the strings of little gold fish and the protective figs of
the ambulant silversmiths in the business district who shouted
to her face you're more of a fox than the blue leticias she wore

around her neck, she carried off everything she found in her
path to satisfy the only thing left from her former status as novice which was her childish poor taste and the vice of asking for
something when there was no need, except that now she didn't
have to beg in the name of God's love in the jasmine-scented
doorways of the viceregal district but she carted off in army
trucks everything that pleased her wishes without any more sacrifice on her part except the peremptory order of send the bill to
the government. It was the same as saying collect from God,
because no one knew for sure from then on whether he existed
or not, he had become invisible, we could see the fortified walls
on the knoll of the main square, the house of power with the
balcony of legendary speeches and the windows with lace curtains and flower pots on the cornices and at night it looked like
a steamboat sailing through the sky, not just from any spot in
the city but also from seven leagues away at sea after they
painted it white and lighted it with glass globes to celebrate the
visit of the well-known poet Rubén Darío, although none of
those signs indicated for certain that he was there, on the contrary, we thought with good reason that those signs of life were
military tricks to try to give the lie to the widespread rumor that
he had succumbed to a crisis of senile mysticism, that he had
renounced the pomp and circumstance of power and had
imposed upon himself the penance of living the rest of his life
in a fearful state of prostration with hair shirts of deprivation in
his soul and all manner of irons of mortification on his body,
with nothing but rye bread to eat and well water to drink, or
nothing to sleep on except the slabs of a bare cell from the cloisters of the Biscayan sisters until he could expiate the horror of
having possessed against her will and having made pregnant
with a male child a forbidden woman who only because God is
great had still not taken her final vows, and yet nothing had

changed in his vast realm of gloom because Leticia Nazareno held the keys to his power and all she needed to do was say that he sent word to send the bill to the government, an ancient formula that at first seemed very easy to evade but which was getting more and more fearful, until a group of determined creditors dared present themselves after many years with a suitcase full of pending bills at the pantry of the presidential palace and we ran into the surprise that no one said yes to us and no one said no but they sent us with a soldier on duty to a discreet waiting room where we were received by a friendly young naval officer with a calm voice and a smiling face who offered us thin and fragrant coffee from the presidential crop, he showed us the white, well-lighted offices with metal screens on the windows and fans on the ceiling, and everything was so bright and human that one wondered in perplexity where the power of that air that smelled of perfumed medicine was, where was the meanness and the inclemency of power in the conscientiousness of those clerks in silk shirts who governed without haste and in silence, he showed us the small inner courtyard where the rosebushes had been cut down by Leticia Nazareno to purify the morning dew from the bad memory of the lepers and the blind men and the cripples who were sent off to die of oblivion in charity homes, he showed us the former shed of the concubines, the rusty sewing machines, the army cots where the harem slaves had slept up to groups of three in cells of shame which was going to be torn down to build the private chapel in its place, he showed us from an inside window the most intimate gallery of government house, the pansy bower gilded by the four o'clock sun on the lattice screen with green stripes where he had just lunched with Leticia Nazareno and the child who were the only people allowed to sit at his table, he showed us the legendary ceiba tree in whose shadow they would hang the hammock with the colors of the flag where he took his siesta on the hottest days, he showed us the milking stables, the cheese vats, the honeycombs, and on coming back along the way he followed at dawn to oversee the milking he seemed to be struck by a bolt of revelation and he pointed out to us the mark of a boot in the mud, look, he said, it's his footprint, we were petrified as we looked at the imprint of a large, coarse sole which had the splendor and the dominion in repose and the stench of old mange of the track of a tiger accustomed to solitude, and in that footprint we saw the power, we felt the contact of his mystery with much more revealing force than when one of us was chosen to see him in person because the higher-ups in the army were beginning to rebel against the newcomer who had managed to accumulate more power than the supreme command, more than the government, more than he, for Leticia Nazareno had come far with her airs of a queen that the presidential high command itself assumed the risk of opening the way to one of you, only one, in an attempt to have him get at least a tiny little idea of what's happening to the nation behind his back general sir, and that was how I got to see him, he was alone in the hot office with white walls and prints of English horses, he was stretched out in an easy chair, under the fan, in the wrinkled white drill uniform with copper buttons and no insignia of any kind, he had his right hand with the velvet glove on the wooden desk where there was nothing but three identical pairs of very small eyeglasses with gold rims, behind him he had a glass-enclosed case with dusty books that looked more like ledgers bound in human skin, on the right he had a large and open window, also with a metal screen, through which the whole city could be seen and all the sky without clouds or birds all the way to the other side of the sea, and I felt a great relief because he showed himself to be less conscious of his power than any of his partisans and he was more homey than in his photographs and also more worthy of compassion because everything about him was old and arduous and he seemed to be minded by an insatiable illness, so much so that he didn't have the breath to tell me to sit down but indicated it to me with a sad gesture of the velvet glove, he listened to my arguments without looking at me, breathing with a thin and difficult whistling, a mysterious whistling that left a dew of creosote in the room, concentrating deeply on the examination of the bills which I described with schoolboy examples because he couldn't grasp abstract notions, so I began by showing him that Leticia Nazareno owed us for an amount of taffeta twice the nautical distance to Santa María del Altar, that is, one hundred ninety leagues, and he said aha as if to himself, and I ended up by showing him that the total debt with the special discount for your excellency was equal to six times the grand prize in the lottery for ten years, and he said aha again and only then did he look at me directly without his glasses and I could see that his eyes were timid and indulgent, and only then did he tell me with a strange voice of harmony that our reasons were clear and just, to each his own, he said, have them send the bill to the government. That was what he was really like during the period in which Leticia Nazareno had remade him from the beginning without the backwoods difficulties of his mother Bendición Alvarado, she made him give up the habit of eating while walking with the plate in one hand and the spoon in the other and the three of them ate at a little beach table under the pansy bower, he opposite the child and Leticia Nazareno between the two teaching them the norms of good manners and good health in eating, she taught them to keep their spines against the chair back, the fork in the left hand, the knife in the right, chewing each mouthful fifteen times on one side and fifteen times on the other with the mouth closed and the head upright paying no attention to their protests that so many rules were like a barracks, after lunch she taught him to read the official newspaper in which he himself figured as patron and honorary editor, she would put it in his hands when she saw him lying in the hammock in the shade of the gigantic ceiba tree in the family courtyard telling him that it was inconceivable that a full-fledged chief of state should not be up on what was going on in the world, she would put his glasses on him and leave him splashing about in the reading of his own news while she trained the boy in the sport of novices which was throwing and catching a rubber ball, and he would come across himself in photographs so ancient that many of them were not of him but of a former double who had been killed by him and whose name he couldn't remember, he would find himself presiding over the Tuesday cabinet meetings which he hadn't attended since the time of the comet, he learned of historic phrases that his ministers of letters attributed to him, he would read as he nodded in the sultriness of the wandering clouds of August afternoons, he would sink little by little into the corn-soup sweat of his siesta muttering this paper is a piece of shit, God damn it, I can't understand how the people stand for it, he muttered, but something had to come out of that unpleasant reading because he would awaken from his short and tenuous sleep with some new idea inspired by the news, he would send orders to his ministers by Leticia Nazareno, they would answer him through her trying to get a glimpse of his thought, because you were what I wanted you to be the interpreter of my highest designs, you were my voice, you were my reason and my strength, she was his most faithful and attentive ear for the sound of the perpetual lava flows of the inaccessible world which besieged him, even though in reality the final oracles that governed his fate were the anonymous graffiti on the walls of the servants' toilets, in which he would decipher the hidden truths that no one would have dared reveal to him, not even you, Leticia, he would read them at dawn on his way back from the milking before the cleaning orderlies had erased them and he ordered the toilet walls whitewashed every day so that no one could resist the temptation to unburden himself of his hidden rancors, there he learned about the bitterness of the high command, the repressed intentions of those who prospered in his shadow and repudiated him behind his back, he felt master of all his power when he succeeded in penetrating an enigma of the human heart in the revealing mirror of the role of the rabblement, he sang again after so many years contemplating through the mist of the mosquito netting the morning beached whale's sleep of his only and legitimate wife Leticia Nazareno, get up, he sang, it's six o'clock in my heart, the sea is where it belongs, life goes on, Leticia, the unpredictable life of the only one of all his women who had got everything from him except the easy privilege of his awakening in bed with her, for he would leave after the last love, hang the runaway lamp by the door of his old bachelor's bedroom, fasten the three bars, the three locks, the three bolts, drop face down onto the floor, alone and with his clothes on, as he had done every night before you, as he did without you until the last night of his dreams of a solitary drowned man, he would return after the milking to your room with its smell of a beast of darkness to continue giving you whatever you wanted, much more than the incalculable inheritance of his mother Bendición Alvarado, much more than any human being had ever dreamed of on the face of the earth, not only for her but also for her inexhaustible relatives who kept arriving from the unknown keys of the Antilles with no other fortune but the flesh that covered them or any other title but their identity as Nazarenos, a harsh family of intrepid males and women who burned with the fever of greed who had taken by storm the monopolies of salt, tobacco, drinking water, the former perquisites with which he had favored the commanders of the various branches of the armed services so as to keep them away from other kinds of ambition and which Leticia Nazareno had been snatching away from them little by little through his orders which he did not give but approved, agreed, he had abolished the barbarous method of execution of being quartered by horses and had tried to put in its place the electric chair which had been given him by the commander of the landing forces so that we too could enjoy the more civilized method of killing, he had visited the horror laboratory at the harbor fort where they chose the most run-down of political prisoners in order to get training in the manipulation of the throne of death whose discharges absorbed the total electrical power of the city, we knew the exact moment of the fatal experiment because we would be left in darkness for an instant holding our breath in horror, we would observe a minute of silence in the waterfront brothels and drink to the soul of the condemned man, not once but several times, because most of the victims remained hanging on the straps of the chair with their bodies looking like a blood sausage and sizzling like a roast but still panting with pain until someone had the mercy to shoot them to death after several frustrated attempts, all in order to please you, Leticia, for you had emptied the dungeons and authorized the repatriation of his enemies once more and promulgated an Easter edict that no one was to be punished for differences of opinion or persecuted for matters of conscience, convinced in his heart in the fullness of his autumn that his fiercest adversaries had a right to share in the tranquillity which he enjoyed on engrossing January nights with the only woman who had merited the glory of seeing him without a shirt and in his long drawers and the enormous rupture gilded by the moon on the terrace of government house, together they looked at the mysterious willows that they had been sent by the king and queen of Babylonia around Christmas time so they could plant them in the rain garden, they enjoyed the sun as it was broken up through the perpetual waters, they took pleasure in the pole star tangled in the branches, they scrutinized the universe on the dial of the small radio through the interference of jeers from fugitive planets, together they would listen to the daily episode of the soap operas from Santiago de Cuba which would leave in their hearts the feeling of a doubt of whether we'll still be alive tomorrow to find out how this misfortune is resolved, he would play with the child before putting him to bed in order to teach him everything it was possible to know about the use and maintenance of weapons of war which was the human science he knew better than anyone, but the only advice he gave him was never issue an order unless you're sure it's going to be carried out, he made him repeat it as many times as he thought necessary so that the boy would never forget that the only mistake that a man invested with authority and power cannot make even once in his lifetime is to issue an order which he is not sure will be carried out, more a piece of advice from a wary grandfather than from a wise father and which the child would never have forgotten even if he had lived as long as he because he taught it to him while he was preparing him to fire for the first time at the age of six a recoil cannon to whose catastrophic report we attributed the fearful dry storm of volcanic thunder and lightning and the awesome polar wind from Comodoro Rivadavia which turned the bowels of the sea upside down and carried off an animal circus set up on the square of the former slave port, we caught elephants in casting nets, drowned clowns, giraffes hanging on trapezes from the fury of the tempest which miraculously didn't sink the banana boat which arrived a few hours later bearing the young poet

Félix Rubén García Sarmiento who was to become famous
under the name of Rubén Darío, luckily the sea calmed down at
four o'clock, the well-washed air filled with flying ants, and he
looked out the bedroom window and saw to the lee of the harbor hills the little white ship listing to starboard and with its
rigging dismantled sailing along out of danger in the backwaters
of the afternoon that had been purified by the brimstone of the
storm, he saw the captain on the quarterdeck directing the difficult maneuvers in honor of the illustrious passenger in a long
dark coat and a checkered vest whom he had never heard of until
the following Sunday night when Leticia Nazareno requested of
him the inconceivable favor of accompanying her to an evening
of poetry at the National Theater and he had accepted without
blinking, agreed. We had been waiting for three hours standing
in the steaming atmosphere of the orchestra seats suffocating in
the full dress which had been required of us urgently at the last
moment, when finally the national anthem began and we turned
in applause toward the box marked with the national coat of
arms where the chubby novice appeared in a hat with curling
feathers and her nocturnal fox tails over a taffeta gown, she sat
down without any greeting beside the young prince in an
evening uniform who had answered the applause with the iris
of the empty fingers of his velvet glove held in his fist as his
mother had told him princes used to do in other days, we saw
no one else in the presidential box, but during the two hours of
the recital we bore the certainty that he was there, we felt the
invisible presence that watched over our destiny so that it would
not be altered by the disorder of poetry, he regulated love, he
decided the intensity and term of death in a corner of the box in
the shadows from where unseen he watched the heavy minotaur
whose voice of marine lightning lifted him out of his place and
instant and left him floating without his permission in the

golden thunder of the trim trumpets of the triumphal arches of
Marses and Minervas of a glory that was not his general sir, he
saw the heroic athletes with their standards the black mastiffs of
the hunt the sturdy war-horses with their iron hoofs the pikes
and lances of the paladins with rough crests who bore the
strange flag captive to honor arms that were not his, he saw
the troop of fierce young men who had challenged the suns of
the red summer the snows and winds of the icy winter night and
dew and hatred and death for the eternal splendor of an immor-
tal nation larger and more glorious than all those he had
dreamed of during the long deliriums of his fevers as a barefoot
warrior, he felt poor and tiny in the seismic thunder of the
applause that he approved in the shadows thinking mother of
mine Bendición Alvarado this really is a parade, not the shitty
things these people organize for me, feeling diminished and
alone, oppressed by the heavy heat and the mosquitoes and the
columns of cheap gold paint and the faded plush of the box of
honor, God damn it, how is it possible for this Indian to write
something so beautiful with the same hand that he wipes his ass
with, he said to himself, so excited by the revelation of written
beauty that he dragged his great feet of a captive elephant to the
rhythm of the martial beat of the kettle-drums, he dozed off to
the rhythm of the voices of glory of the cadenced chant of the
calorific choir that Leticia Nazareno recited for him in the shade
of the triumphal arches of the ceiba tree in the courtyard, he
would write the lines on the walls of the toilets, he was trying
to recite the whole poem by heart in the tepid cowshit olympus
of the milking stables when the earth trembled from the dynamite charge that went off ahead of time in the trunk of the presidential automobile parked in the coach house, it was terrible
general sir, such a violent explosion that many months later all
over the city they were still finding twisted pieces of the armored

limousine that Leticia Nazareno and the child would have used
an hour later for their Wednesday marketing, because the
attempt was against her life general sir, without a doubt, and
then he slapped his forehead, God damn it, how is it possible he
didn't foresee it, what had become of his legendary clairvoyance
because for so many months the graffiti in the toilets were not
against him, as always, or against any of his civilian ministers,
but were inspired by the audacity of the Nazarenos who had
reached the point of nibbling away at the sinecures reserved for
the high command, or by the ambitions of churchmen who were
obtaining limitless and eternal favors from the temporal power,
he had observed that the innocent diatribes against his mother
Bendición Alvarado had become the curses of a macaw, broadsides of hidden rancor which matured in the warm impunity of
the toilets and ended up coming out onto the streets as had
happened so many times with other minor scandals that he himself had taken care to precipitate, although he had never thought
or would have been capable of thinking that they could have
been so ferocious as to place two hundred pounds of dynamite
within the very confines of government house, sneaky bastards,
how is it possible that he was going around so absorbed in the
ecstasy of the triumphal bronzes that his fine nose of a ravening
tiger had not recognized the old and sweet smell of danger in
time, what a mess, he called an urgent meeting of the high command, fourteen trembling military men we were who after so
many years of ordinary behavior and secondhand orders were to
see once more at two fathoms distance the uncertain old man
whose real existence was the simplest of his enigmas, he received
us sitting on the thronelike seat in the hearing room with the
uniform of a private soldier smelling of skunk piss and wearing
small eyeglasses with solid gold frames which we had not seen
even in his most recent portraits, and he was older and more

remote than anyone had been able to imagine, except for the
languid hands without the velvet gloves which did not look like
his natural soldier's hands but those of someone much younger
and more compassionate, everything else was dense and somber,
and the more we recognized him the more obvious it was that
he just barely had one last breath of life left, but it was the breath
of authority without appeal, devastating, difficult even for him
to keep in line like the restlessness of a mountain horse, not
speaking, not even moving his head as we rendered him the
honors of chief supreme general and finally sat down facing him
in the easy chairs arranged in a circle, and only then did he take
off his glasses and he began to scrutinize us with those meticulous eyes that knew the weasel hiding places of our second intentions, he scrutinized them without mercy, one by one, taking all
the time he needed to establish with precision how much each
one of us had changed since the afternoon in the mists of memory when he had promoted them to the highest ranks pointing
to them according to the impulses of his inspiration, and as he
scrutinized them he felt the certainty growing that among those
fourteen hidden enemies were the authors of the assassination
attempt, but at the same time he felt so alone and defenseless
facing them that he only blinked, only lifted his head to exhort
them to unity now more than ever for the good of the nation
and the honor of the armed forces, he recommended energy and
prudence to them and imposed on them the honorable mission
of discovering without too much thought the authors of the
attempt so that they could be submitted to the serene rigors of
military justice, that's all gentlemen, he concluded, knowing full
well that the author was one of them, or all of them, mortally
wounded by the unavoidable conviction that Leticia Nazareno's
life did not depend on God's will then but on the wisdom with
which he could manage to preserve it from a threat that sooner

or later would irremediably be fulfilled, damn it. He made her cancel her public appearances, he made her more voracious relatives get rid of all privileges that might run afoul of the armed forces, the most understanding were named consuls with a free hand and the most bloody were found floating in the mangrove swamps off the channls by the market, he appeared without prior announcement after so many years in his empty chair in the cabinet room ready to put a limit on the infiltration of the clergy into the business of state in order to keep you safe from your enemies, Leticia, and nevertheless he had made more deep soundings in the high command after the first drastic decisions and was convinced that seven of the commanders were unreservedly loyal to him in addition to the general in chief who was the oldest of his comrades, but still lacked power against the other six enemies who lengthened his nights with the unavoidable impression that Leticia Nazareno was already marked for death, they were killing her right in his hands in spite of the measures to have her food tested ever since the day they found a fish bone in the bread, they tested the purity of the air she breathed because he feared they had poisoned the Flit spray, he saw her looking pale at the table, he felt her become voiceless in the middle of love, he was tormented by the idea that they had put black vomit germs in her drinking water, vitriol in her eye drops, subtle and ingenious ways of death that embittered him at every moment during those days and would awaken him in the middle of his sleep with the vivid nightmare that Leticia Nazareno had been bled during her sleep by an Indian curse, upset by so many imaginary risks and real threats he forbade her to go out without the ferocious escort of presidential guards under instructions to kill without cause, but she did go out general sir, she took the child along, he controlled his feelings of evil omens to watch them get into the new armored limousine, he saw them off with signs of exorcism from an inner balcony begging mother of mine Bendición Alvarado protect them, make the bullets bounce off her brassiere, weaken the laudanum, mother, straighten twisted thoughts, without an instant of rest until he heard the sirens on the escort from the main square and saw Leticia Nazareno and the child crossing the courtyard with the first flashes from the lighthouse, she returned agitated, happy in the midst of the custody of warriors loaded down with live turkeys, orchids from Envigado, strings of little colored lights for Christmas nights already announced on the streets by signs made of luminous stars ordered by him to hide his anxiety, he would meet her on the stairs to feel you still alive in the naphthalene dew of the blue-fox tails, in the sour sweat of your tufts of invalid's hair, he helped you carry the gifts to the bedroom with the strange certainty that he was consuming the last crumbs of a condemned jubilation that he would have preferred never having known, all the more desolate as he became more convinced that every recourse he conceived of to alleviate that unbearable anxiety, every step he took to conjure it away brought him mercilessly closer to the frightful Wednesday of my misfortune when he took the tremendous decision of no more, God damn it, if it had to be let it be soon, he decided, and it was like an explosive order that he had not finished putting together when two of his aides burst into his office with the terrible news that Leticia Nazareno and the child had been torn to pieces and eaten by the stray dogs at the public market, they ate them alive general sir, but they weren't the same usual street dogs but hunting animals with frightened yellow eyes and the smooth skin of a shark that someone had set upon the blue foxes, sixty dogs all alike who nobody knew when leaped out from among the vegetable stands and fell upon Leticia Nazareno and the child without giving us time to shoot for fear of killing

them who looked as if they were drowning along with the dogs
in a hellish whirlpool, we could only see the instantaneous signs
of some ephemeral hands reaching out to us while the rest of
the body was disappearing into pieces, we saw fleeting and
ungraspable expressions that sometimes were of terror, other
times of pity, other times of jubilation until they finally sank into
the whirlpool of the scramble and all that was left floating was
Leticia Nazareno's hat with felt violets facing the impassive horror of the totemic vegetable women spattered with hot blood
who prayed my God, this couldn't be possible unless the general
wanted it, or at least unless he didn't know about it, to the eternal dishonor of the presidential guard who without firing a shot
could only rescue the bare bones scattered among the bloody
vegetables, nothing else general sir, the only thing we found
were these medals that belonged to the boy, the saber without
its tassels, Leticia Nazareno's cordovan shoes which no one
knows why appeared floating in the bay about a league away
from the market, the necklace of colored glass, the chain-mail
purse which we deliver here to your own hand general sir, along
with these three keys, the wedding ring of blackened gold and
these fifty cents in ten-cent pieces which they put on the desk
for him to count, and nothing else general sir, it was all that was
left of them. It wouldn't have mattered to him if more had been
left or less, if he had known then that the years he would need
to erase down to the last vestige the memory of that inevitable
Wednesday were not many or very difficult, he wept with rage,
he woke up shouting with rage tormented by the barking of the
dogs who spent the night chained in the courtyard while he
decided what shall we do with them general sir, wondering in
confusion whether killing the dogs might not be killing Leticia
Nazareno and the child who were inside them all over again, he
ordered them to tear down the iron cupola of the vegetable mar-

ket and build in its place a garden with magnolias and quails and a marble cross with a light higher and brighter than the lighthouse to perpetuate in the memory of future generations until the end of time the remembrance of a historic woman whom he himself forgot about long before the monument was demolished by a nocturnal explosion that no one avenged, and the magnolias were eaten by hogs and the memorable garden changed into a dungheap of pestilential slime which he never came to know, not only because he had ordered the presidential chauffeur to avoid passing by the former vegetable market even if you have to travel around the world, but also because he never went out again after he sent the officers off to the solar glass windows of the ministries and kept just the minimal personnel to live in the run-down building where by his orders not the least visible vestige of your urges of a queen was left, Leticia, he kept wandering about the empty house with no known task except the eventual consultations with the high command or the final decision of a difficult cabinet meeting or the pernicious visits of Ambassador Wilson who was accustomed to spend time with him until well into the afternoon under the foliage of the ceiba tree and who brought him candy from Baltimore and magazines with color prints of naked women to try to convince him that he should give him the territorial waters on account for the enormous interest on the foreign debt, and he let him speak on, feigning to hear less or more than he really could hear according to his convenience, he defended himself from the wagging tongue by listening to the chorus of the petite painted bird perched on a lemon limb from the nearby girls' school, he would accompany him to the steps with the first shadows of evening trying to explain to him that he could take anything he wanted except the sea of my windows, just imagine, what would I do all alone in this big building if I couldn't look out now as always at this time at what looks like a marsh in flames, what would I do without the December winds that sneak in barking through the broken windowpanes, how could I live without the green flashes of the lighthouse, I who abandoned my misty barrens and enlisted in the agony of fever in the tumult of the federalist war, and don't you think that I did it out of patriotism as the dictionary says, or from the spirit of adventure, or least of all because I gave a shit about federal principles which God keep in his holy kingdom, no my dear Wilson, I did it all so that I could get to know the sea, so think about some other nuisance, he said, he took leave of him on the stairs with a pat on the shoulder, he went back lighting the lamps in the deserted salons of the former offices where on one of those afternoons he found a strayed cow, he chased her toward the stairs and the animal tripped on the patches in the rugs and fell on her back and tumbled down the stairs and broke her neck to the glory and sustenance of the lepers who fell upon her and carved her up, because the lepers had returned after the death of Leticia Nazareno and were there again along with the blind men and the cripples waiting for the salt of health from his hand in the wild rosebushes in the courtyard, he could hear them singing on starry nights, he would sing with them the song Susana come Susana from his times of glory, he would peek out of the skylight in the granary at five in the afternoon to watch the girls coming out of school and would grow ecstatic over their blue aprons, their knee socks, their braids, mother, we would run in fright from the consumptive eyes of the ghost who called to us from behind the iron bars with the torn fingers of his ragged glove, girl, girl, he would call to us, come let me feel you, he would watch them run off in fright thinking mother of mine Bendición Alvarado how young the young girls of today are, he would laugh at himself, but he would become reconciled with himself when his personal physi-

cian the minister of health would examine his retina with a magnifying glass every time he invited him to lunch, he would take
his pulse, he tried to make me take some spoonfuls of candlewax
to plug up the leaks in my memory, what a mess, spoonfuls of
medicine for me who hasn't had any ailment in this life except
the tertian fevers in the war, shit doctor, he sat eating alone at
the single table with his back to the world as the erudite Ambassador Maryland had told him the kings of Morocco ate, he ate
with knife and fork and his head erect in accordance with the
strict norms of a forgotten teacher, he would go all over the
building looking for the jars of honey whose hiding places
he would forget after a few hours and he would find by mistake
the rolls from the margins of ledgers where he had written in
other times so as not to forget anything when he could no longer
remember anything, he read on one that tomorrow is Tuesday,
he read that there was an initial on your white handkerchief a
red initial of a name that was not yours my master, he read
intrigued Leticia Nazareno of my soul look what has become of
me without you, he read Leticia Nazareno everywhere without
being able to understand how anyone could be so unhappy to
have left that flow of written sighs, and still it was my handwriting, the unique left-handed calligraphy that was found at that
time on the walls of the toilets where he wrote to console himself long live the general, long live the general, God damn it,
completely cured of the rage of having been the weakest military
man on land sea and air because of a fugitive from the cloister
of whom all that remained was the name written in pencil on
strips of paper as he had resolved when he didn't even want to
touch the things his aides put on his desk and he ordered without looking at them to take away those shoes, those keys, everything that might evoke the image of his dead, to put everything
that belonged to them in the bedroom of his wild siestas and

wall up the doors and windows with the final order not to enter that room even on my orders, God damn it, he survived the nocturnal shudders of the dogs chained in the courtyard for many months because he thought that any harm done to them might hurt his dead, he abandoned himself to his hammock, trembling with the rage of knowing who the assassins of his blood were and having to bear the humiliation of seeing them in his own house because at that moment he lacked power against them, he had been opposed to any kind of posthumous honors, he had forbidden visits of condolence, mourning, he was waiting for his moment rocking with rage in the hammock in the shade of the tutelary ceiba tree where my last comrade had expressed to him the pride of the high command over the serenity and order with which the people had withstood the tragedy and he gave a glimmer of a smile, don't be a horse's ass old friend, what serenity, what order, what's happening is that the people didn't give a shit for this misfortune, he went back and forth through the newspaper looking for something besides the news invented by his own press services, he had the little radio put within reach to listen to the same news item from Veracruz to Riobamba that the forces of law and order were close on the track of the authors of the attack, and he muttered of course, you sons of a tarantula, they had identified them beyond the slightest doubt, of course, they had them sur-rounded under mortar fire in a suburban house of ill repute, that's it, he sighed, poor devils, but he stayed in the hammock without displaying even a glimmer of his malice asking mother of mine Bendición Alvarado give me life for this challenge, don't let go of my hand, mother, give me inspiration, so sure of the efficacy of the plea that we found him recovered from his grief when we commanders of the general staff responsible for public order and state security came to give him the news that three of the authors of the crime had been killed in battle with public forces and the other two were awaiting your disposition general sir in the dungeons of San Jerónimo and he said aha, sitting in the hammock with the pitcher of fruit juice from which he poured each of us a glass with the calm pulse of a good marksman, wiser and more solicitous than ever, to the point that he guessed my anxiety to light a cigarette and gave me permission which until then he had never given to any officer on duty, under this tree we're all equals, he said, and he listened without rancor to the detailed report of the crime in the market, how from Scotland they had brought in separate shipments eighty-two newborn bulldogs of whom twenty-two had died in the course of their raising and sixty had been evilly taught to kill by a Scottish trainer who inculcated them with a criminal hatred not only for the blue foxes but for the very persons of Leticia Nazareno and the boy making use of these articles of clothing which they had slipped out little by little from the laundry services in government house, making use of Leticia Nazareno's brassiere, this handkerchief, these stockings, this complete uniform of the boy's which we displayed for him so that he would recognize them, but he only said aha, without looking at them, we explained to him how the sixty dogs had even been trained not to bark when they shouldn't, they were made accustomed to the taste of human flesh, they were kept locked up with no contact with the world for the difficult years of training on a former Chinese farm seven leagues from this capital city where they had life-size figures dressed in the clothing of Leticia Nazareno and the boy whom the dogs also knew from these original pictures and these newspaper clippings which we showed him pasted in an album so that you could get a better idea general sir of the perfection of the work those bastards did, if you could only say that for everybody, but he only said aha, without look-

ing at them, we explained to him lastly that the accused had not
been working on their own, of course, but were the agents of a
subversive brotherhood with headquarters abroad whose symbol was this goose quill crossed over a knife, aha, all of them
fugitives of military penal justice for other previous crimes
against the security of the state, these three who are the dead
ones whose pictures we showed him in the album with the
respective police numbers hanging around their necks, and these
two are the ones who are alive and in jail awaiting your final
and unappealable decision general sir, the brothers Mauricio and
Gumaro Ponce de León, twenty-eight and twenty-three years
old, the first an unemployed army deserter with no fixed domicile and the second a ceramics teacher in the school of arts and
crafts, and to whom the dogs gave such signs of familiarity and
excitement that it alone would have been sufficient proof of guilt
general sir, and he only said aha, but he cited with honors in the
order of the day the three officers who brought the investigation
of the crime to a conclusion and he awarded them the medal of
military merit for services to the nation in the course of a solemn
ceremony in which he named the summary court-martial which
tried the brothers Mauricio and Gumaro Ponce de León and
condemned them to be shot within the next forty-eight hours,
unless they received the gift of your clemency general sir, you are
in command. He remained in the hammock alone and absorbed,
insensitive to the pleas for mercy from all over the world, on the
radio he heard the sterile debate at the League of Nations, he
heard insults from some neighboring countries and some distant
support, he listened with equal attention to the timid reasons of
the ministers in favor of clemency and the shrill motives of those
in favor of punishment, he refused to see the apostolic nuncio
with a personal message from the Pope in which he expressed
his pastoral concern for the fate of two errant members of the

flock, he heard the reports on public order from all over the country which was upset by his silence, he heard the distant shooting, he felt the earth quake from the explosion without origin of a warship anchored in the bay, eleven dead general sir, eighty-two wounded and the ship out of commission, agreed, he said, looking out the bedroom window at the nocturnal bonfire in the cove of the harbor while the two condemned men began to live the night of their eve in the chapel at the San Jerónimo base which was set up as for a wake, he remembered them at that time as he had seen them in their pictures with the bushy eyebrows of their common mother, he remembered them trembling, alone, with the tags of successive numbers hanging around their necks under the always lighted bulb of the death cell, he felt sorry for them, he knew he was needed, required, but he had not made the least gesture that would let the direction of his will peep through when he finished repeating the routine acts of one or more day in his life and he took leave of the duty officer who was to remain on watch by his bedroom to carry the message bearing his decision at any moment he might make it before the first cockcrow, he took leave as he passed without looking at him, good night, captain, he hung the lamp on the door, fastened the three bars, the three locks, the three bolts, sank face down into an alert sleep through whose fragile thin walls he kept on hearing the anxious barking of the dogs in the courtyard, the sirens of the ambulances, the fireworks, the waves of music from some mistaken party in the intense night of the city huddling under the rigor of the sentence, he awoke with the twelve o'clock bells from the cathedral, he woke up again at two o'clock, he woke up again before three with the rattle of the drizzle on the window screens, then he got up off the floor with the arduous maneuvers of an ox first the haunches and then the hind legs and finally the confused head with a string of spittle

from his snout and he ordered first to the officer of the guard
that he take those dogs off where I won't hear them under the
care of the government until their natural demise, secondly he
ordered the unconditional release of the soldiers from the escort
for Leticia Nazareno and the boy, and lastly he ordered that the
brothers Mauricio and Gumaro Ponce de León be executed just
as soon as my supreme and unappealable decision is known, but
not at the execution wall, as had been called for, but under the
punishment that had fallen into disuse, that of being quartered
by horses and their parts exposed to public indignation and horror in the most visible places of his measureless realm of gloom,
poor lads, while he dragged his great feet of a badly wounded
elephant begging with wrath mother of mine Bendición Alvarado, stay with me, don't let go of my hand, mother, let me find
the man to help me avenge this innocent blood, a providential
man whom he had imagined in the delirium of his rancor and
whom he sought with an irresistible anxiety in the depths of the
eyes he found in his path, he tried to find him crouching in the
most subtle registers of voices, in the beating of his heart, in
the least used crannies of his memory, and he had lost the illusion of ever finding him when he discovered himself fascinated
by the most dazzling and haughty man my eyes have ever seen,
mother, dressed like the Goths of yesteryear in a Henry Pool
jacket with a gardenia in the buttonhole, with Pecover trousers
and a brocade vest of silver highlights that he had worn with his
natural elegance in the most difficult salons of Europe holding
the leash of a taciturn Doberman the size of a young bull with
human eyes, José Ignacio Saenz de la Barra, at your excellency's
service, he introduced himself, the last scion of our aristocracy
which had been demolished by the federalist leaders, wiped off
the face of the nation with their arid dreams of grandeur and
their vast and melancholy mansions and their French accents, a

splendid tailend of a breed with no other fortune but his thirty-two years, seven languages, four records in trapshooting at Deauville, solid, slender, the color of iron, half-breed hair with the part in the middle and a dyed white lock, the linear lips of eternal will, the resolute look of the providential man who pretended to be playing cricket with a cherrywood cane so they could take his picture in color with the backdrop of idyllic springtimes of the tapestries in the ballroom, and the instant he saw him he let out a sigh of relief and said to himself that's the one, and that he was. He entered his service under the simple condition that you give me a budget of eight hundred fifty million without my having to give an accounting to anyone and with no authority over me but that of your excellency and in the course of two years I will deliver to you the real assassins of Leticia Nazareno and the child, and he accepted, agreed, convinced of his loyalty and his efficiency after so many difficult tests to which he had submitted him in order to scrutinize the byways of his soul and learn the limits of his will and the chinks in his character before deciding to place in his hands the keys to his power, he submitted him to the ultimate test of the inclement domino games in which José Ignacio Saenz de la Barra assumed the temerity of winning without permission, and he won, because he was the bravest man my eyes had ever seen, mother, he had a patience without pause, he knew everything, he was familiar with seventy-two ways of making coffee, he could distinguish the sex of shellfish, he could read music and Braille, he would stand looking into my eyes without speaking, and I didn't know what to do opposite that indestructible face, those listless hands on the nub of the cherrywood cane with a morning-water stone on the ring finger, that huge dog lying by his feet watchful and ferocious inside the live velvet wrapping of his sleeping skin, that fragrance of bath salts of a body immune to tenderness and death belonging to the most handsome man and the one with the most control my eyes had ever seen when he had the courage to tell me that I was only a military man out of convenience, because military men are just the opposite of you, general, they're men of quick and easy ambition, they like command better than power and they're not in the service of something but of someone, and that's why it's so easy to make use of them, he said, especially one against the other, and all I could think of to do was smile persuaded that he couldn't have hidden his thoughts from that dazzling man to whom he had given more power than anyone he ever had under his regime since my comrade General Rodrigo de Aguilar whom God keep at his holy right side, he made him absolute master of a secret empire within his own private empire, an invisible service of repression and extermination that not only lacked an official identity but was even difficult to conceive of in its real existence, because no one was responsible for its acts, nor did it have a name or a location in the world, and yet it was a fearsome truth that had been imposed by terror over other organs of repression of the state for a long time before its origins and its unfathomable nature had been established in all certainty by the high command, not even you yourself foresaw the reach of that machine of horror general sir, nor could I myself suspect that at the instant in which he accepted the agreement I was at the mercy of the irresistible charm and the tentacular drive of that barbarian dressed like a prince who sent to me at the presidential palace a fiber sack that seemed to be full of coconuts and he ordered them to put it over there in a closet for file papers built into the wall where it would be out of the way, he forgot about it and after three days it was impossible to breathe because of the stench of carrion that penetrated the walls and fogged the mirrors over with a pestilential mist, we looked for the stink in the

198 ❧ Gabriel García Márquez

kitchen and we found in it the stables, we chased it out of the offices with incense and it came out to meet us in the hearing room, with its outpouring of rotted roses it saturated the most hidden crannies where even concealed in other fragrances the tiniest breath of the nighttime plague air mange had reached, and yet it was where we had looked for it least in the sack of seeming coconuts that José Ignacio Saenz de la Barra had sent as the first fruit of the agreement, six heads with the corresponding death certificates, the head of the blind stone-age founding father Don Nepomuceno Estrada, age ninety-four, last veteran of the great war and founder of the Radical Party, dead according to the accompanying certificate on May 14 as the consequence of a senile collapse, the head of Dr. Nepomuceno Estrada de la Fuente, son of the first, age fifty-seven, homeopathic physician, dead according to the accompanying certificate on the same date as his father as the consequence of a coronary thrombosis, the head of Eliécer Castor, age twenty-one, student of letters, dead according to the accompanying certificate as a consequence of various stab wounds from a barroom fight, the head of Lídice Santiago, age thirty-two, clandestine activist, dead according to the certificate as the consequence of an induced abortion, the head of Roque Pinzón, alias Jacinto the Invisible, age thirty-eight, manufacturer of colored globes, dead on the same date as the previous as a consequence of ethyl alcohol intoxication, the head of Natalicio Ruiz, secretary of the clandestine October 17 Movement, age thirty, dead according to the accompanying certificate as a consequence of a pistol shot in the palate because of a broken love affair, six in all, and the corresponding receipt which he signed with his bile all bubbling because of the smell and the horror thinking mother of mine Bendición Alvarado this man is a beast, who would have imagined that with his airs of a mystic and the flower in his buttonhole, he ordered don't send me any more chops, Nacho, your word is enough, but Saenz de la Barra answered that it was a matter between men, general, if you haven't got the stomach to look truth in the face here's your gold and we're the same friends we were before, what a mess, for much less than that he would have had his own mother shot, but he bit his tongue, it's all right. Nacho, he said, do your duty, so the heads kept on coming in those shadowy fiber sacks that looked like bags of coconuts and with his innards all twisted he ordered them taken far away from here while he forced himself to read the details of the death certificates in order to sign the receipts, agreed, he had signed for nine hundred eighteen heads of his fiercest enemies the night he dreamed that he saw himself changed into an animal with only one finger which went along leaving a trail of fingerprints on a plain of fresh concrete, he woke up with a dampness of bile, he eluded his bad dawn mood by taking a head count in the dungheap of sour memories of the milking stalls, so abstracted in his old-man ponderings that he confused the buzzing in his eardrums with the sound of the insects in the rotten hay thinking mother of mine Bendición Alvarado how is it possible that there are so many of them and they still haven't got to the ones who are really guilt, but Saenz de la Barra had made him note that with every six heads sixty enemies are produced and for every sixty six hundred are produced and then six thousand and then six million, the whole country, God damn it, we'll never end, and Saenz de la Barra answered him impassively to rest easy, general, we'll finish with them when they're all finished, what a barbarian. He never had an instant of doubt, he never left a chink for an alternative, he relied on the hidden strength of the Doberman lying in wait eternally who was the only witness to the audiences in spite of the fact that he tried to stop it from the first time he saw José Ignacio Saenz de la Barra

leading the animal with mercurial nerves who only obeyed the
imperceptible mystery of the most dashing but also the least
accommodating man my eyes have ever seen, leave that dog outside, he ordered, but Saenz de la Barra answered him no, general, there's no place in the world where I can enter where Lord
Köchel doesn't enter, so he entered, he remained asleep at his
master's feet while they took the routine account of the severed
heads he got up with a throbbing anxiousness when the
accounting became harsh, his feminine eyes made it hard for me
to think, his human breath made me shudder, I saw him lift up
his steaming snout suddenly with the bubbling of a saucepan
when he pounded on the table with rage because in the sack he
had found the head of a former aide who had also been his
domino crony for many years, God damn it, that's the end of
this mess, but Saenz de la Barra always convinced him, not so
much with arguments as with his soft inclemency of a trainer of
wild dogs, he reproached himself for his submission to the only
mortal who dared treat him like a vassal, alone he rebelled
against his domination, he decided to shake himself loose of that
servitude which was slowly saturating the space of his authority,
this mess is all over right now, God damn it, he would say,
because when all's said and done Bendición Alvarado didn't give
birth to me to take orders but to give them, but his nighttime
decisions fell apart the moment Saenz de la Barra came into the
office and he would succumb to the dazzle of his soft manners
the natural gardenia his pure voice aromatic salts emerald
cufflinks the waxed head his serene walking stick the serious
beauty of the most attractive and most unbearable man my eyes
had ever seen, it's all right, Nacho, he would repeat, do your
duty, and he kept on receiving the sacks of heads, he signed the
receipts without looking at them, he sank with nothing to grasp
on to into the quicksands of his power wondering with every

passage of every dawn of every sea what's happening in the world it's going on eleven o'clock and there isn't a soul in this cemetery house, who's there, he asked, only he, where am I that I can't find myself, he said, where are the teams of barefoot orderlies who unload the donkeys with their greens and chicken cages in the passageways, where are the puddles of dirty water of my foul-mouthed women who replaced the night flowers with fresh ones in the vases and washed the cages and shook rugs off the balconies singing to the rhythm of their dry reed brooms the song Susana come Susana I want to enjoy your love, where are my skinny seven-month runts who shat behind the doors and drew dromedaries in piss on the walls of the hearing room, what happened to my uproar of clerks who found hens laying in the file drawers, my traffic of whores and soldiers in the toilets, the rampaging of my street dogs who ran about bark-ing at diplomats, who has taken my cripples away from the stairs again, my lepers from the rose beds, my insistent adulators from everywhere, he could barely catch a glimpse of his last comrades of the high command behind the compact fence of the new ones responsible for his personal security, he barely had occasion to participate in the meetings of new cabinet members named at the instance of someone who was not he, six doctors of letters in funereal frock coats and wing collars who anticipated his thoughts and decided on matters of government without con-sulting me about them and I am the government after all, but Saenz de la Barra explained to him impassively that you aren't the government, general, you are the power, he grew bored on domino nights even when he faced the sharpest opponents because try as he might to set up the best traps against himself he couldn't lose, he had to submit to the designs of the testers who dunked into his meals an hour before he could eat them, he couldn't find the honey in its hiding places, God damn it, this isn't the power I wanted, he protested, and Saenz de la Barra answered that there isn't any other, general, it was the only power possible in the lethargy of death which in other times had been his paradise and when he had no other chore except to wait for four o'clock to listen to the radio and the daily episode of the soap opera with its sterile loves on the local station, he would listen to it in the hammock with his pitcher of fruit juice untouched in his hand, he would remain floating in the emptiness of suspense his eyes moist with tears over the anxiety to know whether that girl who was so young was going to die or not and Saenz de la Barra would ascertain yes, general, the girl is going to die, then she's not to die, God damn it, he ordered, she's going to keep on living to the end and get married and have children and get old like everybody else, and Saenz de la Barra had the script changed to please him with the illusion that he was giving the orders, so no one died again by his orders, engaged couples who didn't love each other got married, people buried in previous episodes were resuscitated and villains were sacrificed ahead of time in order to please him general sir, everybody was to be happy by his orders so that life would seem less useless when he inspected the building to the metallic clangs of eight o'clock and he found that someone ahead of him had changed the cows' fodder, the lights had been turned off in the barracks of the presidential guard, the personnel were asleep, the kitchens were in order, the floors clean, the butcher blocks scrubbed with creolin without a trace of blood had a hospital smell about them, someone had drawn the bars on the windows and had locked the offices in spite of the fact that it was he and he alone who had the ring of keys, the lights were going out one by one before he touched the switches from the first vestibule down to his bedroom, he was walking in the dark dragging his thick feet of a captive monarch past the darkened mirrors with the single spur wrapped in velvet so that nobody could follow his trail of gold shavings, he went along seeing as he passed the same sea through the windows, the Caribbean in January, he looked at it without stopping twenty-three times and it was the same as always in January like a flowering swamp, he looked into Bendición Alvarado's room to see that her legacy of lemon balm was still in its place, the cages of dead birds, the bed of pain where the mother of her country bore her rotting old age, have a good night, he murmured, as always, even though no one had answered him for such a long time a very good night to you son, sleep with God, he headed toward his bedroom with the runaway lamp when he felt the shiver of the astonished hot coals that were Lord Köchel's eyes in the dark, caught a fragrance of man, the thickness of his dominion, the glow of his disdain, who goes there, he asked, although he knew who it was, José Ignacio Saenz de la Barra in full dress who was coming to remind him that it was an historic night, August 12, general, the immense date on which we were celebrating the first centenary of his rise to power, so that visitors had come from all over the world captivated by the announcement of an event which it was possible to witness only once in the passage of the longest of lives, the nation was celebrating, everybody in the nation except him, since in spite of the insistence of José Ignacio Saenz de la Barra that he live that memorable night in the midst of the clamor and fervor of his people, earlier than ever he drew the three bars of his sleeping dungeon, threw the three bolts, the three locks, he lay face down on the bare bricks with his rough denim uniform without insignia, the boots, the gold spur, and the right arm bent under his head to serve as a pillow as we were to find him pecked away by the vultures and infested with animals and flowers from the bottom of the sea, and through the mist of the sleeping potions he perceived the remote rockets

dared believe word by word when we were awakened by the noise of the trucks loaded with troops in battle gear whose stealthy patrols had been occupying public buildings since before dawn, they took up prone positions under the arcades of the main commercial street, they hid in doorways, I saw them setting up tripod machine guns on the roofs of the viceregal district when I opened the balcony of my house at dawn looking for a place to put the bouquet of wet carnations I had just cut in the courtyard, beneath the balcony I saw a patrol of soldiers under the command of a lieutenant going from door to door ordering people to close the doors of the few shops that were beginning to open on the commercial street, today is a national holiday they shouted, orders from higher up, I threw them a carnation from the balcony and I asked what was going on with so many soldiers and so much noise of weapons everywhere and the officer caught the carnation in midair and replied to me just imagine girl we don't know ourselves either, the dead man must have come back to life, he said, dying with laughter, because nobody dared think such an earthshaking event could have happened, rather, on the contrary, we thought that after so many years of negligence he had picked up the reins of his authority again and was more alive than ever, once more dragging his great feet of an illusory monarch through the house of power where the globes of light had gone on again, we thought that he was the one who had put out the cows as they frisked about over the cracks in the paving on the main square where the blind man sitting in the shade of the dying palm trees mistook the hoofs for military boots and recited those lines of poetry about the happy warrior who came from afar in a conquest of death, he recited them with full voice and his hand outstretched toward the cows who climbed up to eat the balsam apple garlands on the bandstand with their habit of going up and down stairs to eat, they stayed on to live among the ruins of the muses crowned with wild camellias and the monkeys hanging from the lyres of the rubble of the National Theater, dying with thirst and with the clatter of broken pots of spikenards they went into the cool shadows of entranceways in the viceregal district and sank their burning snouts into the pools in inner courtyards and no one dared molest them because we recognized the congenital brand of the presidential iron which the females bore on their flanks and the males on their necks, they were untouchable, even the soldiers made way for them on the narrow turns of the commercial street which had lost its former clamor of an infernal Moorish bazaar, all that was left was a rubble pile of broken ship frames and pieces of rigging in the puddles of burning sludge where the public market had been when we still had the sea and the schooners lay aground among the vegetable stands, there were empty spaces where the Hindu bazaars had stood in his times of glory, because the Hindus had left, they didn't even say thank you to him general sir, and he shouted what the hell, confused by his last senile tantrums, let them go clean up Englishmen's shit, he shouted, they all left, in their place street vendors of Indian amulets and snakebite cures rose up, the frantic seedy jukebox bars with beds for rent in the rear which the soldiers wrecked with their rifle butts while the iron bells of the cathedral announced the mourning, everything had come to an end before he did, we had even extinguished the last breath of the hopeless hope that someday the repeated and always denied rumor that he had finally succumbed to some one of his many regal illnesses would be true, and yet we didn't believe it now that it was, and not because we really didn't believe it but because we no longer wanted it to be true, we had ended up not understanding what would become of us without him, what would become of our lives after him, I couldn't conceive of the world without the man who had made me happy at the age of twelve as no other man was ever to do again since those afternoons so long ago when we would come out of school at five o'clock and he would be lying in wait by the skylights of the stables for the girls in blue uniforms with sailors' collars and a single braid thinking mother of mine Bendición Alvarado how pretty women look to me at my age, he would call to us, we would see his quivering eyes, the hand with the glove with torn fingers which tried to entice us with the candy rattle from Ambassador Forbes, they all ran off frightened, all except me, I stood alone on the street by the school when I knew that no one was watching me and I tried to reach the candy and he grabbed me by the wrists with a gentle tiger's claw and lifted me painlessly up into the air, took me through the skylight with such care that not a pleat in my dress was wrinkled and he laid me down on the hay that was scented with rancid urine trying to tell me something that wouldn't come out of his arid mouth because he was more frightened than I, he was trembling, you could see his heart beating under his jacket, he was pale, his eyes were full of tears as no other man ever had them in all of my life in exile, he touched me in silence, breathing unhurriedly, he tempted me with a male tenderness which I never found again, he made my little buds stand out on my breasts, he put his fingers underneath the edge of my panties, he smelled his fingers, he made me smell them, smell it, he told me, it's your smell, I didn't need Ambassador Baldrich's candy any more to climb through the stable skylight to live the happy hours of my puberty with that man of a healthy and sad heart who waited for me sitting in the hay with a bag containing things to eat, he used bread to soak up my first adolescent sauce, he would put things there before eating them, he gave them to me to eat, he put asparagus stalks into me to eat them marinated with the brine of my inner humors, delicious, he told me, you taste like a port, he dreamed about eating my kidneys boiled in their own ammonia stew, with the salt of your armpits, he dreamed, with your warm urine, he sliced me up from head to toe, he seasoned me with rock salt, hot pepper and laurel leaves and left me to boil on a hot fire in the incandescent fleeting mallow sunsets of our love with no future, he ate me from head to toe with the drive and the generosity of an old man which I never found again in so many hasty and greedy men who tried to make love to me without managing to for the rest of my life without him, he talked to me about himself during the slow digestions of love while we pushed away from us the snouts of the cows who were trying to lick us, he told me that not even he himself knew who he was, that he was up to his balls with general sir, he said it without bitterness, without any reason, as if talking to himself, floating in the continuous buzzing of an inner silence that could only be broken with shouts, no one was more gracious or wiser than he, no one more of a man, he had become the only reason for my life at the age of fourteen when two military men of the highest rank appeared at my parents' home with a suitcase bulging with solid gold doubloons and in the middle of the night they put me aboard a foreign ship along with my whole family and orders never to return to the national territory for years and years until the news burst in the world that he had died without having known that I had spent the rest of my life dying for him, I would go to bed with strangers off the street to see if I could find one better than he, I returned aged and embittered with this drove of sons by different fathers with the illusion that they were his, and on the other hand he had forgotten her the second day he didn't see her climb in through the skylight of the milking stables, he replaced her with a different one every afternoon because by then he couldn't distinguish very well who was who among the troop of schoolgirls in identical uniforms who stuck out their tongues at him and shouted old soursop when he tried to entice them with candy from Ambassador Rumpelmayer, he called them without distinction, without ever wondering if today's had been the same one as yesterday's, he received them all equally, he thought of them all as the same one while he listened half-asleep in the hammock to the always identical arguments of Ambassador Streimberg who had given him an ear trumpet just like the one with the dog of his master's voice with an electrical amplifying device so that he could listen once more to the insistent plan to carry off our territorial waters as surety for the interest on the foreign debt and he repeated the same as always never in a million years my dear Stevenson, anything except the sea, he would disconnect the electric hearing aid so as not to continue listening to that loud voice of a metallic creature who seemed to be turning the record over to explain to him once more what had been explained to me so many times by my own experts without any dictionary tricks that we're down to our skins general sir, we had used up our last resources, bled by the age-old necessity of accepting loans in order to pay the interest on the foreign debt ever since the wars of independence and then other loans to pay the interest on back interest, always in return for something general sir, first the quinine and tobacco monopolies for the English, then the rubber and cocoa monopoly for the Dutch, then the concession for the upland railroad and river navigation to the Germans, and everything for the gringos through the secret agreements that he didn't find out about until after the sudden downfall and public death of José Ignacio Saenz de la Barra whom God keep roasting on an open flame in the cauldrons of his deep hell, we didn't have anything left general, but he had heard the same thing said by all of his treasury ministers ever since the difficult days when a moratorium was declared on the obligation contracted from the bankers of Hamburg, the German fleet had blockaded the port, an English warship had fired a warning shot that opened a breach in the cathedral tower, but he shouted I shit on London's king, better dead than sold down the river, he shouted, death to the Kaiser, saved at the last moment by the good offices of his domino companion Ambassador Charles W. Traxler whose government underwrote a guarantee of the European agreements in exchange for a right of lifetime exploitation of our subsoil and ever since then we've been the way we are owing everything down to the drawers we're wearing general sir, but he took the eternal five o'clock ambassador to the stairs and took leave of him with a pat on the shoulder, never in a million years my dear Baxter, I'd rather be dead than without a sea, overwhelmed by the desolation of that cemetery house where one could walk without running into anyone as if one were under water ever since the evil times of that José Ignacio Saenz de la Barra of my mistake who had cut off the heads of the whole human species except those he was supposed to cut off, those of the authors of the assassination of Leticia Nazareno and the child, the birds refused to sing in their cages no matter how many drops of Cantorina he put in their beaks, the girls in the school next door no longer sang their recess song about the petite painted bird perched on the green lemon limb, life had been going off for the impatient wait to be with you in the stables, my child, with your little palm-nut teats and your clam of a thing, he ate alone under the pansy bower, he floated in the quivering two o'clock heat pecking at his siesta sleep so as not to lose the thread of the television movie in which everything happened according to his orders and completely the opposite of life, because the all-worthy who knew everything never knew that ever since the times of José Ignacio Saenz de la Barra we had first installed an individual transmitter for the soap operas on the radio and then a closed-circuit television system so that only he would see the movies arranged to his taste in which no one died except the villains, love prevailed over death, life was a breath of fresh air, we made him happy with the trick as he had been so many afternoons of his old age with the girls in uniform who would have pleased him until his death if he had not had the bad luck to ask one of them what do they teach you in school and I told him the truth that they don't teach me anything sir, what I am is a waterfront whore, and he made her repeat it in case he hadn't understood well what he had read on my lips and I repeated it letter by letter that I'm not a student sir, I'm a waterfront whore, the sanitation service had bathed her in creolin and rinsed her off, they told her to put on this sailor suit and these nice-girl's stockings and go along this street every afternoon at five, not just me but all the whores of my age recruited and bathed by the sanitary police, all with the same uniform and the same men's shoes and these horsehair braids which look you can put on and take off like a comb, they told us don't be afraid he's a poor foolish old grandfather who isn't even going to lay you but will give you a doctor's examination with his finger and suck on your titties and put things to eat in your pussies, well, everything you do to me when I come, all we had to do was close our eyes in pleasure and say my love my love which is what you like, they told us that and they even made us rehearse and repeat everything from the beginning before they paid us, but I think it's too much of a drag all those ripe bananas in the twitty-twat and all those parboiled malangas up the behind for the four consumptive pesos we've got left after deducting the sanitation tax and the sergeant's commission, God damn it, it's not right to ruin all that food down below if a person doesn't have anything to eat up above, she said, wrapped in the lugubrious aura of the unfathomable old man who listened to the revelation without blinking as he thought mother of mine Bendición Alvarado why do you send me this punishment, but he didn't give any sign that would reveal his desolation taking care rather in every kind of stealthy investigation until he discovered that the girls' school next door had in fact been closed for many years general sir, his own minister of education had provided the funds in an agreement with the archbishop primate and the heads of family association to construct a new three-story building on the shore where the princesses of families of great conceit were safe from the ambushes of the sunset seducer whose body of a beached shad face up on the banquet table began to stand out against the pale mallow of the moon-crater horizon of our first dawn without him, he was under the protection of everything among the snowy African lilies, free at last of his absolute power at the end of so many years of reciprocal captivity in which it was difficult to distinguish who was the victim of whom in that cemetery of living presidents which they had painted tomb-white inside and out without consulting me about it but rather they ordered him around without recognizing him don't come in here sir you'll dirty our whitewash, and he didn't go in, stay up on the second floor sir a scaffold might fall on you, and he stayed there, confused by the noise of the carpenters and the rage of the masons who shouted at him get away from here you old fool you'll get the mixture all shitty, and he got away, more obedient than a soldier during the harsh months of a renovation done without consulting him which opened new windows to the sea, more alone than ever under the fierce vigilance of an escort whose mission didn't seem to be to protect him but to watch over him, they ate half of his meal to avoid his being poisoned, they changed the hiding place of his honey, they put his gold spur on up where a fighting cock has his so it wouldn't bell-ring when he walked, God damn it, a whole string of cowboy tricks that would have made my comrade Saturno Santos die of laughter, he lived at the mercy of eleven flunkies in jacket and tie who spent the day doing Japanese acrobatics, they brought in an apparatus with green and red lights that went on and off when someone within a radius of two hundred feet was carrying a weapon, and we went through the streets like fugitives in seven identical cars which kept changing places, some getting ahead of others along the way so that even I didn't know which one I'm riding in, God damn it, a useless waste of gunpowder on buzzards because he'd pushed the blinds aside to see the streets after so many years of confinement and he saw that no one was reacting to the stealthy passage of funereal limousines of the presidential caravan, he saw the cliffs of solar glass of the ministries that rose up higher than the towers of the cathedral and had cut off the colorful promontories of the Negro shacks on the harbor hills, he saw a patrol of soldiers erasing a sign recently painted with a broad brush on a wall and he asked what it had said and they answered eternal glory to the maker of the new nation although he knew it was a lie, of course, if not they wouldn't have been erasing it, God damn it, he saw an avenue with coconut palms six lanes wide with flower beds down to the sea where the bogs had been, he saw a suburb with villas replete with Roman porticoes and hotels with Amazonian gardens where the public market dump had been, he saw cars moving like tortoises along the serpentine labyrinths of the urban freeways, he saw the crowds dulled by the dog-days sun of high noon on the sun-baked sidewalk while on the opposite side there was no one but the unofficial collectors of the tax for the right to walk in the shade, but no one trembled that time with the omen of hidden power in the refrigerated coffin of a presidential limousine, no one recognized the disillusioned eyes, the anxious

lips, the useless hand that kept giving undestined waves amidst
the shouting of vendors of newspapers and amulets, the ice
cream carts, the three-numbered lottery signs, the everyday
clamor of the street world alien to the intimate tragedy of the
solitary military man who was sighing with nostalgia thinking
mother of mine Bendición Alvarado what has happened to my
city, where is the alley of misery of women without me who
came out naked at dusk to buy blue corvinas and red snappers
and exchange mother curses with the vegetable women while
their clothes were drying on the balconies, where are the Hindus
who shat by the doors of their stalls, where are their pale wives
who soften death with songs of pity, where is the woman who
was changed into a scorpion for having disobeyed her parents,
where are the mercenaries' bars, their brooks of fermented urine,
the everyday look of the pelicans around the corner, and, suddenly, alas, the waterfront, where is it because it used to be here,
what happened to the smugglers' schooners, the iron scarp from
the marines' landing, my smell of shit, mother, what was going
on in the world that no one recognized the fugitive lover's hand
in the oblivion as it left a wake of useless waves of the hand
from the opened panes of the window of an inaugural train that
whistled through fields planted with aromatic herbs where the
swamps with strident malaria birds in the rice paddies had been,
it passed along through the unlikely plains of blue grazing land
frightening herds of cattle marked with the presidential brand
and inside the railroad car of responses to my irrevocable fate
padded with ecclesiastical plush he went along wondering where
was my little old four-legged train, damn it, my boughs with
anacondas and poisonous balsam apples, my uproar of monkeys,
my birds of paradise, the whole nation with its dragon, mother,
where is it all because there used to be stations here with taciturn
Indian women in derbies who sold candy animals through the

windows, they sold mashed potatoes, mother, they sold hens boiled in yellow lard under the arches of a sign made out of flowers eternal glory to the all-worthy that nobody knows where he is, but whenever he protested that that life of a fugitive was worse than being dead they answered no general sir it was peace within order, they told him, and he ended up accepting it, agreed, dazzled one more time by the personal fascination of José Ignacio Saenz de la Barra of my unmothering whom he had degraded and spat upon so many times in the rage of his sleeplessness but he would succumb again to his charms as soon as he entered the office with the light of day leading that dog with the look of human people whom he doesn't leave even to urinate and who has a person's name besides Lord Köchel, and once more he would accept his formulas with a meekness that rose up against himself, don't worry Nacho, he would give in, do your duty, so that José Ignacio Saenz de la Barra would go back once more with his powers intact to the torture he had set up less than five hundred yards from the presidential palace in the innocent colonial masonry building which had been the Dutch insane asylum, a house as large as yours general sir, hidden in an almond grove and surrounded by a field of wild violets, the first floor of which was reserved for the identification and registry services of the civil state and where in the rest of the building the most ingenious and barbarous machines of torture that the imagination could conceive of were installed, so terrible that he hadn't wanted to know about them but advised Saenz de la Barra you keep on doing your duty as best suits the interests of the nation with the only condition that I know nothing and I haven't seen anything and I've never been in that place, and Saenz de la Barra pledged his word of honor to serve you, general, and he had kept it, just as he followed his orders not to go back to martyrizing children under the age of five with electric wires on their testicles in order to force their parents to confess because he was afraid that the infamy might repeat itself during the insomnia of all those nights the same as during the days of the lottery, although it was impossible for him to forget about that workshop of horror because it was such a short distance from his bedroom and on nights of a quiet moon he would be awakened by the fleeting train music of Bruckner thunder dawns that brought on ruinous floods and left a desolation of tattered gowns of dead brides on the branches of the almond trees at the former Dutch lunatic asylum all so that the shrieks of terror and pain of those dying would not be heard on the street, and all of that without collecting a cent general sir, because José Ignacio Saenz de la Barra used his salary to buy the clothing of a prince, shirts of natural silk with his monogram on the chest, kid shoes, boxes of gardenias for his lapel, lotions from France with the family crest printed on the original label, but he didn't have a woman that anybody knew of and no one said he's a fairy and he doesn't have a single friend or a house of his own to live in, nothing general sir, the life of a saint, slaving away at the torture factory until fatigue made him drop onto the couch in the office where he slept as best he could but never at night and never more than three hours at a time, with no guard at the door, no weapon within reach, under the tense protection of Lord Köchel who was bursting his skin from the anxiety caused by eating the only thing they say he eats, that is, the hot guts of the beheaded people, making that boiling-pot sound to awaken him as soon as his look of a human person sensed through the walls that someone was approaching the office, no matter who it is general sir, that man doesn't even trust mirrors, he would make his decisions without consulting anyone after listening to the reports of his agents, nothing went on in the country and no exile in any part of the planet could so much as sigh without José Ignacio Saenz de la Barra's knowing about it immediately thanks to the threads of the invisible web of informers and bribery with which he had covered the whole orb of the earth, that's what he spent his money on general sir, because it wasn't true that the torturers received the salary of ministers as people said, on the contrary, they volunteered for nothing to show that they were capable of quartering their mothers and throwing the pieces to the pigs without any change in their voice, instead of letters of recommendation and certificates of good conduct, they offered testimony of atrocious antecedents so they would be given work under the guidance of French torturers who are rationalists general sir, and consequently are methodical in cruelty and resistant to compassion, they were the ones who made progress within order possible, they were the ones who anticipated conspiracies long before they started incubating in people's thoughts, the distracted customers who were enjoying the coolness of the fan blades in ice cream parlors, those reading the newspaper in Chinese lunchrooms, those who slept in the movies, those who gave their seats on the bus to ladies, those who had learned to be electricians and plumbers after having passed half a lifetime as nocturnal muggers and bandits of the byways, the casual boyfriends of servant girls, the whores on ocean liners and in international cocktail lounges, the promoters of tourist trips from Miami to the paradises of the Caribbean, the private secretary of the Belgian minister of foreign affairs, the tenured chambermaid of the fourth floor of the International Hotel in Mosow, and so many others that no one knows to what far corner of the earth they reach, but you can sleep peacefully general sir, because the good patriots of the nation say that you know nothing, that all of this is going on without your consent, that if general sir knew it he would have sent Saenz de la Barra to push up daisies in the renegades' cemetery at the harbor fort, because every time they learned of a new act of barbarism they would sigh inside if the general only knew, if we could only make him know, if there were some way to see him and he ordered the one who had told him never to forget that the truth is I don't know anything, I haven't seen anything, I haven't talked about these things with anyone, and in that way he regained his calm, but so many sacks of severed heads kept arriving that it seemed inconceivable to him that José Ignacio Saenz de la Barra was daubing himself with blood up to his tonsure without some benefit from it because people are dumb bastards but not that dumb, nor did it seem reasonable to him that while years could pass without the commanders of the three services protesting over their subordinate status, nor did they ask for a raise in salary, nothing, so he had made soundings on his own to try to establish the causes of military compliance, he wanted to find out why they weren't trying to rebel, why they accepted the authority of a civilian, and he had asked the most greedy of them if they didn't think it was time to trim the crest of the bloodthirsty upstart who was tarnishing the merits of the armed forces, but they answered him of course not general sir, it's nothing serious, and since then I no longer know who is who, or who is with whom or against whom in this snare of progress within order that's starting to smell to me like someone playing possum like that other time I don't care to recall with the poor children and the lottery, but José Ignacio Saenz de la Barra calmed his drives with his suave domination of a trainer of wild dogs, sleep in peace, general, he told him, the world is yours, he made him believe that everything was so simple and so clear that he left him again in the shadows of that no man's house which he would cover from one end to the other asking himself with great shouts who the hell am I because I feel as if the reflection in the mirrors is reversed, where the hell am

I because it's going on eleven o'clock in the morning and there isn't a single hen even a stray one in this desert, remember the way it was before, he shouted, remember the uproar of the lepers and the cripples as they fought with the dogs over food, remember that slippery chute of animal shit on the stairs and that hullabaloo of patriots who wouldn't let me walk with their begging throw the salt of health on my body general sir, baptize my body to see if he can get rid of his diarrhea because they all said my laying on of hands had binding virtues more effective than green bananas, put your hand here to see if my palpitations die down because I don't feel like living any more with this eternal earth tremor, fix your eyes on the sea general sir to send the hurricanes away, look up to the skies to make eclipses repent, look down to the earth to drive off the plague because they said I was the all-worthy one who filled nature with respect and straightened the order of the universe and had taken Divine Providence down a peg, and I gave them what they asked of me and bought everything they wanted to sell me not because he was soft-hearted as his mother Bendición Alvarado said but because a person needed an iron liver to refuse a favor to someone who was singing his praises, and now on the contrary there was no one to ask him for anything, no one to say to him at least good morning general sir, did you have a good night, he didn't even have the consolation of those nocturnal explosions that woke him up with a hail of broken glass and blew the doors off their hinges and sowed panic among the troops but which at least let him feel he was alive and not in this silence that buzzes inside my head and wakes me up with its noise, all I am now is a fright painted on the wall of this horror show where it was impossible for him to give an order that hadn't been carried out long before, he found his most intimate desires satisfied in the official newspaper which he still read in the hammock at siesta

time from front to back including the advertisements, there was
no impulse of his feelings or design of his will which did not
appear in print in large letters with the photograph of the bridge
he had not ordered built because he'd forgotten, the opening of
the school to teach sweeping, the milk cow and the breadfruit
tree with a photograph of him with other inaugural ribbons
from the times of glory, and yet he couldn't find peace, he
dragged his great feet of a senile elephant looking for something
that hadn't been lost to him in his house of solitude, he found
that someone before him had covered the cages with mourning
cloths, someone had contemplated the sea from the windows
and had counted the cows before him, everything was complete
and in order, he went back to the bedroom with the candle when
he recognized his own amplified voice in the quarters of the
presidential guard and he looked in through the half-open window and saw a group of officers dozing in the smoke-filled room
opposite the sad glow of the television screen and there he was
on the screen thinner and trimmer, but it was me, mother, sitting in the office where he was to die with the coat of arms of
the nation behind him and three pairs of gold eyeglasses on the
desk, and he was reciting from memory an analysis of the
nation's finances with the words of a sage that he never would
have dared repeat, damn it, it was a more upsetting sight than
that of his dead body among the flowers because now he was
seeing himself alive and listening to himself speak with his own
voice, I myself, mother, I who never had been able to bear the
embarrassment of appearing on a balcony and had never overcome the shyness about speaking in public, and there he was,
so genuine and mortal that he stood perplexed by the window
thinking mother of mine Bendición Alvarado how is this mystery possible, but José Ignacio Saenz de la Barra remained
impassive facing one of the few explosions of rage that he per-

mitted himself in the uncountable years of his regime, it's nothing, general, he said with his softest emphasis, we had to use
this illicit recourse to keep the ship of progress within order
from running aground, it was a divine inspiration, general,
thanks to it we have succeeded in conjuring away the uncertainty of the people over a flesh and blood power who on the
last Wednesday of every month rendered a soothing report on
the acts of his government on the state radio and television, I
assume all responsibility, general, I put this vase with six micro-
phones in the shape of sunflowers here and they recorded the
thoughts you had aloud, I was the one who asked the questions
he answered during Friday audiences without suspecting that
his innocent answers were the fragments of the monthly speech
addressed to the nation, because he'd never used an image that
wasn't his or a word that he wouldn't have said as you yourself
can see with this record that Saenz de la Barra put on the desk
beside these films and this letter in my own hand which I sign
in your presence, general, so that you may decide my fate as you
see fit, and he looked at him disconcertedly because suddenly he
came to the realization that Saenz de la Barra was without the
dog for the first time, defenseless, pale, and then he sighed, it's
all right, Nacho, do your duty, he said, with an air of infinite
fatigue, sitting back in the swivel chair with his gaze fixed on the
accusing eyes of the portraits of the founding fathers, he was
older than ever, gloomier and sadder, but with the same expression of unforeseeable designs that Saenz de la Barra was to recognize two weeks later when he entered the office again without
an appointment almost dragging the dog by the leash and with
the urgent news of an armed insurrection that only his interven-
tion could stop, general, and finally he discovered the imperceptible crack he had been seeking for so many years in that
obsidian wall of fascination, mother of mine Bendición Alva-

rado of my revenge, he said to himself, this poor bastard is shitting in his pants with fear, but he didn't make a single gesture
that would let his intentions show but wrapped Saenz de la
Barra in a maternal aura, don't worry, Nacho, he sighed, we've
got plenty of time to think without anyone's disturbing us
where the hell was the truth in that bog of contradictory truths
that seem less true than if they were lies, while Saenz de la Barra
checked his pocket watch to see that it was going on 7 P.M.,
general, the commanders of the three branches were finishing
dinner at their respective homes with their wives and children,
so not even they could suspect his plans, they will leave dressed
in civilian clothes without an escort through the service entrance
where a taxi called by phone awaits them to trick the vigilance
of our men, they won't see any, of course, but there they are,
general, the drivers, but he said aha, he smiled, don't worry so
much, Nacho, explain to me instead how we have lived up till
now with our skins intact since according to your figures of severed heads we've had more enemies than we had soldiers, but
Saenz de la Barra was only sustained by the tiny throb of his
pocket watch, there were less than three hours left, general, the
commander of the land forces was on his way at that moment
to the Conde barracks, the commander of the naval forces to the
harbor fort, the commander of the air forces to the San Jerónimo base, it was still possible to arrest them because a state
security van loaded with vegetables was following them at a
short distance, but he didn't change his expression, he felt that
the growing anxiety of Saenz de la Barra was freeing him from
the punishment of a servitude that had been more implacable
than his appetite for power, calm down, Nacho, he said, explain
to me rather why you haven't bought a mansion as big as an
ocean liner, why you work like a mule since money doesn't matter to you, why you live like a monk when the tightest women

get all loosened up with the thought of getting into your bedroom, you're more of a priest than any priest, Nacho, but Saenz
de la Barra was suffocating in a cold sweat that he was unable to
hide with his matchless dignity in that crematory oven of an
office, it was eleven o'clock, it's too late now, he said, a coded
message began to circulate at that time over the telegraph wires
to the various garrisons of the country, the rebel commanders
were pinning decorations onto their parade uniforms for the
official portrait of the new government junta while their aides
were transmitting the final orders of a war without enemies
whose only battles were reduced to the control of the centers of
communication and public services, but he didn't even blink at
the eager throbbing of Lord Köchel who had stood up with a
thread of drivel that looked like an endless tear, don't be afraid,
Nacho, explain to me rather why you are so afraid of death, and
José Ignacio Saenz de la Barra with one tug pulled off the celluloid collar softened by sweat and his baritone face was soulless,
it's quite natural, he answered, a fear of death is the ember of
happiness, that's why you don't feel it, general, and he stood up
counting out of pure habit the bells of the cathedral, it's twelve
o'clock, he said, you haven't got anyone left in the world, general, I was the last one, but he didn't move in the big chair until
he perceived the underground thunder of the tanks on the main
square, and then he smiled, don't be mistaken, Nacho, I still
have the people, he said, the poor people as always who before
dawn took to the streets instigated by the unpredictable old man
who over the state radio and television addressed all patriots of
the nation without distinction of any kind and with the most
vivid historical emotion to announce that the commanders of
the three branches of the service inspired by the unchanging
ideals of the regime, under my personal direction and interpreting as always the will of the sovereign people had put an end on

this glorious midnight to the apparatus of terror of a blood-thirsty civilian who had been punished by the blind justice of the mob, for there was José Ignacio Saenz de la Barra, beaten to a pulp, hanging by his feet from a lamppost on the main square with his own genitals stuck in his mouth, just as you had fore-seen general sir when you gave us orders to cordon off the streets to the embassies to stop him from seeking asylum, the people had stoned him general sir, but first we had to riddle with bullets the butcher dog who sucked the guts out of four civilians and left seven of our soldiers badly wounded when the people attacked his living quarters and threw out of the window two hundred brocade vests with the price tags still on them, they threw out some three thousand pairs of Italian boots that had never been worn, three thousand general sir, that's what the government money was spent on, and I don't know how many boxes of buttonhole gardenias and all the Bruckner records with their respective conductor's scores annotated in his own hand, and they also freed the prisoners in the dungeons and set fire to the torture chambers in the old Dutch insane asylum with shouts of long live the general, long live the stud who finally discovered the truth, because they all say that you didn't know anything general sir, that they kept you in limbo abusing your good heart, and even at this moment they're hunting the state security torturers down like rats since we left them without mili-tary protection in accordance with your orders so the people can relieve themselves of so much pent-up rage and so much terror, and he approved, agreed, moved by the bells of jubilation and the music of freedom and the shouts of gratitude from the crowds massed on the main square with large signs saying God keep the magnificent one who redeemed us from the shadows of terror and in that fleeting replica of the times of glory he had the cadet officers who had helped him take off his own chains of a galley slave of power gather in the courtyard and pointing to us according to the impulses of his inspiration he used us to fill in the last high command of his decrepit regime in replacement of the authors of the death of Leticia Nazareno and the child who were captured in their bedclothes when they tried to find asylum in foreign embassies, but he barely recognized them, he'd forgotten their names, he searched in his heart for the burden of hatred he'd tried to keep alive until his death and all he found were the ashes of a wounded pride which was no longer worth maintaining, get them away from here, he ordered, they put them on the first ship to weigh anchor for a place where no one would ever remember them again, poor bastards, he presided over the first cabinet meeting of the new government with the clear impression that those exemplaries chosen from a new generation of a new century were once again the usual civilian ministers with dusty frock coats and weak guts, except that these were more avid for honors than power, more jittery and servile and more useless than all the previous ones in the face of a foreign debt more costly than anything that could be sold in his ravished realm of gloom, because there was nothing to do general sir, the last train on the upland barrens had fallen down an orchid-covered precipice, leopards were sleeping on the velvet seats, the carcasses of the paddle-wheelers were sunk in the swamps of the rice paddies, the news was rotting in the mailbags, the pairs of manatees tricked by the illusion that they were engendering mermaids among the shadowy irises of the round mirrors in the presidential stateroom, and only he was unaware of it, naturally, he had believed in progress within order because at that time the only contact he had with real life was the reading of the government newspaper which they printed only for you general sir, a whole edition of one single copy with the news you liked to read, with the photographs you expected to find,

with advertisements that made him dream of a world different
from the one they had given him for his siesta, until I myself
was able to ascertain with these incredulous eyes of mine that
behind the solar glass windows of the ministries still intact were
the colors of the Negro shacks on the harbor hills, they had built
the palm-lined avenues to the sea so that I wouldn't notice that
behind the Roman villas with identical porticoes the miserable
slums devastated by one of our many hurricanes were still there,
they had sown aromatic herbs on both sides of the railroad
tracks so that from the presidential car the world seemed magni-
fied by the venal waters his mother of my insides Bendición
Alvarado used for painting orioles, and they were not deceiving
him in order to please him as had been done in the later years of
his times of glory by General Rodrigo de Aguilar, or to keep
useless annoyances from him as Leticia Nazareno used to do
more out of pity than love, but to keep him the captive of his
own power in the senile backwater of the hammock under the
ceiba tree in the courtyard where at the end of his years even the
schoolgirl chorus of the petite painted bird perched on a green
lemon limb wasn't to be real, what a mess, and yet the trick
didn't affect him but rather he tried to reconcile himself with
reality through the recovery by decree of the quinine monopoly
and that of other potions essential to the well-being of the state,
but truth came back to surprise him with the news that the
world was changing and life was going on behind the back of
his power, because there wasn't any more quinine, general,
there's no more cocoa, there's no more indigo, general, there
wasn't anything, except his personal fortune which was
uncountable and sterile and threatened by idleness, and still he
wasn't upset by such dire news but sent a message of challenge
to old Ambassador Roxbury in hopes they might find some formula of relief over the domino table, but the ambassador

answered him in his own style of never in a million years, your excellency, this country isn't worth a plug nickel, except for the sea of course, which was diaphanous and succulent and all it needed was a flame underneath to cook the great clam chowder of the universe in its own crater, so think about it, your excellency, we'll accept it on account for the interest of that debt which is in arrears and which won't be paid off even with a hundred generations of leaders as diligent as your excellency, but he didn't even take him seriously that first time, he accompanied him to the stairs thinking mother of mine Bendición Alvarado look at these gringo barbarians, how is it possible that they can only think of the sea as food, he sent him off with the usual pat on the shoulder and he was alone with himself again feeling around among the wisps of illusory mist on the barren plains of power, because the crowds had abandoned the main square, they took away the repetitious placards and put away the rented signs for other identical celebrations in the future as soon as the stimulus of things to eat and drink that the troops distributed during breaks in the ovations was exhausted, they had left the salons deserted and sad again in spite of his order not to close the main doors at any hour so that anyone who wants to can come in, as before, when this wasn't a house of the dead but a palace for the neighborhood, and yet the only ones who stayed were the lepers general sir, the blind men and the cripples who had remained for years and years in front of the building just as Demetrius Aldous had seen them gilding themselves in the sun by the gates of Jerusalem, destroyed and invincible, certain that sooner or later they would come in again to receive from his hands the salt of health because he was to survive all the reverses of adversity and the most inclement passions and the worst attacks of oblivion, because he was eternal, and so it was, he found them again on his way back from the milking as they

boiled cans of kitchen leftovers on the brick fireplaces improvised in the courtyard, he saw them stretched out with their
arms crossed on the mats devastated by the sweat of their ulcers
in the fragrant shadows of the rose beds, he had a common
fireplace built for them, he bought them new mats, and he had
a palm-branch shelter built for them in the rear of the courtyard
so that they wouldn't have to take shelter inside the building,
but four days didn't pass without his finding a pair of lepers
sleeping on the Oriental rugs in the ballroom or a blind man
lost in the offices or a cripple broken on the stairs, he had the
doors closed so that they wouldn't leave a trail of open sores on
the walls or stink up the air of the building with the smell of the
carbolic acid with which the sanitary services fumigated them
although no sooner did he get them out of one place than they
appeared in another, tenacious, indestructible, clinging to their
old fierce hope when nobody hoped for anything any more from
that useless old man who had written reminders in the cracks in
the wall and felt his way along like a sleepwalker through the
winds he found in the misty swamps of memory, he spent hours
of insomnia in the hammock wondering how the hell am I
going to get around the new ambassador Fischer who proposed
to me to disclose the existence of a plague of yellow fever in
order to justify a landing of marines in accordance with the
mutual assistance treaty for as many years as would be necessary
to bring new breath into the dying nation, and he replied immediately never in a million years, fascinated by the evidence that
he was living in the origins of his regime when he had taken
advantage of the same solution to assume the exceptional powers of martial law in the face of a serious threat of civil uprising,
he had declared a state of plague by decree, he planted the yellow
flag on the pole of the lighthouse, he closed the port, Sundays
were suppressed, it was forbidden to weep for the dead in public

and to play music that would make them be remembered and he made use of the armed forces to police the enforcement of the decree and to dispose of those infested according to his will, so that troops with sanitary armbands held public executions of people of the most diverse stations in life, they would mark a red circle on the doors of houses suspected of nonconformity with the regime, they put a branding iron to the foreheads of the lesser lawbreakers, dikes and fags while a sanitary mission urgently summoned from his government by Ambassador Mitchell took charge of keeping the contagion from the occupants of the presidential palace, they gathered up the runt poo from the floor to analyze it with magnifying glasses, they threw disinfectant tablets into the water jars, they fed water worms to animals in their scientific laboratories, and dying of laughter he told them through an interpreter don't be such horses' asses, misters, the only plague here is you people, but they insisted there was, that they had superior orders that there was, they prepared a syrup with preventive powers, thick and green, with which they varnished visitors' bodies all over without distinction of credentials from the most ordinary to the most illustrious, they obliged them to keep their distance in audiences, they standing in the doorway and he sitting at the end of the room where their voices but not their breath could reach him, parleying in shouts with highborn naked people who gesticulated with one hand, your excellency, and with the other covered their bedaubed little dove, and all that to guard from contagion the one who had conceived in the enervation of wakefulness the most banal details of the false calamity, who had invented earthborn lies and spread apocalyptic predictions in accordance with his belief that the less the people understand the more afraid they'll be, and who scarcely blinked when one of his aides, pale with fright, came to attention before him with the news general sir that the plague is causing tremendous casualties among the civilian population, so that through the foggy windows of the presidential carriage he had seen time stopped by his orders on the abandoned streets, he saw the awe-struck look of the yellow flags, he saw the closed doors even on houses where the red circle had been omitted, he saw the gorged buzzards on the balconies, and he saw the dead, the dead, the dead, there were so many everywhere that it was impossible to count them in the clay pits, piled up in the sun on terraces, stretched out over the vegetables in the market, flesh and blood dead people general sir, who knows how many, because there were many more than he would have wanted to see among the hosts of his enemies thrown out like dead dogs in garbage bins, and above the rotting of the bodies and the familiar fetid smell of the streets he recognized the mangy smell of the plague, but he didn't react, he gave in to no entreaties until he felt himself absolute master of all his power again, and only when there didn't seem to be any means human or divine to put an end to the dying did we see appear on the streets a carriage without insignias in which no one perceived at first the icy wind of the majesty of power, but in the interior of funereal plush we saw the lethal eyes, the quivering lips, the nuptial glove which went along throwing handfuls of salt into the doorways, we saw the train painted with the colors of the flag clawing its way up through the gardenias and terrified leopards to the heights of mist of the most precipitous provinces, we saw the hazy eyes through the windows of the solitary railroad car, the afflicted face, the haughty maiden's hand that went along leaving a trail of salt across the mournful barrens of his childhood, we saw the steamboat with its wooden paddle wheel and rolls of mazurkas in chimerical pianolas that bumped its way along among reefs and sandbars and the ruins of the catastrophes caused in the jungle by the dragon's springtime

strolls, we saw the sunset eyes in the window of the presidential
stateroom, we saw the pale lips, the hand without origin which
threw handfuls of salt into villages deadened by the heat, and
those who ate that salt and licked the ground where it had been
recovered their health immediately and were immunized for a
long time against evil omens and the rash of illusions, so that he
was not to be surprised in the twilight of his autumn when they
proposed to him a new disembarkation regime sustained by the
same lie of a political epidemic of yellow fever but he stood up
to the arguments of the sterile ministers who shouted bring back
the marines, general, bring them back with their machines for
fumigating plague-ridden people in exchange for whatever they
want, let them come back with their white hospitals, their blue
lawns, their spinning sprinklers, those people who ended their
leap years with two centuries of good health, but he pounded
on the table and decided no, under his supreme responsibility
until the blunt Ambassador MacQueen answered him that conditions don't warrant any more discussion, your excellency, the
regime wasn't being sustained by hope or conformity or even
by terror, but by the pure inertia of an ancient and irreparable
disillusion, go out into the street and look truth in the face, your
excellency, we're on the final curve, either the marines land or
we take the sea, there's no other way, your excellency, there was
no other way, mother, so they took away the Caribbean in April,
Ambassador Ewing's nautical engineers carried it off in numbered pieces to plant it far from the hurricanes in the blood-red
dawns of Arizona, they took it away with everything it had
inside general sir, with the reflection of our cities, our timid
drowned people, our demented dragons, in spite of the fact that
he had appealed to the most audacious registers of his age-old
cunning trying to promote a national convulsion of protest
against the despoilment, but nobody paid any attention general

sir, they refused to take to the streets either by persuasion or by force because we thought it was a new maneuver on his part like so many others to satiate even beyond all limits his irrepressible passion to endure, we thought just so long as something happens even if they carry off the sea, God damn it, even though they carry off the whole nation along with its dragon, we thought, unmoved by the seductive arts of the military men who appeared in our houses disguised as civilians and begged us in the name of the nation to rush into the streets shouting out with the gringos to stop the implementation of the theft, they incited us to sack and burn the stores and mansions of foreigners, they offered us ready cash to go out and protest under the protection of the troops who were solidly behind the people in opposition to the act of aggression, but no one went out general sir, because nobody had forgotten that one other time they had told us the same thing on their word of honor as soldiers and still they shot them down in a massacre under the pretext that agitators had infiltrated and opened fire against the troops, so this time we can't even count on the people general sir, and I had to bear the weight of this punishment alone, I had to sign alone thinking mother of mine Bendición Alvarado no one knows better than you that it's better to be left without the sea than to allow a landing of marines, remember that they were the ones who thought up the orders they made me sign, they turned our artists into fairies, they brought the Bible and syphilis, they made people believe that life was easy, mother, that everything is gotten with money, that blacks carry a contagion, they tried to convince our soldiers that the nation is a business and that the sense of honor is a bother invented by the government so that soldiers would fight for free, and it was to avoid the repetition of all those ills that I granted them the right to make use of our territorial waters in the way they considered best for the interests of humanity and peace among peoples, with the understanding that said cession not only included the physical waters visible from the window of his bedroom to the horizon but everything that is understood by sea in the broadest sense, or, the flora and fauna belonging to said waters, its system of winds, the inconstancy of its millibars, everything, but I could never have imagined that they would be capable of doing what they did to carry off the numbered locks of my old checkerboard sea with gigantic suction dredges and in its torn crater we saw appear the instantaneous sparkle of the submerged remains of the very ancient city of Santa María de Darién laid low by the whirlwind, we saw the flagship of the first admiral of the ocean sea just as I had seen it from my window, mother, it was identical, trapped by a clump of goose barnacles that the teeth of the dredges had pulled out by the roots before he had time to order an homage worthy of the historic importance of that wreck, they carried off everything that had been the reasons for my wars and the motive of his power and left behind only the deserted plain of harsh lunar dust that he saw as he passed by the windows with a heavy heart crying out mother of mine Bendición Alvarado illuminate me with your wisest lights, because on those twilight nights he would be awakened by the fright that the dead of the nation were standing up in their tombs asking him for an accounting of the sea, he felt their scratching on the walls, he heard their unburied voices, the horror of the posthumous looks that spied through keyholes on the trail of his great feet of a dying saurian in the steaming bog of the last fens of salvation in the shadowy house, he would walk ceaselessly through the cross currents of the tardy trade winds and the false mistrals from the wind machine that Ambassador Eberhart had given him so that he would not think so much about that bad piece of business with the sea, on the top of the reefs he saw the solitary light from the rest home for refugee dictators who sleep like sitting oxen while I suffer, evil-born bastards, he remembered the farewell snoring of his mother Bendición Alvarado in the suburban mansion, her good birdwoman's sleep in the room lighted by the vigil of the oregano, if he were only her, he sighed, happy sleeping mother who never let herself be frightened by the plague, or let herself be intimidated by love or let herself be scared by death, and on the contrary he was so wrought up that even the flashes of the lighthouse without a sea coming at intervals through the windows seemed to him to have been befouled by the dead, he fled in terror from the fantastic starlike firefly that fumigated in its orbit of a spinning nightmare the fearsome outpouring of the luminous dust of the marrow of the dead, put it out, he shouted, they put it out, he ordered the building caulked inside and out so that even the slightest wisp of death's nocturnal mangy air would not creep in through cracks in doors and windows, not even concealed in other fragrances, he remained in the dark feeling his way, breathing with difficulty in the airless heat, feeling himself pass by dark mirrors, walking from fear, until he heard a troop of hoofs in the crater of the sea and it was the moon rising with its decrepit snows, frightening, take it away, he shouted, put out the stars, damn it, by order of God, but nobody ran to him in the former offices, the blind men on the stairs, the lepers pearled with dew who rose up as he passed the stubble of the first rosebushes to implore the salt of health from his hands, and that was when it happened, disbelievers all over the world, shitty idolaters, it came to pass that he touched our heads as he went by, one by one, he touched each one of us on the place of our defects with a smooth and wise hand that was the hand of truth, and the instant he touched us we recovered the health of our bodies and the repose of our souls and we recovered the strength and will to live, and we saw the blind men dazzled by the glow of the roses, we saw the cripples jumping on the stairways and we saw this my own skin of a newborn child which I go about exhibiting in carnivals all over the world so that everyone will know about the miracle and this fragrance of premature lilies from the scars of my sores which I go spreading over the face of the earth for the derision of the unfaithful and as a lesson for libertines, they shouted it in cities and on byways, at dances and parades, trying to infuse in the crowds the terror of the miracle, but nobody thought it was true, we thought it was just one more of the many aulic messages they sent to villages with an entourage of old quacks to try to convince us of the last thing we needed to believe that he had given skin back to lepers, sight to the blind, agility to cripples, we thought that it was the last resort of the regime to call attention to an improbable president whose personal guard was reduced to a patrol of recruits against the unanimous advice of the cabinet who had insisted no general sir, tighter protection was necessary, at least a unit of riflemen general sir, but he had insisted that no one had any need or desire to kill me, you people are the only ones, my useless ministers, my lazy commanders, except that you don't dare and never will dare kill me because you know that afterward you'll have to kill each other, so that all that was left was the guard of rookies for an extinguished house where the cows wandered with no law or order from the first vestibule to the hearing room, they had eaten the flowered lawns on the tapestries general sir, they had eaten the files, but he didn't hear them, he had seen the first cow come up one October afternoon when it was impossible to stay outside because of the fury of the cloudburst, he had tried to chase it away with his hands, cow, cow, remembering suddenly that cow was written with a c, he had seen it another time eating the lampshades at a moment in life when he was beginning to understand that it wasn't worthwhile moving toward the stairs to chase a cow away, he had found two of them in the ballroom exasperated by the hens who were flying up to peck at the ticks on their backs, so that on recent nights when we saw lights that looked like navigational signals and we heard a disaster of large-animal hoofs behind the fortified walls it was because he was going about with a candle fighting with the cows over a place to sleep while outside his public life went on without him, every day in the newspapers of the regime we saw his fictionalized photographs at civil and military audiences in which they showed him to us with a different uniform according to the character of the occasion, every year for so many years on the major holidays of the nation's anniversaries we would hear the repeated harangues on the radio, he was present in our lives as we left home, as we went to church, as we ate and as we slept, when it was public knowledge that he could barely make his way along with his rustic hiker's boots in the decrepit building whose service had been reduced at that time to three or four orderlies who fed him and kept the honey hiding places well supplied and chased away the cows who had made a shambles of the general staff of porcelain marshals in the forbidden office where he was to die according to the prognostications of oracles that he himself had forgotten, they stood hanging on his whimsical orders until he hung the lamp on the door and they heard the noise of the three locks, the three bolts, the three bars of the bedroom rarefied by the lack of sea, and then they would withdraw to their quarters on the ground floor convinced that he was at the mercy of his dreams of a solitary drowned man until dawn, but he would awaken with unforeseen starts, he would browse through his insomnia, dragging his great feet of an apparition through the immense building in darkness disturbed only by the patient digestion of the cows and the obtuse breathing of the hens roosting on the viceroys' coatracks, he heard moon winds in the darkness, he felt the steps of time in the darkness, he saw his mother Bendición Alvarado sweeping in the darkness with the broom of green branches with which she had swept away the leaf storm of the illustrious singed heroes of Cornelius Nepos in the original, the immemorial rhetoric of Livius Andronicus and Cecilius Stratus who were reduced to office trash on the night of blood when he entered the ownerless house of power for the first time while outside the last suicide barricades of the distinguished Latinist General Lautaro Muñoz whom God keep in his holy kingdom were resisting, they had crossed the courtyard under the glow of the city in flames, leaping over the dead hulks of the personal bodyguard of the illustrious president, he shaking from the heat of tertian fever and his mother Bendición Alvarado with no other arm but the broom of green branches, they went up the stairs stumbling in the darkness over the horses of the splendid presidential squiry who were still bleeding from the first vestibule to the hearing room, it was difficult to breathe inside the closed building because of the sour gunpowder smell of the dead horses, along the corridors we saw prints of bare feet stained with horse blood, we saw the marks of palms stained with horse blood on the walls, and in the pool of blood in the hearing room we saw the drained body of a beautiful Florentine woman in an evening gown with a saber thrust through her heart, and she was the wife of the president, and beside her we saw the corpse of a little girl who looked like a toy windup ballerina with a pistol shot in her forehead, and she was his nine-year-old daughter, and they saw the corpse of the Garibaldian Caesar who was President Lautaro Muñoz, the ablest and most capable of the fourteen federalist generals who had succeeded to power through successive coups during eleven years of bloody rivals but also the only one who dared say no in his own tongue to the English consul, and there he was stretched out like a mullet, barefoot, suffering the punishment for his daring with his skull pierced by a pistol shot he had given himself in the palate after having killed his wife and daughter and his forty-two Andalusian horses so that they wouldn't fall into the hands of the punitive expedition of the British fleet, and that was when Commander Kitchener told me pointing to the body you see, general, that's what happens to those who raise their hands against their fathers, don't forget it when you're in your own kingdom, he told him, although he already was after so many nights of insomnia from waiting, so many postponed rages, so many digested humiliations, there he was, mother, proclaimed supreme commander of the three branches of the armed forces and president of the republic for such a time as was necessary for the reestablishment of order and the economic balance of the nation, it had been unanimously resolved by the last field commanders of the federation in agreement with the senate and chamber of deputies in joint session and the backing of the British fleet from my so many and so difficult nights of domino with Consul Macdonall, except that neither I nor anybody else believed it at the beginning, naturally, who could have believed it in the tumult of that frightening night since Bendición Alvarado herself still didn't believe on her bed of putrefaction when she evoked the memory of the son who couldn't find where to begin to govern in that disorder, they couldn't find a piece of grass to cook or to use to warm up that immense unfurnished house in which nothing of value was left except the moth-eaten oil paintings of viceroys and archbishops from the dead grandeur of Spain, everything else had been carried off little by little by previous presidents for their private domains, they didn't even leave a trace of the wallpaper with heroic episodes on the walls, the bedrooms were full of barracks trash, everywhere there were forgotten traces of historic massacres and slogans written with a bloody finger by illusory presidents who lasted one night, but there wasn't even a mat to lie down on to sweat out a fever, so his mother Bendición Alvarado pulled down a curtain to wrap me in and left him lying in a corner of the main stairway while with the broom of green branches she swept out the presidential quarters that the English were finishing sacking, she swept the whole floor defending herself with broom blows from this pack of filibusters who were trying to rape her from behind doors, and a short while before dawn she sat down to rest beside her son who was done in by chills, wrapped in the velvet curtain, the sweat pouring off him on the last step of the devastated main stairway while she tried to bring his fever down with her easy calculations of don't let this disorder get you down, son, it's only a matter of buying a few leather stools the cheapest you can find and they'll be painted with flowers and animals, I'll paint them myself, she said, it's only a matter of buying some hammocks for when visitors come, those especially, hammocks, because in a house like this there must be a lot of unannounced visitors at all hours, she said, we'll buy a church table to eat on, we'll buy iron utensils and pewter plates so they can suffer the bad life of soldiers; we'll buy a decent jug for drinking water and a charcoal stove and that's it, after all it's the government's money, she said to console him, but he wasn't listening to her, depressed by the first mallow light of dawn which was lighting up the hidden side of truth in living flesh, conscious of being nothing but a pitiful old man who was shaking with fever sitting on the stairs thinking without love mother of mine Bendición Alvarado so that was the whole mess, damn it, so power was that house of castaways, that human smell of burned horses, that desolate dawn of another twelfth of August just like all the others was the date of power, mother, what kind of a mess have we got ourselves into, suffering the original upset, the atavistic fear of the new century of darkness that was rising up in the world without his permission, the cocks were crowing at sea, the English were singing in English gathering up the dead from the courtyard when his mother Bendición Alvarado ended her merry accounting with the remnant of relief I'm not frightened by the things we have to buy and the chores we have to do, what frightens me is the number of sheets to be washed in this house, and then it was he who leaned on the strength of his disillusionment to try to console her with sleep easy, mother, in this country no president lasts long, he told her, and not only did he believe it then but he kept on believing it for every instant of his very long life of a sedentary despot, all the more as life convinced him more and more that the long years of power don't bring any two days that are just alike, that there would always be a hidden intention in the proposals of a prime minister when he released the dazzling display of truth in the routine Wednesday report, and he would only smile, don't tell me the truth, counselor, because we'll run the risk that it will be believed, thwarting with that single phrase a whole laborious strategy of the cabinet to try to get him to sign without asking questions, for he had never seemed more lucid to me than during the time of the rumors that he urinated in his pants during official visits without noticing it, he seemed more severe as he sank into the backwaters of decrepitude with the slippers of a terminal case and the eyeglasses with only one temple which was tied on with a piece of thread and his manner had become more intense and his instinct more certain in putting aside what was inopportune and signing what was needed without reading it, God damn it, because when all's said and done nobody pays any attention to me, he smiled, see how I ordered them to put up a barrier in the vestibule so the cows wouldn't climb up the stairs, and there it was again, so boss, so boss, it had stuck its head through the office window and was eating the paper flowers on the altar of the nation, but he limited himself to smiling you see what I'm talking about, counselor, what's got this country all fucked up is the fact that no one has ever paid any attention to me, he said, and he said it with a clearness of judgment that seemed impossible at his age, even so Ambassador Kippling said in his suppressed memoirs that around that time he had found him in a pitiful state of senile unawareness which did not even permit him to take care of himself in the most childish acts, he told how he found him soaked in an incessant and salty matter which flowed from his skin, that he had acquired the huge size of a drowned man and he had opened his shirt to show me the tight and lucid body of a dry-land drowned man in whose cracks and crannies parasites from the reefs at the bottom of the sea were proliferating, he had a ship remora on his back, polyps and microscopic crustaceans in his armpits, but he was convinced that those sproutings from reefs were only the first symptoms of the spontaneous return of the sea that you people carried off, my dear Johnson, because seas are like cats, he said, they always come home, convinced that the rows of goose barnacles in his crotch were the secret announcement of a happy dawn in which he was going to open his bedroom window and would see again the three caravels of the admiral of the ocean sea who had grown weary of searching the whole world over to see if what they had told him was true who had smooth hands like his and like those of so many other great men of history, he had ordered him brought before him, by force if necessary, when other navigators told him they had seen him mapping the innumerable islands of the neighboring seas changing their old names of military men to the names of kings and saints while he sought in native sci-ence the only thing that really interested him which was to dis-

cover some masterful hair-restorer for his incipient baldness, we
had lost all hope of finding him again when he recognized him
from the presidential limousine disguised in a brown habit with
the cord of Saint Francis around his waist swinging a penitent's
rattle among the Sunday crowds at the public market and
sunken into such a state of moral penury that it was impossible
to believe that he was the same one we had seen enter the audience room in his crimson uniform and gold spurs and with the
solemn gait of a sea dog on dry land, but when they tried to get
him into the limousine on his orders we couldn't find a trace
general sir, the earth had swallowed him up, they said he had
become a Moslem, that he had died of pellagra in Senegal, and
had been buried in three different tombs in three different cities
in the world although he really wasn't in any of them, condemned to wander from sepulcher to sepulcher until the end of
time because of the twisted fate of his expeditions, because that
man was a fraud general sir, he was a worse jinx than gold, but
he never believed it, he kept on hoping that he would return
during the last extremes of his old age when the minister of
health used pincers to pull out the ox ticks he found on his body
and he insisted that they weren't ticks, doctor, it's the sea coming back, he said, so sure of his judgment that the minister of
health had thought many times that he wasn't as deaf as he made
one believe in public or as unraveled as he seemed to be during
uncomfortable audiences, although a thorough examination had
revealed that his arteries had turned to glass, he had beach-sand
sediment in his kidneys, and his heart was cracked from a lack
of love, so the old physician took refuge behind the shield of old
comradeship to tell him that it's time now to hand over the tools
general sir, at least decide in whose hands you're going to leave
us, he told him, save us from being orphaned, but he asked him
with surprise who told him I'm thinking about dying, my dear

doctor, let other people die, God damn it, and he finished in a
joking vein that two nights ago I saw myself on television and I
looked better than ever, like a fighting bull, he said, dying with
laughter, because he had seen himself in a fog, nodding with
sleep in front of the screen, and with his head wrapped in a wet
towel in accordance with the habits of his more recent nights of
solitude, he was really more resolute than a fighting bull before
the charms of the wife of the ambassador of France, or maybe
Turkey, or Sweden, what the hell, they were all so much alike
that he couldn't tell them apart and so much time had passed
that he couldn't remember himself among them with his dress
uniform and a glass of champagne untouched in his hand during
the festivities for the anniversary of August 12, or at the com-
memoration of the victory of January 14, or the rebirth of
March 13, how should I know, because in the rigamarole of
historic dates of the regime he had ended up not knowing which
was when or what corresponded to what nor did he get any use
from the little rolled pieces of paper that with so much good
spirit and so much care he had hidden in the cracks in the walls
because he had ended up forgetting what it was he was supposed
to remember, he would find them by chance in the hiding places
for the honey and he had read one time that April 17 was the
birthday of Dr. Marcos de León, we have to send him a tiger as
a gift, he had read, written in his own hand, without the slightest idea of who he was, feeling that there was no punishment
more humiliating or less deserved for a man than betrayal by his
own body, he had begun to glimpse it long before the immemorial times of José Ignacio Saenz de la Barra when he became
aware that he only knew who was who in group audiences, a
man like me who had been capable of calling the whole population of the most remote village in his realm of gloom by their
first and last names, and yet he had reached the opposite

extreme, from the carriage he saw among the crowd a boy he knew and he had been so surprised at not remembering where he had seen him before that he had him arrested by the escort while I tried to remember, a poor man from the country who spent twenty-two years in a jail cell repeating the truth established on the first day in the court transcript, that his name was Braulio Linares Moscote, that he was the illegitimate but recognized son of Marcos Linares, a fresh-water sailor, and Delfina Moscote, a breeder of jaguar hounds, both with an established domicile in Rosal del Virrey, that he was in the capital of this country for the first time because his mother had sent him to sell two dogs at the March poetry festival, that he had arrived on a rented donkey with no other clothes except those he was wearing at dawn on the same Thursday they had arrested him, that he was at a stand in the public market drinking a mug of black coffee as he asked the girls behind the counter if they knew of anyone who wanted to buy two cross-bred dogs for hunting jaguars, that they had answered no when the bustle of drums began, cornets, rockets, people shouting here comes the man, there he comes, that he had asked who was the man and they had answered him who else could it be, the one who gives the orders, that he put the dogs in a crate so that the counter girls could do him the favor of watching them for me until I get back, that he climbed up on a window ledge to be able to see over the crowd and he saw the escort of horses with gold caparisons and feathered crests, he saw the carriage with the dragon of the nation, the greeting by a hand with a cloth glove, the pale visage, the taciturn unsmiling lips of the man who gave the orders, the sad eyes that found him suddenly like a needle in a pile of needles, the finger that pointed him out, that one, the one up on the window sill, arrest him while I remember where I've seen him, he ordered, so they grabbed me and hit me, beat me with the flats of their sabers, roasted me on a grill so that I would confess where the man who gave the orders had seen me before, but they had been unable to drag any other truth out of him except the only one there was in the horror chamber of the harbor fort and he repeated it with such conviction and such personal courage that he ended up admitting he had been mistaken, but now there was no way out, he said, because they had treated him so badly that if he hadn't been an enemy he is now, poor man, so he rotted away alive in the dungeon while I wandered about this house of shadows thinking mother of mine Bendición Alvarado of my good times, be with me, look at what I am without the shelter of your mantle, shouting to himself that it wasn't worth the trouble having lived so many splendid days of glory if he couldn't evoke them to seek solace in them and feed himself on them and continue surviving because of them in the bog of old age because even the most intense grief and the happiest moments of his great times had slipped away irrevocably through the loopholes of memory in spite of his naïve attempts to impede it with little plugs of rolled-up paper, he was punished by never knowing who this Francisca Linero aged ninety-six was, the one he had ordered buried with the honors of a queen in accordance with another note written in his own hand, condemned to govern blindly with eleven pairs of useless spectacles hidden in the desk drawer to hide the fact that he was really conversing with specters whose voices he couldn't even decipher, whose identities he guessed by instinctive signs, sunken in a state of abandonment whose greatest risk had become evident to him in an audience with his minister of war in which he had the bad luck to have sneezed once and the minister of war said your health general sir and he had sneezed again and the minister of war again said your health general sir, but after nine consecutive sneezes I didn't say your health general sir again but I

felt terrified by the threat of that face twisted in a stupor, I saw
the eyes sunken in tears that spat on me without pity from the
quicksand of his throes, I saw the tongue of a hanged man on
the decrepit beast who was dying in my arms without any witness of my innocence, without anyone, and then the only thing
that occurred to me was to get out of the office before it was
too late, but he stopped me with an authoritative wave between
two sneezes not to be a coward Brigadier General Rosendo Sac-
ristán, stay where you are, God damn it, I'm not such a damned
fool as to die in front of you, he shouted, and that's how it was,
because he kept on sneezing up to the edge of death, floating in
a space of unconsciousness peopled by fireflies at midday but
clinging to the certainty that his mother Bendición Alvarado
would not give him the shame of dying from a sneezing attack
in the presence of an inferior, never in a million years, better
dead than humiliated, better to live among the cows than among
men capable of letting a person die without honor, God damn
it, for he hadn't gone back to arguing about God with the apostolic nuncio so that he wouldn't notice that he was drinking his
chocolate with a spoon, nor back to playing dominoes for fear
that someone would dare lose to him out of pity, he didn't want
to see anyone, mother, so that no one would discover that in
spite of the close vigilance of his personal conduct, in spite of
his impression of not dragging his flat feet which after all he had
always dragged, in spite of the shame of his years he felt himself
on the edge of the abyss of grief of the last dictators in disgrace
whom he maintained more prisoners than protected in the
house on the cliff so that they wouldn't contaminate the world
with the plague of their indignity, he suffered it alone on that
evil morning when he had fallen asleep in the pool in the private
courtyard while he was taking his bath of medicinal waters, he
was dreaming about you, mother, he was dreaming that it was

you who made the cicadas who were bursting from so much buzzing over my head among the flowering almond boughs of real life, he dreamed it was you who painted with your brushes the colored voices of the orioles when he awoke startled by the unforeseen belch of his insides in the bottom of the water, mother, he awoke congested with rage in the perverted pool of my shame where the aromatic lotuses of oregano and mallow floated, where the fresh blossoms from the orange tree floated, where the hicatee turtles floated aroused by the novelty of the gold and tender flow of rabbit droppings from general sir in the fragrant waters, what a mess, but he survived that and so many other infamies of old age and had reduced his service personnel to the minimum in order to face them without witnesses, no one was to see him drifting through the no-man's-house for days and nights on end with his head wrapped in rags soaked in liniment moaning with despair against the walls, surfeited with pain, maddened by the unbearable headache of which he never spoke even to his personal physician because he knew that it was only just one more of the so many useless pains of decrepitude, he would feel it arrive like a thunderclap of stones long before the heavy storm clouds appeared in the sky and he ordered nobody to bother me as soon as he felt the tourniquet tighten on his temples, nobody come into this building no matter what happens, he ordered, when he felt the bones of his skull creak with the second turn of the tourniquet, not even God if he comes, he ordered, not even if I die, God damn it, blind with that pitiless pain which did not even give him an instant of respite to think until the end of the centuries of desperation when the blessing of the rains fell, and then he would call us and we would find him newborn with the little table ready for dinner opposite the mute television screen, we served him roast meat, beans with fatback, coconut rice, slices of fried plantains, a dinner inconceivable for his age which he let grow cold without even tasting it as he watched the same emergency film on television, aware that the government was trying to hide something from him since they had repeated the same closed-circuit program without noticing that the film was backward, God damn it, he said, trying to forget what they wanted to hide from him, if it were something worse he would have known it by now, he said, snorting over the dinner he had been served, until it struck eight on the cathedral clock and he arose with the untouched plate and threw the meal down the toilet as every night at that time for so many years to hide the humiliation that his stomach rejected everything, to while away with the legends of his times of glory the rancor that he felt toward himself every time he fell into some detestable act of the carelessness of an old man, to forget that he was only alive, that it was he and no one else who wrote on the walls of the toilets long live the general, long live the stud, and that he had sneaked out a healer's potion to do it as many times as he wanted and in one single night and even three times each time with three different women and he paid for that senile ingenuousness with tears more from rage than grief clinging to the chain of the toilet weeping mother of mine Bendición Alvarado of my heart, despise me, purify me with your waters of fire, fulfilling with pride the punishment of his naïveté because he knew only too well that what he lacked then and had always lacked in bed was not honor but love, he needed women less arid than those who served my comrade the foreign minister so that he would not lose the good habit since they closed the school next door, fleshy boneless women for you alone general sir, sent by plane with official exemption from customs from the shopwindows of Amsterdam, the film festivals of Budapest, the sea of Italy general sir, look at what a marvel, the most beautiful in the whole world whom he would find sitting with singing-teacher decorum in the shadows of the office, they got undressed like artists, they lay down on the felt couch with the strips of their bathing suits printed like a photographic negative on their warm golden honey skin, lying beside the enormous concrete ox who refused to take off his military uniform while I tried to encourage him with my most loving means until he wearied of suffering the pressures of that hallucinating beauty of a dead fish, and he told her it was all right, child, go become a nun, so depressed by his own indolence that that night at the stroke of eight he surprised one of the women in charge of the soldiers' laundry and threw her down with his claws on top of the laundry tubs in spite of the fact that she tried to get away with the frightened excuse that I can't today general, believe me, it's vampire time, but he turned her face down on the laundry table and planted her from behind with a biblical drive that the poor woman felt in her soul with the crunch of death and she panted so big general, you must have studied to be a donkey, and he felt more relieved with that moan of pain than with the most frenetic dithyrambs of his official adulators and he assigned the washerwoman a lifetime pension for the education of her children, he sang again after so many years when he gave the cows their fodder in the milking stalls, bright January moon, he sang, without thinking about death, because not even on the last night of his life would he allow himself the weakness of thinking about anything that didn't make common sense, he counted the cows twice again while he sang you are the light of my darkened path, you are my northern star, and he discovered that four were missing, he went back into the building counting along the way the hens sleeping on the viceroys' coatracks, covering the cages with the sleeping birds which he counted as he put the cloth covers over them forty-eight, he set fire to the droppings scattered by the cows during the day from the vestibule to the audience room, he remembered a remote childhood which for the first time was his own image shivering on the icy barrens and the image of his mother Bendición Alvarado who stole the innards of a ram away from the garbage-heap buzzards for lunch, it had struck eleven when he covered the whole building again in the opposite direction lighting his way with the lamp as he put out the lights down to the vestibule, he saw himself one by one fourteen generals walking with a lamp repeated in the dark mirrors, he saw a cow collapsed on her back in the rear of the mirror in the music room, so boss, so boss, he said, she was dead, what a mess, he went through the sleeping quarters of the guard to tell them that there was a dead cow inside a mirror, he ordered them to take it out early tomorrow, without fail, before the building fills up with vultures, he ordered, inspecting with the light the former offices on the ground floor in search of the other lost cows, there were three of them, he looked for them in the toilets, under the tables, inside every mirror, he went up to the main floor searching the rooms room by room and all he found was a hen lying under the pink embroidered mosquito netting of a novice from other times whose name he had forgotten, he took his spoonful of honey before going to bed, he put the bottle back in the hiding place where there was one of his little pieces of paper with the date of some birthday of the famous poet Rubén Darío whom God keep on the highest seat in his kingdom, he rolled the piece of paper up again and left it in its place while he recited from memory the well-aimed prayer of our father and celestial lyrophorous master who keepeth afloat airplanes in the heavens and liners on the seas, dragging his great feet of a hopeless insomniac through the last fleeing dawns of green sunrises from the turns of the lighthouse, he heard the winds sorrowing for the sea that had gone away, he heard the lively music of a wedding party that was about to die struck from behind by some carelessness of God, he found a strayed cow and he cut off its path without touching it, so boss, so boss, he went back to his bedroom, seeing as he passed by the windows the block of lights of the city without a sea in every window, he smelled the hot vapor of the mystery of its insides, the secret of its unanimous breathing, he contemplated it twenty-three times without stopping and he suffered forever as ever the uncertainty of the vast and inscrutable ocean of people sleeping with their hands on their hearts, he knew himself to be hated by those who loved him most, he felt himself illuminated by the candles of saints, he heard his name invoked to straighten the fortunes of women in childbirth and to change the destiny of those dying, he felt his memory exalted by the same ones who cursed his mother when they saw the taciturn eyes, the sad lips, the hand of a pensive bride behind the panes of transparent steel in the remote times of the somnambulant limousine and we would kiss the mark of his boot in the mud and we sent him fetishes for an evil death on hot nights when from our courtyards we saw the wandering lights in the soulless windows of government house, no one loves us, he sighed, looking into the old bedroom of the lifeless birdwoman painter of orioles his mother Bendición Alvarado her body strewn with sawdust, have a good death mother, he said to her, a very good death son, she answered him in the crypt, it was exactly twelve o'clock when he hung the lamp on the doorway wounded inside by the fatal twisting of the tenuous whistles of the hernia, there was no space in the world except that of his pain, he ran the three bolts of the bedroom for the last time, closed the three locks, the three bars, he suffered the final holocaust of his scant micturition in the portable latrine, he stretched out on the bare floor in the pants of rough burlap which he wore at home ever since he had put an end to audiences, the

striped shirt without the artificial collar, and the slippers of an
invalid, he lay face down with his right arm doubled under his
head as a pillow and he fell asleep immediately, but at ten minutes after two he awoke with his mind aground and his clothes
soaked in the pale and warm sweat of the eye of a cyclone, who's
there, he asked shaken by the certainty that someone had called
him in his sleep by a name that was not his, Nicanor, and once
again, Nicanor, someone who was able to get into his room
without taking down the bars because he came and went as he
wished going through the walls, and then he saw her, it was
death general sir, his, dressed in a penitent's tunic of pita fiber
cloth, with a long-poled hook in her hand and her skull sown
with the tufts of sepulchral algae and flowers of the earth in
the fissures of her bones and her eyes archaic and startled in the
fleshless sockets, and only when he saw her full length did he
understand that she had called him Nicanor Nicanor which is
the name by which death knows all of us men at the moment of
death, but he said no, death, it still wasn't his time, it was to be
during his sleep in the shadows of the office as it had always
been announced in the premonitory waters of the basins, but
she replied no, general, it's been here, barefoot and with the
beggar's clothes you're wearing, although those who found the
body were to say that it was on the floor of the office with
the denim uniform without insignia and the gold spur on the
left heel so as not to go against the auguries of their Pythians, it
had been when he least wanted it, when after so many long years
of sterile illusions he had begun to glimpse that one doesn't live,
God damn it, he lives through, he survives, one learns too late
that even the broadest and most useful of lives only reach the
point of learning how to live, he had learned of his incapacity
for love in the enigma of the palm of his mute hands and in the
invisible code of the cards and he had tried to compensate for

that infamous fate with the burning cultivation of the solitary vice of power, he had made himself victim of his own sect to be immolated on the flames of that infinite holocaust, he had fed on fallacy and crime, he had flourished in impiety and dishonor and he had put himself above his feverish avarice and his congenital fear only to keep until the end of time the little glass ball in his hand without knowing that it was an endless vice the satiety of which generated its own appetite until the end of all times general sir, he had known since his beginnings that they deceived him in order to please him, that they collected from him by fawning on him, that they recruited by force of arms the dense crowds along his route with shouts of jubilation and venal signs of eternal life to the magnificent one who is more ancient than his age, but he learned to live with those and all the miseries of glory as he discovered in the course of his uncountable years that a lie is more comfortable than doubt, more useful than love, more lasting than truth, he had arrived without surprise at the ignominious fiction of commanding without power, of being exalted without glory and of being obeyed without authority when he became convinced in the trail of yellow leaves of his autumn that he had never been master of all his power, that he was condemned not to know life except in reverse, condemned to decipher the seams and straighten the threads of the woof and the warp of the tapestry of illusions of reality without suspecting even too late that the only livable life was one of show, the one we saw from this side which wasn't his general sir, this poor people's side with the trail of yellow leaves of our uncountable years of misfortune and our ungraspable instants of happiness, where love was contaminated by the seeds of death but was all love general sir, where you yourself were only an uncertain vision of pitiful eyes through the dusty peepholes of the window of a train, only the tremor of some taciturn lips, the fugitive wave of a velvet glove on the no-man's-hand of an old man with no destiny with our never knowing who he was, or what he was like, or even if he was only a figment of the imagination, a comic tyrant who never knew where the reverse side was and where the right of this life which we loved with an insatiable passion that you never dared even to imagine out of the fear of knowing that we knew only too well that it was arduous and ephemeral but there wasn't any other, general, because we knew who we were while he was left never knowing it forever with the soft whistle of his rupture of a dead old man cut off at the roots by the slash of death, flying through the dark sound of the last frozen leaves of his autumn toward the homeland of shadows of the truth of oblivion, clinging to his fear of the rotting cloth of death's hooded cassock and alien to the clamor of the frantic crowds who took to the streets singing hymns of joy at the jubilant news of his death and alien forevermore to the music of liberation and the rockets of jubilation and the bells of glory that announced to the world the good news that the uncountable time of eternity had come to an end.

1968–1975

Insights,
Interviews
& More ...

Meet Gabriel García Márquez

> [Gabriel García Márquez] spent his first eight years in his maternal grandparents' home, listening to their nonstop stories, superstitions, and folk beliefs.

IN LATE FEBRUARY 1997, just before his seventieth birthday, Gabriel García Márquez announced that he was once again exiling himself to Mexico City. His native Colombia, he said, was a country "uncomfortable... uncertain, and troubling for a writer." Most of his fellow Colombians, who familiarly and affectionately refer to their Nobel laureate as "Gabo," went ahead with the birthday celebrations without the guest of honor. Reminiscences and remembrances of his long career filled newspapers and radio and television programs. But Gabo had headed north.

García Márquez's now-here, now-there relationship with Colombia is not new. He has been back and forth between Colombia, Mexico, and other countries since 1956. His first twenty-eight years, however, were entirely Colombian. García Márquez was born in the northern coastal town of Aracataca on March 6, 1927. He spent his first eight years in his maternal grandparents' home, listening to their nonstop stories, superstitions, and folk beliefs.

Because of their way of storytelling (especially that of his grandmother) he was unable to distinguish between the real and the fabulous. They recounted the most improbable happenings with the same facial and vocal expressions with which they recounted fact. His grandfather also took him to circuses and other entertainments and introduced him to the miracle of ice (an episode that introduces *One Hundred Years of Solitude*). The author would later remark "I feel that all my writing has been about the experiences of the time I spent with my grandparents."

After his grandfather's death in 1936, García Márquez moved to Sucre, where his father was a pharmacist. The boy was soon sent to a boarding school in Barranquilla. At the age of twelve he entered a Jesuit secondary school in Zipaquirá, not far from Bogotá. In 1946 he followed his parent's wishes and enrolled in the law program of the Universidad Nacional in Bogotá. He quickly lost interest in his studies, however, and took to roaming the city and writing. During these years he made two life-changing discoveries. On a visit to his parents, he met his future wife (then-thirteen-year-old Mercedes Barcha Pardo), who pledged her undying love. And he read Kafka's *Metamorphosis* in Jorge Luis Borges's translation. *Metamorphosis* reinforced his grandmother's storytelling technique, recounting "the wildest things with a completely natural tone of voice," he later recalled. In the meantime he had begun his writing career. In 1946 his first story, "The Third Resignation," was published in the newspaper *El Espectador,* followed by ten other stories over the next few years.

In 1948 he transferred to the Universidad de Cartagena, where he began his career as a ▶

> On a visit to his parents, he met his future wife (then-thirteen-year-old Mercedes Barcha Pardo).

Meet Gabriel García Márquez *(continued)*

journalist reporting for Cartagena's *Universal.* By this time he had read Hemingway, Joyce, Woolf, and Faulkner (the last of whom was to have a lasting influence). In 1950, not long after becoming a reporter for Baranquilla's *El Heraldo,* he accompanied his mother back to his grandparents' home to prepare it for sale. This return to his "haunted" childhood inspired him to write his first novella, *La Hojarasca (Leaf Storm,* U.S., 1972). The novella was rejected by the first publisher to whom he submitted it, forgotten, and then not published until 1955. But his career as a journalist would continue throughout his life. "I've always been convinced," he later told one interviewer, "that my true profession is that of a journalist."

Back in Bogotá in 1952, he joined the *El Espectador* staff as a reporter, story writer, and film critic. His as-told-to series, "The Truth About My Adventure, by Luis Alejandro Velasco," about the shipwreck of a Colombian destroyer carrying illegal cargo (published in book format as *Relato de un Naufrago* in 1970), infuriated the government. As a result he was sent by the newspaper to Italy. He eventually settled in Paris, where he wrote the initial drafts of *El Coronel Ne Tiene Quien le Escriba (No One Writes to the Colonel,* U.S., 1968) and *Este Pueblo de Mierda,* which would be published in 1961 as *La Mala Hora (In Evil Hour,* U.S., 1979). The story "Un Dia Despues del Sabado" ("One Day After Saturday") brought him his first award (the Colombian Association of Writers and Artists Award) in 1954. Suddenly out of a job because the Colombian government closed down *El Espectador,* he worked as a freelance journalist

> 66 His as-told-to series . . . about the shipwreck of a Colombian destroyer carrying illegal cargo infuriated the government. 99

in Paris and London. Returning to Caracas, Venezuela, he met up with an old friend with whom he spent 1957 touring eastern Europe in search of solutions to Colombia's problems.

Nineteen fifty-eight found García Márquez working for *Momento* magazine in Caracas. But he managed to slip back into Colombia to marry Mercedes. (They would have two children: Rodrigo in 1959 and Gonzalo in 1962.) By this time he had become favorably impressed by Fidel Castro's Cuban revolution and in 1959 helped found the Colombian branch of Castro's news agency (Prensa Latina). Thus began a friendship that has continued, with occasional criticism from García Márquez, to this day. After stints in Havana and New York City (through 1961), he resigned from Prensa Latina and moved the family to Mexico City. The city was to become his semipermanent home. In 1961, *El Coronel Ne Tiene Quien le Escriba* and *La Mala Hora* were published, the latter receiving Colombia's Premio Literario Esso. The story collection *Los Funerales de la Mama Grande (Big Mama's Funeral)* followed in 1962.

On a 1965 family vacation in Acapulco, as he later wrote, "All of a sudden—I don't know why—I had this illumination on how to write the book." "The book" was *Cien Años de Soledad (One Hundred Years of Solitude,* U.S., 1969), which he completed over the intensely focused and impoverishing eighteen months that followed, and which appeared to universal acclaim in 1967. Popularity and fame were his. And, as translations appeared in country after country, the term "magical realism" entered readers' vocabularies around the world.

Barcelona, Spain, was the next stop. ▶

66 He had become favorably impressed by Fidel Castro's Cuban revolution and in 1959 helped found the Colombian branch of Castro's news agency (Prensa Latina). 99

Meet Gabriel García Márquez *(continued)*

There García Márquez worked on *El Otoño del Patriarca* (*The Autumn of the Patriarch*, U.S., 1976). In the years since 1980 other novels, novellas, nonfiction works, stories, plays, and screenplays have appeared, among them: *Cronica de una Muerte Anunciada* (*Chronicle of a Death Foretold*, U.S., 1983) in 1982; *El Amor en los Tiempos del Colera* (*Love in the Time of Cholera*, U.S., 1988) in 1985; *La Aventura de Miguel Littín, Clandestine en Chile* (*Clandestine in Chile*, U.S., 1987) in 1986 (which brought down the wrath of the Chilean military dictatorship); *El General en Su Labertino* (*The General in His Labyrinth*, U.S., 1990) in 1989 (which was his amazing fictional study of the final days of South America's great hero—referred to as "The Liberator"—Simón Bolívar); *Doce Cuentos Peregrinos* (*Strange Pilgrims: Twelve Stories*, U.S., 1993) in 1992; and *Del Amor y Otros Demonios* (*Of Love and Other Demons*, U.S., 1993) in 1995. His journalism culminated in 1996 with his account (published in the United States as *News of a Kidnapping*) of the kidnappings of ten prominent Colombians by agents of drug trafficker Pablo Escobar.

Whether in fiction or nonfiction, in the epic novel or the concentrated story, Gabriel García Márquez is now recognized (in the words of Carlos Fuentes) as "the most popular and perhaps the best writer in Spanish since Cervantes." He is one of those very rare artists who succeed in chronicling not only a nation's life, culture, and history, but also those of an entire continent, and a master storyteller who, as the *New York Review of Books* once said, "forces upon us at every page the wonder and extravagance of life."

> His journalism culminated in 1996 with his account ... of the kidnappings of ten prominent Colombians by agents of drug trafficker Pablo Escobar.

William Kennedy's "Stunning Portrait of a Monstrous Caribbean Tyrant"

From the *New York Times Book Review,*
October 31, 1976

IN 1968 WHEN HE BEGAN TO WRITE this majestic novel, Gabriel García Márquez told an interviewer that the only image he had of it for years was that of an incredibly old man walking through the huge, abandoned rooms of a palace full of animals. Some of his friends remember him saying as far back as 1958, when as a newsman he was witnessing the fall of Marcos Pérez Jiménez in Venezuela, that he would one day write a book about a dictator. He has since spoken of the influence of the life of the Venezuelan *caudillo,* Juan Vicente Gómez, on this book. He himself lived for years under the Rojas Pinilla dictatorship in his native Colombia. He covered the trial of a Batista butcher in the early days of Castro's Cuban takeover. He lived in Spain during the interminable rattlings of Franco's elusive death, when that country was a hospitable journey's end for deposed Latin dictators.

He has added to these times of his own life fragments from the long history of dictators— the deaths of Julius Caesar and Mussolini, the durability of Stroessner, the wife-worship of Perón, what seems to be a close study of the times of Trujillo and the United States and English gunboat-puppeteering of so many bestial morons into the dictator's palace. He has absorbed and reimagined all this, ▶

66 Some of [García Márquez's] friends remember him saying as far back as 1958 that he would one day write a book about a dictator. 99

and more, and emerged with a stunning portrait of the archetype: the pathological fascist tyrant.

García Márquez (his surname is García; Márquez is his mother's name) began this novel in 1968 and said in 1971 that it was finished. But he continued to embellish it until 1975 when he published it in Spain. Now Gregory Rabassa, who translated the author's last novel, *One Hundred Years of Solitude,* and who on the basis of these two books alone stands as one of the best translators who ever drew breath, has given us the superb English equivalent of García Márquez's magisterial Spanish.

The book, as is to be expected from García Márquez, is mystical, surrealistic, Rabelaisian in its excesses, its distortions and its exotic language. But García Márquez's sense of life is that surreality is as much the norm as banality. "In Mexico surrealism runs through the streets," he once said. And elsewhere: "The Latin American reality is totally Rabelaisian."

And so his patriarch, the unnamed General (his precise rank is General of the Universe) of an unnamed Caribbean nation, lives to be anywhere between 107 and 232 years old, sires 5,000 children, all runts, all born after seven-month gestations. He is a bird woman's bastard, conceived in a storm of bluebottle flies, born in a convent doorway, gifted at birth with huge, deformed feet and an enlarged testicle the size of a fig, which whistles a tune of pain to him every moment of his impossibly long life. The graffiti on the walls of the servants' toilet give him oracular insight

66 García Márquez's sense of life is that surreality is as much the norm as banality. 99

8

into traitorous cohorts, one of whom he serves roasted for dinner to a gathering of his generals.

He has such power that when he orders the time of day changed from three to eight in the morning to deliver himself from darkness, the roses open two hours before dew time. His influence is so indelible that eventually his cows are born with his hereditary presidential brand. His venality is such that he rigs the weekly lottery, using children under seven to draw the winning three numbers, and he always wins all three. To quiet the children about their enforced complicity, he imprisons them. When they number 2,000 and the Pope anguishes publicly over their disappearance and the League of Nations investigates it, he isolates the children in the wilderness after a Nazi-like deportation in boxcars, and finally drowns them at sea, denying they ever existed.

But his most fantastic depredation is the sale of the Caribbean Sea to the gringos who have kept him in power. The United States ambassador orders in giant suction dredges and nautical engineers, who carry off the sea "in numbered pieces to plant it far from the hurricanes in the blood-red dawns of Arizona, they took it away with everything it had inside general sir, with the reflection of our cities, our timid drowned people, our demented dragons," and they leave behind a torn crater, a deserted plain of harsh lunar dust. To replace the breezes that were lost when the sea went away, another U.S. ambassador gives the General a wind machine.

The novel is unendingly bizarre and fevered, but ultimately not difficult. Yet it is ▶

> **[The General's] most fantastic depredation is the sale of the Caribbean Sea to the gringos who have kept him in power.**

William Kennedy's "Stunning Portrait of a Monstrous Caribbean Tyrant" *(continued)*

difficult to enter: a densely rich and fluid pudding that begins at the end and makes Faulknerian leaps forward and backward in time. Sentences at times run on for three pages, with dialogue neither quoted nor paragraphed. García Márquez has compounded the problems by making the novel a puzzle of pronouns, consistently changing narrative points of view in mid-sentence. For instance: ". . . he saw more infamy and more ingratitude than had ever been seen and wept over by my eyes since the day I was born, mother . . ." The he, the my, and the I all refer to the General.

The narration is largely within the General's mind, but García Márquez also enters other minds with brief intensity, often speaks in the collective voice of all people in the blasted nation; and so, through relentless immersion of the reader in these exquisitely detailed perspectives, he illuminates the monster internally and externally and delivers him whole. As with *One Hundred Years of Solitude,* the reader also bathes luxuriously in panoramic prose, this work even more poetic than the last. There is no conventional plot, only chronologically scrambled episodes that take the General from birth to death through an unspecified modern era in which the king and queen of Babylonia co-exist with closed-circuit television. He is traced through assassination attempts, atrocities, comically senile sexual perversity, through marriage to a nun and a ridiculous war with the church to have his mother canonized, through meaningless, empty politics that have nothing to do with his untouchable power, through

> 66 As with *One Hundred Years of Solitude,* the reader bathes luxuriously in panoramic prose, this work even more poetic than the last. 99

doomed palace revolts and the rise and fall of a mad secret police chief who keeps sending him sacks of heads of presumed enemies.

The General deteriorates from a deformed, charismatic stud into a mindless blood beast imprisoned on the "throne of illusions" that his power creates, unable to say what is true now, or what was true in the beginning. He comes to think of himself as God and names his son Emanuel.

A reader grows somewhat weary at times over the excesses, the repetition and predictability of certain sections—that old man walking endlessly through the palace corridors, kicking lepers and beggars in the courtyard, tending the resident cows on the stairs and taking the concubines by surprise, and there is a yearning for some pithy understatement. But García Márquez is as exorbitant as Melville and Dostoyevsky. He believes not only that excess is good for you, but that it is essential, that a book must have an immensity about it in the same way life is enormous—and dense and mysterious and as repetitiously predictable as the General's vengeance for an affront. How else, his novel implicitly asks, could the story of interminable dictatorship be told?

This novel, of necessity then, has none of the life-celebrating quality that made *One Hundred Years of Solitude* so universally embraced. There is nothing to celebrate in the General's long and tortured life. He is given endless opportunity to persuade us that his anguish and grief and bafflement are real. But we are never persuaded. He is not even pitiable. He is a spectacle, the embodiment ▶

William Kennedy's "A Stunning Portrait of a Monstrous Caribbean Tyrant" *(continued)*

of egocentric evil unleashed, maniacally violent, cosmically worthless and, despite pretensions to eternity, as devoid of meaning as anything else in an absurd world. His main contribution to life, finally, is fear; but fear such as thunder, cancer or madness may provoke, fear based on irrational possibility, on the oblique ravages of a diabolical deity.

The book is a supreme polemic, a spiritual exposé, an attack against any society that encourages or even permits the growth of such a monstrosity. García Márquez objectifies the monster and at novel's end attempts to explain it as the consequences of the General's incapacity to love: ". . . he had tried to compensate for that infamous fate [of being unable to love] with the burning cultivation of the solitary vice of power, he had made himself victim of his own sect to be immolated on the flames of that infinite holocaust, he had fed on fallacy and crime, he had flourished in impiety and dishonor and he had put himself above his feverish avarice and his congenital fear only to keep until the end of time the little glass ball [his personal symbol of the nation] in his hand without knowing that it was an endless vice the satiety of which generated its own appetite until the end of all times general sir. . . ."

But the monster is not reducible to a single cause, any more than civilization is explainable through the invention of the wheel. The cause is beyond reductive statements, even when they exfoliate into such resplendent prose. The General presumes to have love of a kind for his goddess mother and his lusty wife. But he loves them the way he loves and softly caresses his wounded testicle: as an extension of himself. Given time, he will annihilate anything that is not of, by, from, or for himself. Could lovelessness alone explain such blood-drenched misanthropy?

The incapacity to love seems to stand, rather, as another fact of the General's life, like the whistle of his hernia, or the seed of his unknown father, or his discovery that a lie is more comfortable than doubt. And these facts, under the hand of this master novelist, accumulate not to explain anything simply, but to embody a most complex and terrible vision of Latin America's ubiquitous, unkillable demon. ∾

Have You Read?
More by Gabriel García Márquez

ONE HUNDRED YEARS OF SOLITUDE

One of the twentieth century's enduring works, *One Hundred Years of Solitude* is an internationally beloved novel and the ultimate achievement in a Nobel Prize–winning career.

García Márquez tells the story of the rise and fall of the mythical town of Macondo through the history of the Buendía family. It is a rich and brilliant chronicle of life and death and the tragicomedy of humankind. In the noble, ridiculous, beautiful, and tawdry story of the Buendía family, one sees all of humanity; in the history, myths, growth, and decay of Macondo, one sees all of Latin America.

"*One Hundred Years of Solitude* is the first piece of literature since the Book of Genesis that should be required reading for the entire human race."

—William Kennedy,
New York Times Book Review

COLLECTED NOVELLAS

Leaf Storm, Gabriel García Márquez's first novella, introduces the mythical village of Macondo. It is a desolate town beset by torrents of rain, where a man must fulfill a promise made years earlier. *No One Writes to the Colonel* is a novella of life in a decaying tropical town in Colombia with an unforgettable central character. *Chronicle of a Death Foretold* is a dark and profound story of three people joined together in a fatal act of violence.

Have You Read? *(continued)*

"García Márquez has extraordinary strength and firmness of imagination and writes with the calmness of a man who knows exactly what wonders he can perform."

—Alfred Kazin,
New York Times Book Review

IN EVIL HOUR

Written just before *One Hundred Years of Solitude,* this fascinating novel of a Colombian river town possessed by evil points to the author's later flowering and greatness.

"An openly political novel posing the people of the land against the forces of oppression . . . it has the virtues of wit and compassion."

—Jonathan Yardley,
Washington Post Book World

INNOCENT ERÉNDIRA AND OTHER STORIES

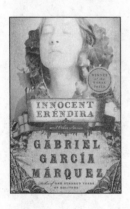

This collection of fiction, representing some of García Márquez's earlier work, includes eleven short stories and a novella, *Innocent Eréndira,* in which a young girl who dreams of freedom cannot escape the reach of her vicious and avaricious grandmother.

"It is the genius of the mature García Márquez that fatalism and possibility somehow coexist, that dreams redeem, that there is laughter even in death. Not being a genius, I don't know how he does it, but I am grateful."

—John Leonard,
New York Times

LEAF STORM AND OTHER STORIES

Leaf Storm is the first book García Márquez wrote. He began it when he was nineteen. It was published eight years later. In this early effort we see the colorful historical background that forms the basis for his later work.

"To call these allegories would be to suggest that they are 'symbolic' somehow and perhaps plainly stated. They are not; the texture is that of the prose poem, and the intention a restatement of religious belief. But the feeling one comes away with is that of enchantment, which is a sense of having endured terror and magic."
　　　　　　　—Paul Theroux, *Chicago Tribune*

NO ONE WRITES TO THE COLONEL AND OTHER STORIES

Written with compassionate realism and wit, the stories in this mesmerizing collection depict the disparities of town and village life in South America—the frightfully poor and outrageously rich, memories and illusions, and lost opportunities and present joys.

"A rare combination of grace and vibrancy. Every scene, every gesture signs life and denies death. . . . He is an absolute master."
　　　　　　　—*New York Times*

gabriel garcía márquez

collected stories

COLLECTED STORIES

Collected here are twenty-six of the author's most brilliant and enchanting short stories, presented in the chronological order of their publication in Spanish and drawn from three volumes: *Eyes of a Blue Dog, Big Mama's Funeral,* and *The Incredible and Sad Tale of Innocent Eréndira and Her Heartless Grandmother.* Combining mysticism, history, and humor, the stories in this collection span more than two decades, illuminating the development of García Márquez's prose and exhibiting the themes of family, poverty, and death that resound throughout his fiction.

"The stories are rich and startling in their matter, and confident and eloquent in their manner.... They are—the word cannot be avoided—magical."

—John Updike, *The New Yorker*

Don't miss the next book by your favorite author. Sign up now for AuthorTracker by visiting www.AuthorTracker.com.